ORIGINS OF THE CURSED DUELIST

EXTENDED EDITION

CHRISTOPHER D. SCHMITZ

Tree Shaker books

TREESHAKER BOOKS

Copyright © [Year of First Publication] by [Author or Pen Name]

All rights reserved.

No portion of this book may be reproduced in any form without written permission from the publisher or author, except as permitted by U.S. copyright law.

I would like to thank my amazing kickstarter partners and superfans who helped bring this project to life:

Aliee M Zapernick, Hunter Martin, Matthew Morgan, Jacob Baird, Brendan Papz, Scott Casey, Shelby Land, Randall Fickel, Ellen Pilcher, Gerald P. McDaniel, Billye L Herndon, Floyd W, Realm Makers, Alex M, D. Gould, Rick Heinz, Sharrie Randall-Gaskins, Katherine Shipman, Anja Peerdeman, Glenn Moyer, Douglas Van Dyke Jr, James S. O'Brien, Vickie Grider, Matthea W. Ross, Perry St.Laurent, Alyssa Kritz, Rachel Newhouse, Melanie B, Leslie Twitchell, Tabatha Robinson, Shanda Douglas, Andy Newman, Caitlin Millsaps, Michael W Welch, Admiral Jeebus, Kendall Marx, Nikki Gregg, Bree Moore, Joni Caplan, Dean F. Sutherland, Michael Antony Bernabo, James R McGinnis Jr, H Anderson, Aramanth, John Idlor, Emma Adams, Pamacii, Keino Somers, K Stoker, Andrew Lafferty, Roos van Dijk, Nick Mandujano III, Angela R. Watts, Jan Kilnear, Peter Younghusband, Allie Burton, Rebecca Buchanan, Belinda Crawford, Rafi Spitzer,

Joshua C. Chadd, Sara Ontiveros, Ian Cummings, Joshua Gerdes, Christa Rickard

Special Offer

Stay up to date on the world of Arcadeax... you'll get access to a bunch of special freebies, bonus content, and the author's newsletter. You can unsubscribe at any time.
To get access to this exclusive group, just follow this link:

https://www.subscribepage.com/duelist

and add your email to be added immediately!

CURSE OF THE FEY DUELIST

Contents

1. Chapter 1 — 1
2. Chapter 2 — 9
3. Chapter 3 — 26
4. Chapter 4 — 41
5. Chapter 5 — 52
6. Chapter 6 — 72
7. Chapter 7 — 88
8. Chapter 8 — 104
9. Chapter 9 — 119
10. Chapter 10 — 131
11. Chapter 11 — 144
12. Chapter 12 — 158
13. Chapter 13 — 170
14. Chapter 14 — 181
15. Chapter 15 — 193
16. Chapter 16 — 201

17.	Chapter 17	206
18.	Chapter 18	217
19.	Chapter 19	228
20.	Chapter 20	239
21.	Chapter 21	243
	Fullpage Image	247
		286
	Glossary	287
		292
		293
	About Author	294

Chapter One

G ENESTA'S ELVEN EARS TWITCHED. She stared in disbelief at a human child. He was covered in blood, his chest heaving with rage. The boy looked around with feral, frenzy-filled eyes.

A massive, muscular orc towered at her left. Male, by his appearance, the orc laughed and gave a yank of the leather thong that connected to the torq around her neck. The creature had leashed her, owned her as a slave.

Rhylfelour was the devious war chief of the Broken Hand clan, a tribe of orcs belonging to the Demonsbreak, a collective of unseelie orcs with a dark past. The orc grinned at her and then at the boy.

The orc tethered Genesta to a tree before approaching the young one.

"What is your name, child of Adam?" Rhylfelour asked.

The boy backed away from him, nearly tripping over the corpse of Urzgug. Urzgug had been one of Rhylfelour's clan mate. He had bled out from the many wounds the confused child had given him.

"I am not a child," the nameless one insisted. "I'm twelve years old... almost. I turn twelve in... in..." His eyes turned aside, searching for the information which he couldn't seem to remember.

"You're young," Rhylfelour spat. "But I did not ask your age. And I don't care. What do they call you?"

The boy clutched his knife even tighter as Rhylfelour looked him over. Near the boy's feet lay the remnants of several pieces of fruit; the human had been eating from the tree behind him. Dark, wine-colored juice stained the human's lips.

"Is even your name left to you, child?" Genesta called.

Two young eyes snapped to her, now realizing she was there. "My name... my name is Remy," the boy said after some effort. "Remington Keaton."

Like her captor, Genesta also looked over at the boy. Remy wore a strange fabric for his pants, a knit she'd never seen before, and his shirt was gone, destroyed in the fight with Urzgug. Urzgug had grabbed the boy when they'd stumbled upon him. Thinking he'd found a helpless human child to toy with, he'd wrecked the shirt before Remy dropped it and produced a fancy, gilded blade and eviscerated his assailant.

"Your memories?" Genesta asked.

"N-not here," Remy stammered after a pause spent looking around. "I don't think I am on Earth, even."

Rhylfelour chortled a gust of laughter.

"I barely remember," said Remy. "Like trying to see bits of a dream that was so vivid the night before. My home... just a glimpse of Mother and Father..."

Rhylfelour pointed to the tree. "That one's fruit will scramble the brain, kid. They call it the Aphay tree... And you're in the worst place you could be."

Remy bristled. He, too, detected the threat in Rhylfelour's voice. Genesta arched a brow. The child seemed more competent than the other human children she'd seen. Not that she'd met many. They did not survive long in Arcadeax. The fey folk resented anything from realms outside of their own.

"You fell into a real shit-hole, kid," Rhylfelour continued. "This is the faewylds: the parts between kingdoms, between the seelie kingdom of Summer and the unseelie realm of Winter. Specifically, you're in the Grinning Wood where all manner of nasties live. Sometimes powerful, important tuatha dumped their victims here so that those things will erase their problems. The beasties usually do a good job of cleanup."

"Kingdoms? Tuatha?"

The orc explained, "The seelie and unseelie are kingdoms—tuatha are its residents. The faewylds are another neutral kingdom of Arcadeax, and you are at my mercy."

Remy brandished his dagger. "That other one thought I was helpless, too," he said, bobbing his head towards Urzgug's bloody corpse.

Rhylfelour gave him a look of annoyed admission. "Urzgug often acted like an idiot. But I am interested in where you got that fancy weapon?"

Remy could only shrug. "I... I just *have* it. I know that it's mine. I remember that much."

"It is a dúshlán blade," Genesta said. "Fetiche magic—that's the power of the gods and the realm itself acting on your behalf. Someone has done you a great wrong, child. Someone imbalanced the scales of cosmic justice despite knowing better. The blade is linked to your pain and to the one who wronged you. It cries out for vengeance and will tell you when that person is near. It will glow as it cries out for vengeance."

Remy stared at the knife's edge for a moment, and then his eyes shifted to the menacing orc. The blade did not currently glow.

Rhylfelour said, "You killed Urzgug; he was more than an acquaintance of mine. He was my apprentice."

"He tried to kill me. I defended myself," Remy said.

"Correct. Arcadeax is a dangerous place. There is no shortage of things that will attempt to kill a ddiymadferth—a weak and useless bottom feeder like yourself. You took an apprentice from me, and I demand an even exchange."

Remy took a step back from the orc.

Rhylfelour was tall, even for an orc. He had thick arms that boasted corded muscle below his olive skin, but not so much that he lacked mobility or could be easily outmaneuvered. The orc carried a traditional battle ax upon his back, but also wore a sword at his hip. Rhylfelour seemed to understand that brute force was not a solution to every problem, and he'd adequately equipped for them.

Perhaps the most intimidating thing about Rhylfelour was the spark of hideous intelligence that burned within his eyes. Genesta knew he was calculating, devious, and ruthless in addition to being an incredibly strong brute. And she was a part of his growing empire: an unwilling one, certainly, but she was a seer and had delivered the prophecy that he would someday rise to take the unseelie kingdom's Rime Throne. The orc wanted that more than any other thing in all of Arcadeax.

"Are you trying to recruit me?" Remy looked from Rhylfelour to Genesta. "Some kind of human, orc, and elf alliance?"

"No. The elf is not my equal," Rhylfelour chuckled, "and neither are you." He drew his sword. It was an elven longsword made for a seelie soldier. Genesta had watched Rhylfelour murder its owner long ago. The blade looked dainty in his massive paws, but it was nimble, precise. "The elf girl is special. An untrained aes sidhe—an elvish spell caster, but with the rarest of gifts. Genesta has visions of the future. I... *liberated* her three years ago."

Genesta bit her lip. That much was true, but the seelie court's council of mavens ruled over any folk with arcane abilities. Mavens policed the realm and ruled from the tower of Suíochán Naséan with the blessing of Oberon.

And above all else, the high maven feared the abilities of seers, which is why any that were discovered were locked away beneath their Radiant Tower. The elf had seen his attack coming while being transported to the maven's stronghold. She'd said nothing. Rhylfelour was the lesser of evils.

"Like you, Genesta is bound to me," Rhylfelour hissed. "I will either train you to be Urzgug's replacement, or I will kill you."

Remy gulped. He set his feet and held the dúshlán. The boy radiated fear, but he refused to back down.

Rhylfelour snarled and lunged, pulling back to a feint in the last moment and baiting Remy forward. The orc caught him off guard and swung his sword. Using the flat of the blade, he knocked the dagger from the human's hand.

He sidestepped the bewildered Remy and tripped him so that the boy fell to the damp, peaty sod.

Genesta winced as Rhylfelour turned the boy to his back and stepped on him, pinning him to the ground. The orc pointed the tip of his sword at Remy's neck.

But instead of ending the human's life, Rhylfelour laughed. "Good... good. That is the fighting spirit I am looking for. Skills you can be trained for—they can be learned. Heart cannot."

Remy struggled beneath the orc's powerful foot, thrashing like a wild beast. He obviously did not share the creature's amusement. Between ragged, tearful gasps, he snarled, "I... will... kill you!"

Rhylfelour raised an eyebrow. "Will this child be the death of me?" he asked Genesta.

She paused a moment, as if considering the impact of her answer. Her eyes widened. She saw something—or wished for her captor to believe it—and waited long enough to make Rhylfelour think she'd altered an answer for personal gain.

Genesta nodded enthusiastically. "Yes. This child will kill you. He is of no value—leave him to die in the faewylds."

"Interesting." The orc's toothy grin crawled ever wider. "I am on to you, seer. You'll need to master this game if you hope to best me some day and escape to freedom. This game is what elevated me to leader of my clan... And combined with the strength of my will, it shall eventually earn me the throne."

Genesta blanched. She knew the orc was right—and she knew that Rhylfelour knew it, too.

He slowly applied more pressure, threatening to crush the child's ribcage. [Swear an oath of fealty to me and you shall live,] he said in the high speech.

Remy squirmed, trying to escape the pain.

[Swear it,] he said more forcefully.

"He does not know the olde tongue," Genesta cried, trying to save Remy's life. "And neither do I."

Rhylfelour laughed. "Sometimes I forget that you are practically ddiymadferth, too," he spat the word. It was a derogatory term usually reserved for humans, and it was one of the worst profanities they fey used. "You were an impoverished bruscar sidhe before I found you. Never forget that you were a poor member of the poorest caste... But I will teach it to you as well."

She bowed her head. He'd been claiming to do as much for some time now, but was more likely to follow through if he had more than one student.

The orc turned his attention back to the child whose eyes burned with hate as they locked on his aggressor and then glanced aside at his dúshlán blade, which lay just beyond his reach.

"Repeat these words after me and you shall live," Rhylfelour said. He spoke an oath slowly in the high tongue so that the child could repeat the alien words.

Remy looked at Genesta.

"The words will bind you," she told him, recognizing the pain in his eyes. "It is impossible to lie while speaking in high speech, and oaths made in it will magically enforce their keeping."

Rhylfelour spoke the first word of the oath again, growling it insistently. When Remy refused to repeat it, Rhylfelour applied more pressure—enough that one of Remy's ribs cracked audibly.

The human cried out, but spoke the word. And then repeated the next. And then the next, until the oath was made.

Finally, Rhylfelour laughed and let the boy go. He hurried over and snatched up his dagger, but did not move to strike the orc with it. He could not.

"Come along," the orc said, leaving Urzgug's body behind for the carrion birds. "I will teach the language to you both. And in the morning, son of Adam, I will teach you how to hold that dagger properly."

Chapter Two

Remy grew strong and lithe as a teenager.

He'd become strong, despite Rhylfelour habitually under feeding the human, even despite demanding a rigorous training regimen over the course of the following eight years. Remy managed to still pack on a decent amount of mass. Of course, much of the bulges on his arms were due to scar tissue build up rather than muscles.

Rhylfelour only knew one way to train his apprentices. Pain was the greatest teacher. And Remy had endured a great deal of Rhylfelour's scholarly tutelage.

For nearly a decade, Remy's life had become one gray smear of time. Day turned to night and back today again in Rhylfelour's endless pursuit of breaking Remy. When Rhylfelour did not personally instruct the human in the art of hand-to-hand combat, he had other fey creatures take over instruction, passing on the sum of their knowledge.

Rhylfelour's goal was to make Remy into a weapon. *His weapon.*

Most of those creatures in Rhylfelour's camp were from the hideously twisted pseudo-elf race of orcs, but there were many other creatures of tuathan heritage present as well.

Remy learned stealth from a faceless bodach, he learned survival from a dryad, and every night he was drilled on languages including the olde tongue. After every training session with the orc, Remy was forced to repeat the vow Rhylfelour had forced upon him below the Aphay tree.

[I swear my allegiance to Rhylfelour, son of Jarlok and warlord chief of the Broken Hand orcs.]

"Ddiymadferth," Rhylfelour snapped at Remy, using the personal insult. "Saddle the horses. We ride for Capitus Ianthe before nightfall."

"This late?" Remy asked.

Rhylfelour backhanded the young man and sent him sprawling. "Do not think to question me, human."

Remy wiped a small trickle of blood away from the corner of his mouth and then turned to stand. He breathed deeply and did his best to calm the roiling emotions inside of him. "If we leave for Capitus Ianthe now, we may not arrive safely," he risked explaining to the orc. "You have many enemies. And every week there are more. We should not risk your safety by heading out so late... let us delay until the morning."

Rhylfelour raised his hand again as if to strike, but held back the blow when Remy did not flinch. He glared down his nose at him instead and ordered, "I have issued the command. Saddles. I do not wish to delay."

Remy nodded. He still had bruises from the last time he'd questioned Rhylfelour. Several minutes later, the horses were ready, and Remy mounted one. The larger of the two awaited Rhylfelour, who arrived a minute later.

The orc swung his leg up, and over as he slid into the saddle.

"Where are the rest?" Remy asked, anticipating the warlord would bring a contingent of security with him.

Most of the territory controlled by the twelve orc tribes of the Demonsbreak were inside the boundaries of the unseelie realm, but some extended into the faewylds. The warlords paid tribute and had allegiances with whomever sat on the thrones of their respective realms: Queen Mab had ruled the faewylds from her Briar Throne for as long as Oberon had ruled the seelie court and its Gilded Throne; the unseelie's Rime Throne had changed hands frequently since Oberon's brother, King Wulflock, disappeared and left power vacuum ages ago.

Rhylfelour had his ambitions set upon the Rime Throne, and everybody knew it. But he had to contend with members of both the unseelie court and the faewylds to continue his pursuit of it—and he also had to deal with the other eleven orcish warlords and their factions.

Remy had seen him negotiate deals with many of the other orcs he'd cowed into submission. At least two holdouts remained who actively plotted to kill his master. So far, the usual orcish assassination attempts had proved too inept to bother Rhylfelour.

"There are no others. Just you and me," Rhylfelour said.

Remy choked back a grin and wondered if this was his chance. The unseelie realm was dangerous, but it had rules. The faewylds were a wilder kind of danger. It, too, had rules, but the place had an untamed sort of savagery that infused it with chaos and could tip the scales on the unprepared.

Maybe I'll get lucky and one of the warlord's enemies will kill him in the middle of the night.

Rhylfelour looked down at the human. His eyes lingered on the dúshlán blade tucked in Remy's belt. "Speak your oath," he commanded.

Remy did as ordered, perfectly articulating the repetitively trained words In the high tongue. Remy could not kill Rhylfelour; unless the orc asked for it, he could even raise a hand against him when training. Arcadeaxn magic was potent stuff.

"Then I am satisfied. There is no danger to me," the orcish warlord said.

The two of them set out on horseback riding north for several hours. An hour before dusk approached, they crossed into the faewylds. They rode another couple of hours before stopping for the night.

Remy did not know where Capitus Ianthe was. He barely knew where Wildfell, Queen Mab's capitol city, was. Capitus Ianthe was a kind of caravan and the primary domain of Mab's successor, Princess Maeve. Maeve, like Mab, was a tylwyth teg, which was one of the breeds of the elven sidhe. There were longer eared and had a look of ferality about them. Unlike the sidhe, the tylwyth teg put on no airs or feigned false sorts of civility. They were wildfey in every sense... And Remy had no idea what Rhylfelour had in mind by a visit to Maeve's city, but it must've had something to do with his obsession for the Rime Throne.

The human built a small fire just big enough to cook some of the provisions which they brought with them. Remy hurried into the bush and set a few small traps, hoping to snare a fresh meal by morning. He returned to find Rhylfelour digging a small hole next to the mat, which he rolled out to sleep upon.

A few paces away, the orc had tethered the horses with enough lead that they could graze. Saddles, saddlebags, and their other provisions, including their weapons, lay nearby.

Remy raised an eyebrow at that. He thought it foolish that Rhylfelour would leave the weapons out of their reach. They were in a dangerous land and Rhylfelour had more enemies than Remy could count.

Rhylfelour grinned at the human as if he could read Remy's mind. Inside the small trench near Rhylfelour's mat, the orc placed a dagger. He laid twigs and leaves over that and then scattered the fine sand over the top to hide the hole.

Remy wanted to ask about it, but the orc gave him a short shake of his head to quiet him.

They ate in silence, which Remy was grateful for. Rhylfelour was prone to nasty, cutting remarks. As invested as he was in Remy's training for combat, he had very little interest in building the human up as a person. Instilling a dose of self-loathing made it easier to control folk.

But Remy refused to believe anything Rhylfelour had ever told him about himself. Remy may have lost all of his memories from before the Aphay tree, but he knew that Rhylfelour was a liar at his core... and whatever knowledge about Remy's past existed in this world existed beyond Rhylfelour's control.

They sat by the fire and listened to the night air as they ate. Burning sticks crackled as tiny embers scattered skyward. Remy looked across the halo of light and spotted a crow watching him quizzically. It perched upon a fallen log, nearby, and gave a couple tentative hops to the ground and nearer the human.

The crow cocked his head, addressing them with dark eyes. Rhylfelour watched the human and the bird.

Remy peeled off a piece of sinewy meat from the piece he was chewing on. He tossed it halfway between him and the bird. The crow hopped two more steps and then pecked at the morsel before snatching it up and swallowing.

It looked back at the human again as if waiting for another treat. Remy shrugged at the bird; the food was gone. But he'd heard that crows like shiny things for their nests. He produced a polished button from a pocket. It was broken and of little value.

Remy tossed the prize to the bird, who looked at it and then back to Remy before picking up the glinting material and flying away.

Rhylfelour shook his head with a low chuckle. "Stupid boy. Crows talk to each other, don't you know? Once you're known as someone who gives them prizes, they will only keep coming."

"Who cares? So, a crow likes me. Big deal."

"No, fool. *All* crows will think that of you," Rhylfelour said. And then the orc laid down and closed his eyes.

Remy did likewise. He watched the embers die down to little more than a murky orange glow. There was plenty of light from the stars and the moon overhead, and it was late, but sleep eluded Remy.

The warlord's hubris seemed to scream in the night. Remy could not understand why Rhylfelour took such a chance by sleeping out in the open air of the faewylds.

As he tossed and turned, he heard something. Rustling grass in the glade or leaves in a grove was no uncommon thing. His ears were attuned to the different sounds distinguishing a field mouse shaking foliage from larger creatures stalking through the underbrush. A snapping twig and delicate footfalls distinctly alerted him of the latter. Remy cocked an ear and tried to simulate the breathing pattern of someone who was asleep.

Damn you, Rhylfelour... I did not come all the way out into the faewylds to get murdered for you!

Remy prepared himself, thinking through all the different scenarios. If someone was here to kill them, they were probably targeting the orc. The human was of little value, though this could prove the exact situation Remy had hoped for. With a little luck, he could be free of Rhylfelour forever.

And then he spotted a set of yellow eyes peering through the tall heather. They were on the opposite side of the trail leading to Capitus Ianthe. They glinted enough in the moonlight that Remy identified them as belonging to an orc.

The sound of metal sliding across leather stood the hairs up on Remy's neck as the intruder pulled a blade from its scabbard. Then the assassin crept out of the brush and darted directly for them. A murderous glint burned in his eyes.

Rhylfelour leapt up and to the ready, surprising his attacker. He caught his fellow orc's weapon arm by the wrist, and they twisted into a tumbling heap, each wrestling for control of the other.

Remy was on his feet in a flash. He reached down and put one hand on his dúshlán. The human bit his tongue to make sure he did not audibly cheer for Rhylfelour's opponent... But he made sure to stay out of the way and hope that the invading orc proved strong enough to murder Rhylfelour, but was also inept enough to let Remy live.

Rhylfelour knocked the intruder's weapon far beyond the reach of either combatant. They rolled through a pile of hot coals that had earlier been a fire. They snarled and struck each other, but Rhylfelour's skills proved far superior. He demonstrated exactly why he had attained warlord status.

Cockily, Rhylfelour looked sidelong at Remy and scanned him. He rolled his eyes and recognized that the human had stayed back, hoping this was his moment of freedom. Rhylfelour plunged his hand into the secret compartment where he'd stashed his dagger.

Remy finally understood. This entire trip had been a trap for the hunter orc. They'd played the part of both bait and trap.

Rhylfelour retrieved the short blade and jammed it into his enemy's head. It made a sickly cracking sound as it penetrated both thick bone of the creature's skull and plunged deeper into brain tissue.

The hunter went limp, curling his arm and convulsing as if stroking out. It tried to talk, to beg for mercy. Rhylfelour's strike had crippled the creature, but not killed him.

Turning him over, Rhylfelour rummaged through his enemy's belongings and then stripped him. He took stock of the assassin, identifying all the ceremonial tattoos upon the creature's skin. The warlord grinned deviously.

"Exactly as I suspected," Rhylfelour said.

Remy noticed what the warlord had found. Several of the tattoos were marks of allegiance to rival orc tribe: ironically a tribe known as Fractured Skull. It was one of the holdout tribes that had been trying to depose Rhylfelour. An assassination attempt against Rhlfelour from the tribe, at least a failed one, would give him grounds to seek retribution and potentially consolidate power.

This was all part of the plan, Remy realized. *We were never headed for Capitus Ianthe.*

Rhylfelour bent and used his blade to carve on the hide of the failed assailant. He skinned portions of him and kept the tattooed flesh as trophies—markers of proof against his political opponents. There were much like the duelist ribbons used as social credit in the seelie realms—only far more macabre.

Remy stared at the struggling orc as his master began saddling his horse.

"Come along, ddiymadferth. The deed is accomplished; we ride for home," Rhylfelour said.

"You're just going to leave him here?" Remy asked. The creature kicked his legs impotently, trying to turn himself over. Bare patches where his hide had been cut away bled profusely, but they began clogging with dirt. The orc writhed in agony.

Rhylfelour shrugged. "Kill him if you like. Feed him to your crow, but we leave now."

Remy gritted his teeth, but then bent low and used his dúshlán to end the creature's suffering. A quick stroke across the jugular splashed orcish blood across the campsite.

The human hurried and packed up the camp. He saddled his horse and then climbed aboard his back and followed the warlord.

Dawn approached with the crimson band across the horizon. There is just enough light to see the gathering of crows circling the sky above the campsite which they'd left behind.

Rhylfelour looked back and noted the carrion birds. He looked at Remy, his human protégé, and said, "I told you. And now they'll expect you to continue feeding them... And so will I."

Remy detected a hint of threat and the voice. "What do you mean?"

"An assassin for an assassin. This is what I train you for, and Chief Ogguhar has made a grave mistake sending his son to do what no one else has been able to."

Remy gave him an inquisitive look.

"Kill me," Rhylfelour chuckled. He looked back to the words and spat in the high speech, [Aderyn Corff.]

Remy knew what it meant. *Corpse Bird.*

"That is what you will be," Rhylfelour insisted as the light began to crest over the distant hills. "My assassin. My corpse bird. My Aderyn Corff."

Hot on the orc's heels, Remy approached the warlord's stronghold.

Using the labor of slaves, Rhylfelour had erected a stone structure capable of repelling an invasion force for weeks. Palisade walls provided the first layer of defense, followed by a slope upwards where row after row of tents housed non orc tuatha. These were the first wave of his forces: sidhe conscripts, mostly elves, fauns, a few trolls, and many others.

Inside that circle were the orcish forces followed by a short bastion defended by Rhylfelour's more valuable living assets, of which Remy was considered one.

The inner-most ring was at the peak of the slope. There, Rhylfelour had built a simple block fortress. Inside that he kept a harem of oricsh whores, and his prized possession: Genesta, his sidhe seer. He'd forced her to play madam to his coterie of green-skinned breeding fodder. Only a few confidants knew her true function and value to the warlord.

Genesta walked down the steps and greeted Remy on his arrival. She cast a sidelong look at the warlord, who loosened his pants as he passed them and entered the building after returning. Killing his enemies always got Rhylfelour's blood up.

On the far side of the courtyard, a new collection of slaves had arrived. They were caged like chattel. Rhylfelour did a brisk trade in slaves. Aside from providing allies with indentured soldiers and mercenary support, he'd built his empire on the slave trade.

Unseelie sidhe barons of the winter court owned land and charged rents to tenants. Some demanded tributes on production, but orcs did not own a wealth of lands or investments.

Nonetheless, the factions of the Demonsbreak carved profits out of flesh and demanded both gold and respect for their empires. Of course, Rhylfelour had been helped by owning a slave who could measure the future success of any venture.

Genesta gave Remy a hug. "I am glad you survived," she said to Remy.

He squinted, recognizing she was responsible for Rhylfelour's knowledge of the assassin. "You told the old bastard about his murder?"

She nodded. "I had to... And who are you calling old? He and I are comparable aged."

Genesta had aged fast. She was relatively young for an elf, but the stresses of her life had taken a massive toll. The elves of the high noble courts retained their youth seemingly forever. By all accounts, Oberon still looked like a young man, though he was thousands of years old; the same went for Queen Mab. As far as Remy understood, the royal sidhe had access to food that preserved them. Ceremonial feasts enjoyed by the sidhe courts weren't just high-quality buffets; they included certain foods and drink infused with ambrosius, which prolonged life and preserved the body.

Remy did not know exactly what the stuff was, only that it worked. He'd never met Oberon, but he'd seen Mab once in passing. She was the seelie king's equal, and she looked only a couple of years older than Remy. Whatever ambrosius was, it was effective.

He put Genesta's condition out of his mind. Remy was just thankful to have a friend. She still clung to him tightly. "And here I thought you could tell the future? You should have known I would survive."

"It does not work like that, child," Genesta said. "You know that I can only see potential futures and outcomes, which are most likely. I had hoped that Rhylfelour would meet his end and that you might escape, allowing you to flee to the seelie side of Arcadeax." Her voice turned dour. "It was not very likely. In fact, it was the least likely outcome, but I still held out hope."

Remy's eyebrows pinched. "It was more likely that I would die than escape? So much for hope."

Genesta shrugged. "I hoped *and* clung to faith. Those two do not always walk hand-in-hand. But I placed faith in the training which Rhylfelour provided... It may yet prove to be the only valuable accomplishment of his life."

Remy looked over his shoulder and studied the wall of slaves somberly. "Those folk might beg to differ." There was nothing he could do for them.

Some of the slaves were wildfey, but most were a few humans. Two of them, both young boys, were no older than Remy had been when Rhylfelour had taken him. They were tied to a post a little distance away from the others. An older woman watched them with pain in her eyes; Remy assumed she was their mother.

"What's special about those two?" Remy asked.

Genesta shook her head. "The warlord is pleased with you. He intends to send you out soon: oath bound to complete missions on his behalf."

Remy realized the implications, and he turned to his friend with shocked eyes. "These are... my replacements?"

She nodded solemnly.

Remy looked down at his arms. They were unmarked. Slave owners traditionally branded their property so that it could not be taken from them. But more importantly, so that escaped slaves could be located and returned for rewards and enabling their owners to punish to the slave. The wildfey mattered less. They typically had places to return to, and depending on what kind they were, they might have had hide or fur to cover markings... But humans? Humans belong to nowhere and it was difficult to hide a slaver's brand. Rhylfelour had opted to never brand Remy. He had considered the oath to be enough. That, and his constant threats carried more weight than a brand ever could.

Not only would the orc's trackers come after him if he ever escaped, but Rhylfelour employed a notorious slave taker known as Syrmerware Kathwesion, who was known for his violence. He poorly treated the product, and fear of encountering him kept the rest in line. The slave taker's gang was responsible for nearly ninety percent of all slaves gathered for market. Rhylfelour only controlled sales and distribution—driving product was all Syrmerware Kathwesion's domain.

Remy watched the two young humans. He took a couple of steps toward them when Rhylfelour exited the brothel. Still pulling his pants up, Ryhlfelour barked at the human to get his attention. "Aderyn Corff."

It was the first time that Remy had heard him use a word that might be considered anything less than an insult. Remy turned to look at his master.

High overhead, a trio of crows circled the courtyard. They landed nearby and tilted their heads, addressing Remy with their curious, intelligent gazes.

"Get some rest. I will have a new task for you in the morning." Rhylfelour said.

Remy bowed his head, careful not to look aside, or at anything at all. He knew how little it took to upset the warlord, especially after the warlord was done whoring with his orcish sows. And then Remy headed to his little shack which adjoined the orc's main fortress.

Remy stared at Rhylfelour.

The warlord sat in a crude, high-backed chair. The macabre furniture was lashed together at the joints and made from bones and other ossein material. Rhylfelour tore flesh with his teeth and picked at the few vegetables and fruits on his plate.

On either side of the long banquet table, Rhylfelour's most trusted henchmen were gathered. Remy had a place amongst them, though he wondered if it was just so that Rhylfelour could keep an eye on him. The human was placed as far away from the warlord as he could be seated, but without placing him at the opposite head position of the table.

As the orc chewed, he drummed the fingers of his right hand. Like most orcs, Rhylfelour had a minor deformation. He had six fingers on that hand. Upon each digit he wore a ring: each one was the signet for the different orc chieftain of the Demonsbreak and he'd taken the ring from each one who owed Rhylfelour their allegiance.

Remy had witnessed Rhylfelour secure most of those rings. The warlord had sent his marauders to accomplish great feats on behalf of the other chieftains, or Rhylfelour had bested them in combat or bedded their females, stealing the signets after he cuckolded them.

Rhylfelour was willing to do whatever he had to in order to secure the fealty of his bannermen, however ruthless, or however friendly. Upon his extra finger, Rhylfelour wore two bands, doubling up on that digit, and his own ring hung on a chain at his neck. Only the orc's thumbs remained unadorned—and he wanted the rings of the remaining two orc tribes for them.

Abruptly, Rhylfelour tossed aside the bone he was gnawing on and fixed Remy with a stern gaze. "Aderyn Corff. I'm sending you on a task this afternoon."

One of the warlord's lieutenants sat among the band of killers. He looked from the human to the orc and shot him a cockeyed glance. "Aderyn Corff?"

Rhylfelour chuckled and shook his head. "You will hear that name spoken of soon, and often. The fame will spread foreign and abroad. *The corpse bird.* Aderyn Corff's training is complete." He stared mirthfully at Remy. "Today, his cage will open, and my death bird will fly."

Chapter Three

Remy left his master's feast hall. He had stuffed a few crumbs within his pocket, and when he entered the courtyard, he spotted the crows that had followed him from the faewylds.

He tossed the scraps to the birds, and they hurried over and gobbled them up. The lead crow cawed loudly, as if in thanks. Or perhaps it was swearing its own oath of fealty?

The collection of slaves that Rhylfelour had stored in the courtyard had been moved sometime that morning. They likely been shipped elsewhere to fulfill an order, or else they had been branded and relocated to the slave markets in one of the unseelie cities.

Only the two boys remained in the courtyard. Remy turned away from his crows and walked over to them. They both wore the forlorn expressions of kids who'd seen their known lives come to an end. Just that morning, they'd watched their mother be carted off to some unknown fate, likely to never be seen again.

Remy bit his lip. Because his own memories had been wiped out years ago, Remy could barely sympathize. He imagined the internal torture they must have endured. Even if you could not identify with it personally, empathy was possible for him—but not for the orcs. They would give no mercy.

It's a blessing I cannot remember my past. Small favors from the Dagda, I suppose.

The brothers did not recoil from Remy as they had shied back from Rhylfelour or his taskmasters.

As he approached them, Remy could feel many eyes sweep over him, weighing the importance of the man. Despite being Rhylfelour's pet ever since the day the orc had brought him into his camp, there were but few who trusted him, and none of those were orcs. However, Remy knew that trust and the binding oaths made in the magical tongue were not dependent upon each other.

Remy assumed there were many in Rhylfelour's camp who waited for the warlord's human apprentice to free his slaves and cost them all their livelihood. Protecting his master's property was not a condition of his oath.

"My name is Remy." Remy kept his voice low. "The orc warlord is your master now."

One of the boys looked at him. Worry flooded his gaze. "Our mother. Will we ever see her again?"

"Probably not. I am sorry." Remy shook his head. "But for now, you must focus on surviving."

"See, Shadarkith? He does not care. He is loyal to that bastard orc chief."

Remy did not think the whelp's comments could sting. Somehow, that one did.

"No, Ekai. He's here to help us... See how the other orcs look at him? He's an outsider."

Remy kept his voice very low. He stated matter-of-factly, "Rhylfelour will make you take an oath in the old tongue. It doesn't matter if you understand the words or not, they will bind you to his service and prevent you from harming him. Were it not so, I would have cut his neck ages ago. I'm trying to give you enough information so that you'll survive."

"Survive?" Shadarkith asked.

"I think he means to train you. To teach you to be an assassin," Remy said. "I was about your age when he began training me."

Both the boys' heads snapped to attention. They focused on something beyond Remy.

Rhylfelour appeared in the doorway and stomped his way over to the humans. Remy bowed his head and backed away. The orc had a wicked gleam in his yellow eyes as he fixed them upon his two new protégés.

One of the warlord's kitchen scullions emerged carrying two plates. They were both piled up with the goodly selection of vegetables, fruits, grains, and leftover gristle parts of the meat. This was the same food, high-quality stuff, that had come directly from the warlord's table.

Rhylfelour took one of the plates and then directed the servant to bring the other to Genesta. He kept her existence secret even from his most trusted group of brigands.

She'd been too free to volunteer information when Rhylfelour had taken Remy from the faewylds, and that was the only reason

Remy knew her secret. But those in Rhylfelour's inner circle would be hungry enough for power that they'd use that information against the warlord.

The orc placed the food upon a nearby crate. The kids were half starved, and the aroma of the food caught their attention. Though they tried to act as if they were disinterested in any gifts from the creature that had enslaved them, their hunger was obvious.

Rhylfelour took a key and unshackled both Shadarkith and Ekai. "If you try to run, my trackers will find you. As you've not yet proved yourselves of any value, they are not instructed to return you in any specific condition."

Both boys had the gangly build of youth, and their muscles were wiry and raw. Humans did not have it easy in Arcadeax. The family had probably been scooped up by Syrmerware Kathwesion in one of his excursions through the realm, or possibly in the faewylds.

Most humans lived beyond the reaches of the unseelie. Those that dared dwell within the realm and had secured their own freedom carried some form of identification of that distinction. Freedoms did humans no good if their status was not registered with the throne and if they became regular targets of collectors like Kathwesion.

"Your task is simple. I am here to establish a baseline: to understand what I am working with. To help me see that, you will fight each other." Rhylfelour nodded towards Remy. "Do you see Aderyn Corff? He started with a great deal of natural talent. He'd already murdered my previous apprentice, even though he was much like you, ddiymadferth. He had no brother to fight... He faced *me*."

Shadarkith looked at his brother. Ekai returned the glance. "I do not want to fight him."

"If neither will fight, then neither will eat. There is only one plate here. Between you two, the victor shall feast. The other shall go hungry."

Ekai looked at the food, and then at his sibling. He launched himself at Shadarkith and the fight began. There became a rolling mass of arms and legs, squealing and screaming with adolescent fury. Both voices strained with anguish, but not for physical pain.

Rhylfelour looked at Remy. "Your task, Aderyn Corff, is to bring me the head and the ring of my enemy. You know of whom I speak. I know I have taught you well. Use every skill at your disposal. See it done."

Remy nodded solemnly. "How long do I have?"

"As long as it takes. However, if I even think about attempting to flee, you'll wish I had murdered you beneath the Aphay tree all those years ago. Strike from the shadows. Make all due haste, but let Chief Ogguhar feel the sting of your blade."

Remy bowed low. He knew the importance of the ring. Once the warlord owned all twelve, Queen Rhagathena would have to entertain his proposal as legitimate. They'd give him undisputed control of an army of orcs. That would make the spider queen sit up and take note. The full might of the orcish species might not be enough to wrest the Rime throne from the sidhe dukes and barons who each privately vied for its control... But it would certainly make Rhagathena entertain the proposal.

"I shall leave at once and I'll return within a ten-day," Remy said. Then he stomped off towards the stables. The three crows whom he had befriended finished pecking at the soil and leapt into the sky and followed.

Remy stayed off the main roads as his horse took him cross-country. He angled directly for the heart of Chief Ogguhar's territory. Whenever he did pass another traveler, he only addressed them with a curt nod in passing and maintained an air of authority and confidence. So long as he acted like he belonged wherever he was, he was allowed to pass. But that did not mean he would risk an encounter. Too many wished for trouble, though Remy desired only anonymity.

Ever present behind him, the crows followed.

By the third day he'd come close enough to Ogguhar's encampment that he detoured into the rugged lands surrounding it. Remy took his horse by the reins and stalked further into the woods, careful to remain unseen.

Only a small fraction of the trees bore leaves here. Most had succumbed to a kind of creeping blight. Their withered stalks had shed bark skins leaving behind only skeletal hands that reached for the sky. Even the undergrowth seemed to have stymied and yielded to low moss and the thorny bracken of the fen.

Remy explored until he found a rocky outcropping that ascended to a high point overlooking the orc camp. He tethered his horse in a nearby glen that remained hidden, and then he pitched a tent at the overlook's perch.

The human lay on his belly where he'd crawled to the edge of the cliff. Remy watched the camp, searching for any signs of the chief. It did not take long to find him.

Ogguhar was an obese and officious creature. He always adorned himself with war-paint—ready for battle at any given notice. His word was law in his camp, and he lorded it over the orcs of the Fractured Skull tribe. He used no honor guard or personal soldiers. While he had appointed many lieutenants, Ogguhar was his own orc and trusted none to safeguard him but himself.

If Remy had been an orc, he was not sure if he'd resent the power this creature wielded or revere him. But that question was moot; Remy was a human, and the only thing he was certain of was that he would kill Chief Ogguhar within the next three days.

Remy looked to his left. The crow had landed and perched nearby. It seemed to address Remy with an intelligent tilt of his head.

"Corax?" Remy asked, giving a name to the bird.

It angled its beak and blinked with a slow shutter of its horizontal, nictitating eyelids. Then Corax also turned and watched the chief. The bird had picked up on Ogguhar as Remy's mark.

Remy gave a little smile and continued his surveillance. In response, one of Corax's friends flew down and shadowed Ogguhar the rest of the day, providing an easy marker of the chief's location.

The next day, Remy continued his watch. He searched for patterns, places he could slip through the orc's defenses and make a kill. That whole second day, Ogguhar batted at the occasional crow, trying to wave it off. In one comical moment, a bird had even landed on him and briefly pecked at Ogguhar's neck before flying off.

On the morning of the third day, Ogguhar had a saddled horse brought to him. Like Rhylfelour, Ogguhar rode a large war stallion which might have looked comically huge if ridden by a human or one of the sidhe. Under Ogguhar, it looked like the only appropriate mount.

Remy had explored all the trails nearby over the last two nights while under the cover of darkness. He knew exactly where the chief was headed, or at least which attack points he would pass by, and soon.

The human hurried stealthily through the withered woodlands and came to a crossroads which he knew Ogguhar must travel through, regardless of his destination. Remy prepared his trap and then hid behind 2 giant stones which protruded from the ground. Either of them easily dwarfed the assassin.

Keeping his eyes to the sky, Remy watched until he spotted Corax. The bird following his mark at a steady distance. When he could finally hear the clopping of hooves approaching, Remy leapt out onto the road. He readied his bow and nocked an arrow.

"Hold the road," Remy barked.

Ogguhar stopped his horse, but he sat atop it and laughed. "Who are you? Some common highwayman? Don't you know who I am? You would *be lucky* if I left you—"

Remy interrupted him. "I am Aderyn Corff."

Ogguhar understood the meaning of the name and scoffed, "The corpse bird? Ha."

"I was not sent for your gold, except for that bit around your finger. Rhylfelour requires only that... and your life."

The orc chieftain recognized something wild in Remy's eye. Something that understood the degree of training that Rhylfelour had invested in him. He whirled his horse in the other direction and spurred it into a sprint.

A thin line was tied around Remy's left leg. He yanked it stiffly and tighten the lanyard which stretched across the road behind. The speeding charge ran through the tripwire.

It flung Remy from his feet and the man landed on the road in a rolling heap. Remy would never have been able to disable a sprinting warhorse with the strength of his own legs, but it was enough to make the steed reel and fall as well. It righted itself moments later and hurried away—but it was now riderless.

Remy popped to his knees and snapped off his arrow. It lodged in Ogguhar's back with a thick and meaty thud.

Grabbing his dagger, Remy cut the line tied around his leg and returned to the road in a dead sprint. He fired two more arrows; one of them glanced off the chieftain's arm and the other hit him in the torso again.

Ogguhar turned to face his attacker, but Remy was already jumping onto him, jabbing his blade into the vital spots. The human aimed for blows that would cripple the massive warrior most quickly.

The orc chief collapsed to his knees before he realized the irony of the situation. He'd paid the human no heed, and his assassin had granted no mercy. Three crows landed upon him, loudly crowing in anticipation of fresh meat.

Ogguhar breathed with heavy and labored gasps, fading fast. He swung his arms in vain, impotent efforts to at least wound his opponent. Lethargic from losing so much blood, the orc's strikes were sluggish. Remy easiled evaded them. He could have managed that even before Rhylfelour had trained him. Remy took a step back, waiting for Ogguhar to collapse.

Once the orc tipped to his side, Remy strolled up behind him. He whispered to him, "Rhylfelour wanted me to make this slow, but I shall grant you this one mercy: a quick death."

Remy ended the orc chieftain's life. He had no desire to make him wallow in misery and pain. Neither did he report that he'd killed Ogguhar's son a few days previously.

The unseelie had shaped him into a killer, but that did not mean Remy had to be cruel; it did not make him enjoy the task. Remy may have become a tool of unseelie powers, but they could never have *him*. They could cage him with mystic oaths and force his hands to enact evil, but they could not bend his soul. Remy clung to that knowledge as he dragged the knife against tender flesh.

The human produced a bag and then took Ogguhar's head, as Rhylfelour had commanded. He severed the finger, ring and all, and took that as well. Then he hurried away, returning to his horse and leaving the warm remains to the crows.

As soon as he was back in the saddle, he heard their loud caws in the distance. Corax proclaimed a celebration to others of his kind and a murder formed in the distance, a thick swarm of carrion birds descending to feast.

Remy rode hard for Rhylfelour's stronghold and reached the orc's fortress by the midpoint of day nine. The creatures at the gate watched his approach from a tower near the gate and bid the sentries open it so that he passed unmolested at full speed.

The horse had worked up a lather, and it shook the froth from its face and mane as Remy slid off it in the warlord's courtyard. Rhylfelour stood there, towering over the two young boys whose training had already begun.

One of the brothers held a stick in his hands. His bare arms were covered in welts and bruises. Remy remembered the brutality of the orc's lessons. Rhylfelour had stressed how important it was to learn how to predict an incoming strike and then block.

Rhylfelour's free hand held a switch of his own, but the warlord was not focused on defense lessons. With his other hand balled into a fist, he'd been beating the other adolescent human.

"I said speak the oath," Rhylfelour roared.

Ekai lay on the ground, only semiconscious. His left eye was swollen shut and blood trickled from his mouth and nostrils.

"Just say it, Ekai," Shadarkith insisted.

"I... I will... will not."

"Then this will continue," the orc hissed. He struck him twice more and Rhylfelour muttered at Remy, "This one is even more stubborn than you were at this age."

Rhylfelour struck the boy again, and Ekai finally went limp.

Shadarkith's breath caught in his throat. He stifled his whisper and wiped away a tear.

Remy bristled as he approached. Rage filled him, and he desired to murder the warlord then and there. He wanted to scoop up the two young boys and steal them away, rescuing them from the fate that had already taken Remy. He knew that Rhylfelour would show no mercy. Tears only encouraged violence by the orc. Above all, Rhylfelour would not allow Ekai a moment's respite until he spoke the oath.

Rhylfelour turned at his corpse bird's approach, leaving Shadarkith to tend his brother. "You have what I desire?"

It took an act of will for Remy to tear his eyes away from the young ones. When he finally did, he threw the severed head of the orc's rival chief. With a dull thud, it landed in the dirt near his master's feet.

"And the ring?"

Remy threw him the severed finger with the band still on it.

Rhylfelour practically giggled as he added the gold ring to his collection. He turned the circlet several times and admired how it looked on his hand. Paying his pet humans no further attention, he called over his shoulder, "No more training today." Taken with a good mood, he walked purposefully towards his harem.

Genesta sat with Remy as he bound up young Ekai's wounds. He'd moved the boy closer to the fire and tried to nurse him back to consciousness, but Ekai would not be roused.

"Is he going to be okay?" Shadarkith had asked. It was still early in the night.

With a grimace, Remy said, "We can only hope."

Since then, and halfway through the night, Shadarkith would say nothing except to occasionally mumble, "I kept trying to tell him… just speak the oath…"

Rhylfelour had long since retired. His mood had improved even more since whoring. Whatever his orcish mistresses did to him, it was foul enough that Genesta removed herself from the premises to avoid all stain and thought of it.

Remy bit his lip and hung his head as he rested one hand on the chest of the severely beaten boy. "I should've stopped him. I should have done something."

"Should you have?" Genesta asked with a rhetorical tone. "Likely, yes."

"But could I have?" Remy asked.

Ekai's chest rose and fell shallowly. A pall hung over those seated around the fire.

"You are trained, are you not? Do you believe yourself capable of killing Rhylfelour?" Genesta asked.

Remy nodded. "I believe I have the skill. More so now after killing Ogguhar. Orcs look intimidating, but they are neither more nor less fragile than any other species of tuatha."

"Then you have the power," Genesta said.

Remy tilted his head and furrowed his brow.

"No," Genesta said. "I don't mean some sort of special magic. I merely mean that you possess the *ability*. Although I do believe that the Dagda favors you, and he would likely expect you to exercise your gifts wisely. What I mean is this: having power is meaningless if you choose to never wield it."

A crow hopped out of the shadows from nearby. It gave a light-footed skip and moved closer to Remy and the boy under his care.

Remy frowned as he looked at Genesta. "But the oath? How can I act when I am bound?"

"Being oath bound is *not the same* as being impotent."

They sat together in silence for another few minutes. And then Ekai took a deep and ragged breath. It rattled as he exhaled, and then it stopped altogether.

Shadarkith wept, but he did so silently. Waking Rhylfelour or one of the warlords lieutenants would only earn him further stripes.

Remy's jaw set and he gritted his teeth. Anger welled enough for the orc warlord that he would gladly commit the murder were it within the bounds of his oath.

The crow took two hops closer to the body and looked at Remy. It blinked inquisitively.

"No, Corax. This one is not for you. I will bury him properly and respectfully."

Corax uttered a quiet chirp and then flapped his wings, flying off to wherever it was he nested at night.

Remy reached for a shovel which leaned nearby and then scooped up Rhylfelour's latest victim.

Genesta asked, "Do you want to be someone's slave all your life, or are you willing to fight?"

As Remy laid the child over his shoulder, his brother mumbled again, "I kept trying to tell him…"

"No," Remy insisted to Shadarkith. Passion bled ragged heat into his voice. "Ekai did the right thing. He was stronger than you or I. He resisted." He squeezed the haft of the spade shovel and headed for the gates so we could find softer soil to bury the child under. As he went, he spoke another oath, this one to himself. "Rhylfelour will die… and somehow, oaths be damned, it shall be by my hand."

Chapter Four

Remy awoke with a start.

Genesta gasped nearby. Her back stiffened as if taken by a seizure and her eyes moved rapidly beneath their lids.

Remy rushed over and grabbed her, draping his body across hers so that no onlookers would see her caught in the ecstasy of a vision. Seers could not simply look into the future and at will—portents came upon them when they were triggered. Every seer was different and not everyone experienced visions the same way.

So far as he knew, none of those with the gift of future-sight could rely on perfect accuracy. They saw potential, probably scenarios, and often knew what futures were most likely based on changing events.

Remy only knew that the warlord would demand whatever knowledge he could gain from her, even when the elf was loath to give it. Holding it back was the only way left for her to fight him.

"What's happening to her?" asked Shadarkith.

Remy hissed, shushing him. "Quiet. Don't let anyone see."

Shadarkith goose stepped closer and watched as Remy cradled the shivering elf. "She... she's a seer? One of the aes sidhe?"

Rare as that gift was, people must have spoken enough of it amongst the human wildfolk for Shadarkith to correctly identify Genesta's condition.

"Say nothing. She does not want the warlord to know when the sight comes on her."

A few minutes later, with the morning light cresting on the horizon, Genesta blinked and looked up at Remy. "Rhylfelour's plan... it is working. I have seen it. Over and over... Many different futures, and in all of them, the spider queen, Queen Rhagathena, offers Rhylfelour what he wants."

Remy found a nearby jug of water and offered it to her.

She drank thirstily, and then continued. "She is troubled. Something is..." Her eyes searched the clouds as if she tried to find words to describe countless unspeakable visions. Words were so seldom useful when trying to describe things seen in the dreamscape. "Something is eating her power like locusts devouring a field. She will offer Rhylfelour the throne in exchange for a great task."

The door to Rhylfelour's stronghold swung open with a loud sound. The orc warlord emerged and looked directly at the motley collection.

Before anymore could be overheard, Genesta looked at Remy. "He will put this task upon you." And then she clammed up.

Rhylfelour stomped over to his pets. "Where is the stubborn one? The obstinate child?"

Remy's eyes remained downcast. "He died last night. You may check with your guards; I buried him beyond the walls."

The orc chuffed a sigh of disappointment, but then he shrugged. "Whatever refuses to bend must be broken. If folk will not be made useful for battle, they'll be good for fertilizer."

It took every ounce of will for Remy to hold his ground and his tongue. He'd earned enough goodwill from the warlord these last several years, and all of it was currency he'd saved up. Some day he would cash it in to purchase for the murder of Rhylfelour. *But now is not the time*, Remy told himself. *The strike must be perfect; it cannot miss.*

Rhylfelour turned his gaze to the remaining brother. His voice was deep and menacing. "What about you, little ddiymadferth? Will you be a useful tool?"

Shadarkith immediately burst out in tears. He visibly tried to stop them from coming, tried to control himself, but could not. Remy assumed that while he was away, Shadarkith had learned what Remy had at his age: tears earned orcish beatings.

"Your elf is a seer," he offered up.

Remy set his jaw, but feigned ignorance.

"Is she, now?" Rhylfelour asked. "How do you know?"

The fact that Genesta was aes sidhe was not common knowledge. Shadarkith did not know, but Rhylfelour had killed others who were far stronger when they'd discovered her secret.

"Did she say something?" Rhylfelour asked.

Shadarkith nodded. Tears dripped off his nose. "She said... she said that you would take the throne and be offered the crown."

The news made Rhylfelour smile, but he'd already known that his daily actions brought him one step closer to that possibility.

"She said that it was a certainty and that the spider queen would seek you out soon," Shadarkith continued.

"That is excellent news." Rhylfelour turned and headed back for his home. "Someone will be by to feed you momentarily," he promised Shadarkith.

Remy kept his face neutral. He could not blame the child for breaking, but it unnerved him that Shadarkith could be flipped so easily.

Shadarkith practically melted onto the ground, whimpering and wallowing in his weakness. But he was thankful that a small mercy was on its way—at least he would eat.

Remy stared daggers at the orc's backside as he departed.

In the distance someone yelled, "Rider approaching!"

And in the distance, Corax bellowed a caw, greeting the sun.

The messenger was a stern looking unseelie sidhe. The elf's ears ended in sharp points, and his dark eyes surveyed everything within the warlord's courtyard.

He remained atop his horse and in the saddle. He'd not even dismounted to speak with Rhylfelour. He merely heralded the queen's coming.

Rhylfelour waited for her upon the stairs. He'd already taken the precaution of locking his aes sidhe prisoner within the walls of his harem. Remy and Shadarkith stood near the edge of the yard. The young boy's eyes grew wide as two long lines of soldiers clomped their way into the innermost ring of Rhylfelour's domain. Clad in plate armor, they provided a barrier against threats to the spider queen.

Remy stood on his toes to see the procession. Shadarkith climbed a small crate to do the same.

An oversized carriage drawn by two chargers pulled into the center of the courtyard, and only then did the elven herald crawl down from his horse. He approached the coach and opened the large double doors.

Remy watched as a gorgeous elf woman emerged from the carriage.

She had raven hair and large eyes; there were no sclera to them. They were black and shone like polished agates. Glinting light from the late morning rays sparkled on those orbs, reflecting like the diamond-shaped scales hanging from the chain around her neck. The chest pieces barely covered her ample bosom.

The unseelie realm was always cold, but the temperature did not seem to bother her, despite her immodest garb. Then Queen Rhagathena emerged more fully. Where the hips and legs of a normal sidhe female would have been, the rest of her monstrous body begun.

Like some sort of centaur's terrible dream, she had the body of a giant spider. Motuled blacks and reds streaked down her thorax and to the tips of her legs, which terminated in sharp points.

Her herald bowed low, and Rhagathena grinned. Her mouth was filled with dainty points, much like feline incisors. However, they hid behind a captivating smile that quirked playfully. Her face tempted Remy to ignore Rhagathena's lower half.

She needs no web with a smile like that, Remy realized. She should have been terrifying, but she was somehow tempting, despite her visage.

Her herald announced her. "Presenting Queen Rhagathena, Ruler of the Rime Throne and the unseelie, Lady of Arctig Maen, and Anansi of the Spinefrost Ridge, mistress of the N'arache-folk."

Rhagathena turned her attention to Rhylfelour. "My dear warlord, I have sought you out with great intention and for a specific purpose. Will you invite me in?"

Rhylfelour kept himself calm and collected. Every word and every movement were premeditated. He may have been a bloodthirsty orc, but Rhylfelour had spent his life aiming for this specific audience. He'd devoted decades to educating himself with both knowledge of the realm and of social graces.

"Why, of course, my Queen? Won't you come and dine? You may find our service lacking somewhat here, at least compared to Hulda Thorne, or your court at Arctig Maen, but my staff shall make every effort to produce their finest."

Rhagathena gave a courtly nod and then approached the warlord. Only her personal attendant and two personal guards accompanied her. A few moments later, they entered the halls of Rhylfelour's fortress.

"What just happened?" Shadarkith asked.

Remy looked at him. He tried to keep the uncertainty from his face. "This is the beginning of the end. Everything up until now has been preparation for the game at hand."

Shadarkith did not understand that.

Remy did not bother explaining. Even if he had more specific knowledge as to Rhylfelour's aims, Shadarkith was barely more than a child and would not understand. Besides, he'd already proved himself untrustworthy with too much knowledge.

But the assassin knew: the warlord was more going to assign him a new task... a task for the queen. Probably several. Each would be a name, or a target.

Rhylfelour had shaped Remy into a weapon of death, and now he intended to use it. He would use Remy to acquire the thing that he wanted most: the hand of Rhagathena, the spider queen, and a seat that accompanied it—the Rime Throne.

Remy did not see Rhylfelour for two days. The orc had kept mostly out of sight as he reveled within the confines of his fortress. He'd never entertained such high-class members of the upper castes.

Rhagathena had invited a few of the noteworthy members of her court to call on them. They were mostly sidhe nobles. Unlike the seelie, so far as Remy knew, prominent houses were mostly directed by sidhe, but also included many creatures of all manner. Boggarts, trolls, goblins, and more made-up strange collections in the unseelie hierarchy of nobles.

Elves were fewer in the domain of the Winter Court than in their seelie counterpart, but that lesser number commanded an equal amount of power—concentrating it more in the hands of those sidhe allies who had sided with the winter court during the great schism: the ancient war fought between the fey forces and those of the infernal domain, the forces of Hell. The creatures of the seelie kingdom had sided with the fiendish outsiders.

The ancient alliances no longer existed, but it was not difficult to imagine how the unseelie forces aligned with the infernals in temperament and goals. Not that the summer court was much better, but they'd resisted the thralls of Hell and now guarded the fiendish gates. They kept alive the arcane seals that repelled the infernal princes by refreshing them with the sacrifice of the teind, the Hell Tithe.

The spider queen had left earlier on the second day, along with the Elven nobles who brought friends and vassals to call on the warlord. Rhagathena's departure had rendered all of Rhylfelour's underlings mute for the time being.

He'd gathered his forces, but everyone awaited his next word. Finally, the orc emerged and summoned his most trusted lieutenants. That included Remy.

"My fellow tuatha," he said with an uncharacteristic smile, "and my token human, in two days we ride for the enclave. I've sent a summons for the other orc chiefs of the Demonsbreak."

Rhylfelour surveyed the faces of those gathered. None made any presumption to understand what he was talking about. They knew what the enclave was. It was the ancestral meeting location for the orcish clan leaders, and also a council gathering. But none knew why he was calling for it.

"The queen has need of me. She requires the strength of my arms. It has come to her attention that I've been trying to unify all the orc clans under one banner."

Rhylfelour gave a nod of acknowledgment towards Remy. "Thanks to my corpse bird, I am one ring away from that becoming a reality and from my empire becoming critically useful to the Rime Throne."

"What does the queen require of the Broken Hand Clan?" one of the orcs asked.

"Her borders have been harassed of late... not the usual fighting between Oberon's border guard and hers. There have been roving gangs of bandits from the faewylds and the roads near their post in the Selvages. The heaviest activity comes from the lands near Krogga," the warlord spat.

Krogga was the only remaining orc. He commanded the Severed Foot Clan.

"Apparently, Chief Krogga has proved reluctant to hunt down those wildfey responsible." Rhylfelour glanced slowly around the room.

Remy gulped. It did not take an expert to see the implications. Krogga's lands were nearest the roads closest to the seelie passage. Severed Foot was the gateway to the Selvages: the no-man's-land between the realms of the winter and summer courts. A giant chasm stretched for much of it. On both sides of the rift, the region was technically part of the faewylds.

If Rhagathena wanted to bring a major force through there, it made sense that she would want to clear the area of any third-party interference. Many bridges crossed the chasm and regulated traffic going between, those passageways were guarded by garrisons on either side. Remy also believed bandits were choking supply lines between Hulda Thorne and those defensive outposts.

Remy crossed his arms and listened to the warlord prattle on about his dreams for orc-kind to emerge to dominance alongside the sidhe in the unseelie courts. The human didn't buy it. Everything about the spider queen set his teeth on edge and triggered every danger sense he possessed.

He imagined Chief Krogga also saw what he did: most likely, Queen Rhagathena wanted to reignite the old wars with Oberon. Another conflict would only mean the death of orcs. Lots of orcs. The Severed Foot was closest to the front lines, and they would likely see the heaviest losses.

Of course, Krogga won't hunt down a bunch of wildfey bandits—those fey are probably the last few folk holding back a full-blown war from developing.

Rhylfelour barked something at Remy which he didn't understand. The human turned his attention to the warlord and cocked his head.

"Be prepared, my death bird," the orc told him. "This time, Chief Krogga will yield, or he shall meet your crows."

Remy nodded.

The human may have admired Krogga for his resistance to the pressures of the warlord, but Remy had little say in the matter. If Rhylfelour ordered him to kill the last orc chief, he would have to obey that command or die in his refusal... And Remy could never fulfill his promise to himself if he was dead.

Remy would do whatever he had to do in order to stay alive until that time... until the moment was right. Then could he kill Rhylfelour.

Chapter Five

The trip to the Demonsbreak enclave did not begin for several days. Prior to that, much of it was spent packing and preparing. They had to give time for the messengers to deliver their summons for the enclave to the other orc warlords.

Orcish territories were scattered mostly on the west side of the winter court's capitol, Hulda Thorne. Rhagathena's royal stronghold, Arctig Maen, was at the city's center. Their proximity to the front lines for any future battle against Oberon and the forces of Summer's court was the first and most obvious reason Remy suspected the Sspider queen was manipulating Rhylfelour. Not that Remy cared, except that the orc had wrapped him up so tightly in oaths and duty that there would be no escape for Remy if Rhylfelour's forces were suddenly directed to open combat against the seelie kingdom.

Rhylfelour stood in the morning sky five days after dispatching his messengers. He summoned one of his smiths to bring a flaming brand. Orcs held down Shadarkith and Rhylfelour pressed the red-hot iron against his flesh.

He'd decided at the last minute to brand the young human because of the enclave. If ever there would be a time when planning escape was ideal, it would be when the most talented members of the clan's army were away.

The child screamed in agony. His howls fell upon deaf ears and even Remy turned his face away. He could afford for Rhylfelour to believe that he cared about the plight of the young one—or anyone, in fact.

"Take care of this whelp," Rhylfelour barked at one of the orcish whores standing in the courtyard.

Remy had seen their "care." Those females were anything but maternal. The females dragged the boy into their charge as Rhylfelour and his inner circle mounted their horses.

This enclave was important, and Rhylfelour was not about to go without his prized possession: the Elvish seer.

The procession rode out with minimal pomp and circumstance. Corax and his wing-mates followed Remy, flying overhead, and watching greedily as the army of Rhylfelour's best one hundred troops passed beyond the outer palisade gates of the warlord's domain.

Rhylfelour was a realist. He put little stock in ceremony and ritual, except for when it served a purpose. His intentions for this enclave were single fold. Either the orc clans unified under his rule, or he would destroy those who dissented. The outcome would be the same either way.

After several hours in the saddle, the line of travelers thinned and stretched. It split into small clusters of travelers who talked, or in some cases fought.

So long as Genesta stayed within earshot of Rhylfelour, she had enough free rein to ride beside Remy.

"The bastard decided to brand the child anyway," Remy noted once he felt confident they could speak plainly.

Genesta nodded. "He will train the child much as he did you, but the boy presents a greater opportunity."

Remy cocked his head.

"He is one of your kind. Shadarkith is a son of Adam, a human. Rhylfelour suspects you have some kind of baseline affinity for him—at least a desire to protect him from harm," Genesta said.

"Damn it," Remy said. He sighed, knowing the orc was correct. "That makes things more difficult."

Genesta stared at him until he continued his reasoning to its conclusion.

Remy said plainly, "He'll make sure that I obey every command, and not just to the letter of the law, as is fey tradition, but the spirit of the law. Even when I perform Rhylfelour's commands, if he does not like *how* I carry them out, he will injure the child. And even if I die trying to please the orcish bastard, he will have trained my replacement in the meantime."

Genesta nodded solemnly. "You've spoken truly."

He looked at her and caught a glimmer in her eyes, which she tried to hide. "You've seen something. What is it?"

"What you described... You are right. It certainly *will* lead to the death of you." She looked at him just as one of the warlord's lieutenants began writing towards them to prevent this sort of intermingling. "The warlord's orders will certainly get you killed." She whispered the last part, "unless you kill him first."

And then one of the orcish handlers assigned to Genesta made her tighten the distance she kept with Rhylfelour, moving her too near for them to speak candidly.

It took several more days for the procession to reach the enclave. As they approached, they spotted other similar large gatherings on the distant horizon. Each of the tribes sent their strongest warriors as escorts for their chieftains and they sized each other up as they collectively arrived for the assembly.

Legions of orcs from different factions camped in the larger circle around the enclave's meeting space. Warriors met to wrestle each other, pitting the strength of tribe versus tribe; orcs bet on their peers, or against them, for sport.

At the bottom of the gentle slope, several pillars had been erected in the valley. Runes covered them, devoting one of each of the twelve monuments to the different orc tribes.

The enclave operated by ancient rules, and each convoy could send in only twelve representatives from each faction. The number was significant to the creatures, as were their clan names. Collectively, they were called the Demonsbreak in honor of the event which had spawned the tribes' creation.

Rhylfelour led the Broken Hand. The recently deceased Ogguhar had been from Fractured Skull, and Chief Krogga led Severed Foot.

As they passed the boundary of the stones, Rhylfelour brandished an ancient, withered hand that had been tied to a lanyard. He hung it around his neck. The macabre symbol was a marker of a great victory won by the orcs in ancient times. The engraved symbols on each clan leader's signet ring depicted the body part a clan was named after—that was the source of any true power: their ownership of a demonic cadaver that was hacked to pieces long ago by their ancestors, hence the name of Demonsbreak.

Remy glanced at Rhylfelour's trophy. What the orcs accomplished in ancient times had been a legendary feat. They had still been strong allies with the seelie during the infernal wars, albeit reluctantly, and they'd fought against the demonic invaders.

One of Hell's princes had laid waste to the battlefield and nearly wiped them off the map, but the orcs had rallied and charged the enemy. When all was said and done, only twelve orcs remained. They stood above their felled enemy and hacked apart his smoldering remains. Each took one twelfth of his body as a trophy.

While there were several groups of orcs living as wildfey, the twelve orc tribes of the unseelie drew their origins to that battle.

Each of the groups dismounted as they passed their tribe's signal stone.

Remy watched Rhylfelour glower at chief Krogga, his enemy. In the early days, the species had a basic respect for each other and followed a tribal code of conduct. It insured fair treatment amongst their kind, even if it permitted barbaric activities against outsiders.

But now? The species had become entrenched in winter court politics over the generations. Ever deeper betrayals worsened relationships, and great brutalities drove rifts between the clans.

Rhylfelour was the worst offender.

The dozen smaller parties assembled at the very heart of the enclave where a bonfire had been built. At the head of each walked the tribal chief, also known as Warlord. Their lesser officers and advisers walked behind them as the twelve came together.

A nervous-looking orc from Fractured Skull glanced around. He bowed his head and wilted slightly at the sight of Rhylfelour.

"Ogguhar's successor, no doubt?" Rhylfelour suggested. He vainly turned his new ring a full circle upon his finger. "Your predecessor resisted an oath of fealty. I trust you will not make that same mistake?"

A defiant fire seemed to light in the young orc's eyes. Before he could open his mouth to say anything, Corax descended from the clouds and perched upon Remy's shoulder. The bird looked greedily from creature to creature.

The emissary from Fractured Skull gulped at the site. "The death bird," he said. "So, the rumors are true?"

Rhylfelour nodded slowly. "Aderyn Corff is one of mine."

The newcomer bowed his head slightly and agreed to a tribute as Rhylfelour's vassal.

Remy looked around at the orcs within the inner circle of the enclave. They traded knowing looks with each other. Rhylfelour had been the last to arrive, and apparently Ogguhar's replacement had spread rumors of the cursed crow who had marked the former chief for death prior to his murder.

Krogga hissed. Of all the others assembled, he was the only other leader besides Rhylfelour to still wear a ring. "This whole charade is ridiculous. What is the meaning of calling an enclave?" Krogga demanded.

"One purpose, and one alone," Rhylfelour said. "To insist that the twelve unify as one body under my rule."

Krogga chuffed with a derisive sort of laughter. He leaned forward and annunciated carefully. "No."

The other orcs stared at their feet with awkward silence. They each owed too much to the would-be-king.

"Then you leave us no choice," Rhylfelour said. "You should leave the enclave and relinquish your hold over those demonic remains. Go. Take your clan and go your separate way. Head for the faewylds, or delve the dvergr tunnels or contend with the trow for all I care."

Krogga stared hard at Rhylfelour. He narrowed his gaze and said it again. "No." His words were adamant, and his eyes were burned.

"No?"

"Are you deaf, you half-breed son of a ddiymadferth whore?" Krogga leveled an insult. "I said no. You may think you're tough.

But you've got no stones, boy. You're a twisty snake in the grass, playing the spider queen's game of shells and shadows. Dealing daggers and favors in the dark. Broken Hand has forgotten the strength of our kind and traded it for favors. You've aspirations for the throne... but Severed Foot remembers. We remember our strength and what we are."

Rhylfelour leveled an accusatory glare. "And what is that?"

Krogga grinned. "Survivors."

"Flippant, given my resources," Rhylfelour threatened, shooting a glance to Remy... to Aderyn Corff.

"All I need to do is outlast you," Krogga hissed. "And then the orcish enclave will return to what it was before you corrupted our body."

"I offered you peace," Rhylfelour roared. "All you need to do is leave your trophy and ring behind, and you have my guarantee that Severed Foot can depart unmolested just like any other wildfey."

In response, Krogga held aloft the shriveled foot and lower leg of the ancient infernal prince that had once decimated their ancestors. "This? No. The foot remains where it belongs... and it will stay there until you're long eaten by worms."

Krogga turned with his entourage and stomped away.

"Give it to me," Rhylfelour roared.

The remaining orcish holdout bellowed, "Over my dead body!"

Rhylfelour and the other warlords watched Krogga go, and he muttered below his breath, "So be it."

The orc clenched his hand into a fist and turned to Remy. "You heard him. You know my desire, human. Bring me the head and the ring of Warlord Krogga. Severed Foot must be brought into the fold." Rhylfelour looked to the sky and spotted the full moon beginning its rise. "I don't care what it takes—but end that creature's life by the next full moon. Swear this to me."

Remy scowled and clenched his jaw. He caught sight of the subtle nod that Genesta gave him.

He closed his eyes and sighed, focusing on the task at hand—becoming the killer, a man of singular, deadly focus. He opened them again as Aderyn Corff. Shifting into the olde tongue he said, [I swear it.]

Remy followed the war chief as he departed the enclave. Given the nature of how things had gone at the orc gathering, Severed Foot's security was extremely high.

Shadowing them from a distance, Remy made certain he was not seen. If anything, Krogga's most trusted lieutenants only ever spotted the circling of crows as the human tracked them.

Remy assumed that Corax learned to discern the assassin's target based on the amount of focus he'd put upon him. He knew that crows were smart... But he never figured that would translate to some sort kind of death mark once Rhylfelour unleashed him upon a target.

The return took twice as long as expected, but Krogga finally arrived safely within his own region. Here, Remy's nerves were on high alert for danger. The slightest discovery would likely lead to the human's death.

Remy had no intention of dying for the warlord who had enslaved him. Not unless it also bought Rhylfelour's death.

For six days, Remy watched Krogga's village. It was not all that different from Rhylfelour's domain, although instead of resting upon hillock, it was in a large forest glade. Trees were long ago clear-cut except for several large and ancient arbors which had been rimmed with lumber and turned into towers to form lookouts. Pike-topped palisade walls as they stretched between thick trunks.

Each day, Remy slinked between copses of old growth until he could find a tree tall enough to climb. He did not find any discernible defensive patterns for which to exploit, as he had on his last mission.

In the absence of weaknesses, he looked for a different approach. Remy stayed another week watching each night. The orc chieftain's guards remained ever vigilant, even in the early hours.

Krogga's house was stately but small. He was not a creature prone to opulence. His indulgences were small and negligible, and he kept neither harem nor entourage for his own pleasure. Half a dozen small shacks, each a guardhouse, provided quarters for his protectors. Those tiny structures formed a ring around their warlord's home. At least one soldier remained awake and tasked with Krogga's personal protection at all times.

What Remy did find was that chief Krogga arose about the same time every night to avoid his bladder bowels. There was a small, fenced area hiding a midden heap inside that highly secure zone.

Remy knew that he had found his best chance to complete his mission.

With stealth like a cat, Remy descended his lookout tree.

Finding his way through the dark, he returned to his own small encampment. The human planned to sleep through most of the day and then carry out Rhylfelour's orders, returning on the following night.

He found his camp and noticed the small string line that he'd run to alert him of intruders was down.

Remy crept through the underbrush, which provided a visual barrier and kept out most animals. Just within, he spotted his small canvas tent. It had been trampled into the ground. His horse, what remained of it, lay dead at the center where a small fire had been built. Remy did not build fires when he was trying to remain unseen.

A cluster of tiny elf-like creatures huddled around Remy's horse. They were covered in blood and gore, and they tore heaps of flesh off the poor horse. Greedily, they chomped and gulped down mouthfuls of horse meat, either tearing pieces free with their hands or using their sharp, jagged teeth to bite chunks free. One of the vile, bearded little men removed his hat and rolled it around in the pooling blood to freshen its deep rouge.

Powries, Remy cursed to himself. Known by most simply as redcaps, the horrible little folk were a kind of goblin creature. They looked like weathered, elderly humans, except that they stood no taller than Remy's waist. In addition to their telltale hats, they wore boots made with iron straps that held the iron soles of their shoes in place. They were one of the few fey-folk who could touch the stuff.

Iron inflicted such pain on the rest of the tuatha that the sidhe lords, Oberon of the seelie, his long-lost brother Wulflock who had led the unseelie, and even Mab of the faewylds, had decreed it a crime against Arcadeax itself to use the stuff to harm another.

But redcaps were cranky little bastards. They didn't care about royal decrees and barely observed laws. They practically enjoyed the scorn others heaped upon them and gave it right back tenfold. However, redcaps were likely to use their iron boots to leave a mark no fey victim could ever forget.

Remy didn't know if it was true, but he'd heard that pain inflicted upon the fey by iron never healed and never stopped burning. It wasn't a concern for a human, except that he knew if he used a ferrous weapon, he'd be hunted down by every empire and tortured for his crimes.

He reached past the thorny hedges and retrieved one of the pikestaffs these creatures typically wielded. They boasted a jagged triangle of iron at the tip.

The redcaps didn't spot him. They were too engrossed in their gluttonous orgy of blood and meat. One by one, Remy stole their weapons and hid them behind the spiny bracken. And then, snatching the last one, Remy took up that last spear and rushed into the circle.

Placing the sharp tip against the throat of the enemy he believed to be their leader, based purely upon the size of his cap, Remy backed the creature up against the fire. The other goblins rushed around looking for the weapons but found none.

"Hold. Easy boys," the powrie leader told his crew. He made hand motions to calm them. "If the long shanks wanted us dead, he'd have cut my throat by now."

"Your name," Remy demanded, tensing his posture as he gripped the shaft of the redcap's weapon.

"Redcomb," he said. "I take it this was your horse?"

Remy narrowed his gaze. He had heard of this redcap. He was considered a warrior in his own right and something of a hero to all powrie-kind. By most metrics, he was a simple raider and an occasional mercenary. The human's heart twinged. There are many who might say the same thing about him.

"I have heard of you," Remy said.

Redcomb's gaze lifted and noted Corax as the bird descended and found a perch on the sturdy shrubs. Two other crows followed suit, and Corax watched the scene with greedy eyes.

Recognition dawned on Redcomb's face. "And I have heard of you, Aderyn Corff. Heard ye been killing orcs."

Remy nodded to acknowledge him.

"You have me at a disadvantage. Ye've gotten the better of me and after I have incurred a debt by eating your horse." Using only his eyes, Redcomb stopped one of his powrie followers who tried creeping up on Remy's blind spot. "I said stop it, boys. He ain't a fey, and your boots will do no good."

The human glanced aside at the presumptuous goblin. The powrie seem to pout, but backed off.

"Then let us discuss repayment," Remy said.

Redcomb nodded, and Remy set aside the weapon. The fey took matters of settling debt very seriously, and if the goblin admitted one was owed, it took precedence over anything else.

"I'm willing to strike a deal that absolves you of your debt," Remy told him. "I need information about the Severed Foot clan, camped yonder."

The powrie captive spat. He obviously had no love for orcs. "We may be able to strike a bargain... I'm eager to, in fact."

"Excellent. If we reach an accord, I shall even return to you your weapons," Remy said.

Eager to make a binding packed which would restore their defenses to them, Redcomb switched to the old tongue. [Tell us what you require.]

Thanks to the information gained from Redcomb, Remy had learned about secret paths into the orc village. The redcaps had their bone to pick with the orcs and had also been scouting the area.

Krogga had been on high alert since the enclave. While his personal security detail remained ever vigilant, the same was not the case for the average member Severed Foot clan. Apathy had crept in enough that it would allow Remy a certain amount of invisibility if he'd tried to sneak past.

The redcaps routinely raided small storerooms, and supply shacks, belonging to the orcs. Several months back, one of Redcomb's kin had been killed when a soldier found him trespassing there.

Redcomb normally operated on the south-most side of the unseelie, but he and his forces were in the area looking to wreak havoc as retribution for his kinsman. Once learning of Remy's intentions, he gladly partnered with the human.

Presently, Remy slinked through the shadows and narrow passageways between lean to's and all shacks. Even the highest quality orc villages were only pale imitations of the elaborate structures commissioned by the sidhe lords. It had been considered extravagant when Rhylfelour hired dwarven masons, the coroniaid cousins of the dvergr, to construct his private residence. The quality between orcish and dwarven craftsmanship was not even on the same spectrum.

Remy was almost afraid to bump into the stick buildings as he snuck between them and into the darkened alleys. After skulking through several maze-like passages and ducking out of view from some late night revelers, he was able to arrive unseen near Krogga's domicile.

Hiding behind one of the smaller dormers, Remy approached the guard who was on duty from behind. Remy managed such stealth that he'd approached quieter than a whispering breeze. He locked an arm around the guard's neck from behind.

All of Krogga's guards were massive, muscular things. Remy was thicker and much stronger than most sidhe—only the strongest of elves could have surpassed him. But an orc? They were typically on par when it came to brute force—and often even stronger.

The guard might have grabbed his attacker and turned the tables if Remy had not dragged a razor-sharp blade across his throat. Remy's grapple was mostly meant to gently lay the eliminated soldier on the ground with as little noise as possible.

He dragged the body into the darkness a moment after. One by one, he crept into the quarters of the guards and made sure they would never awaken. And then he vanished into the shadows and waited.

Nearly an hour had passed while the human assassin stood motionless within the black. And then he heard the gentle sounds of footfalls as they moved lazily towards him. The shambler who made them was obviously half-asleep.

Remy saw the dull yellow of Krogga's eyes. Hiding behind half drooping lids, they reflected the brilliant moonlight.

The chieftain walked so close from him that Remy could have reached out and touched him. Instead, he let Krogga shuffle past and turn to squat over the midden heap.

After, Krogga's eyes opened wide when they spotted the silver glint of Remy's keen blade beneath the night sky.

Krogga had no obvious weapons on him. He backed up against the privacy fence, unprotected and alone.

"They cannot hear you," Remy said. "They're all dead."

"You. You are the one that the other, foolish tuatha call the Corpse Bird. Rhylfelour holds your reins."

Remy offered him a dour smile. "I suppose that is true, in a sense."

Krogga asked, "And you are here for my ring and my life." He'd not phrased it is a question. It was a foregone conclusion.

The old orc, seemingly out of nowhere, pulled a blade. It was nearly identical to Remy's... it was a dúshlán.

Remy dropped into a defensive crouch and pulled his own, but the enemy warlord did not attack with his. Instead, he stared at his blade as if wishing the runes etched upon them would glow.

"Pity," Krogga said. "I suppose this means your master is nowhere nearby."

"Rhylfelour?" Remy stared at the blade. "Your dúshlán is linked to Rhylfelour?"

Krogga nodded resolutely, and then he tossed the blade to the grass between him and the assassin.

"You're not even going to fight me?" Remy asked.

The venerable orc shrugged. "I've been fighting a long time, lad. Seems my life has been nothing but fighting and waiting."

Remy flashed him an inquisitive look. "Waiting?"

"For the return of the King. Rhagathena is a pretender to the Rime Throne. She is no true queen. Someday, the true unseelie king will return. King Wulflock: Brother of Oberon and protector of the realm."

Remy cut the distance between them by half. Krogga did not react. The human retrieved the orc's dúshlán blade.

"Do it then, lad. I'll even spare you some of the trouble of looting my corpse." Krogga turned his head to the fence and spotted a crow perched there, waiting for the kill. The orc frowned, twisted his ring, and removed it from his finger. He tossed it to Remy.

"You also carry one of the mystic blades?" Krogga asked, recognizing the weapon in Remy's hand.

The human nodded.

"As owner of a dúshlán you know the burden that comes with bearing one."

Remy shrugged. "Actually, I do not. I know this blade cries out for blood... But I know not whose it belongs to. My memories were taken from me when I stumbled into this realm from another. I was a mere child. It's how I came to be forced into Rhylfelour's service."

The orc's brows rose. "So, you do not serve him willingly?"

Slowly, Remy shook his head. "Were I not oath bound, I would have killed him already."

Krogga grinned. "Then perhaps your presence is tied to my own fate... to my own revenge. Unless you seek to prosper your patron?"

Remy shook his head again. "He *will* die... and by my own hand."

"Will you make me a promise, then?"

The human narrowed his gaze.

"My dúshlán," he said. "Satisfy its hunger. It yearns for Rhylfelour's blood as much as you do. Rhylfelour will die by your hand... yet by *my* blade."

Remy drew the orc's dúshlán from its scabbard. In it, he could feel the weight of all Rhylfelour's evil—of every murder and rape, of every robbery and wrongdoing, tied up in the person of that beastly warlord. In creating a dúshlán for him, Arcadeax itself had pledged that Rhylfelour deserved death.

The human nodded with grim determination.

And then Krogga drew down the neck of his shirt to expose the arteries of his neck and he kept his eyes closed as Remy approached. He would never open them again.

Remy approached, blade drawn... But in his mind, he imagined that the life he took that night belonged to his real enemy: Rhylfelour, chief of the Broken Hand orcs.

A harsh cry of a crow split the night and hundreds of the carrion birds flew through the dusky sky, answering Corax's call to the feast. The late patrols of the Severed Foot guards shook as they heard the cawing and watched the birds fly past.

An orc suggested they check on their chief. And then a watchtower rang alarm bells near the front gates.

One orcish body tumbled over the edge of his post and fell to the main gate's road as a trio of redcaps anointed their hats with the fresh blood of a kill. They threw a lever to release a counterweight, and the doors opened wide.

"Another redcap," barked an orcish guard. "This time there are three of them." He drew his sword.

And then, through the gates, poured a small horde of the diminutive creatures. They rushed inside the palisade walls with their iron tipped weapons. Bloodthirsty powries rushed into the fray.

Orcs howled in pain as the tiny raiders slashed and burned flesh with their illegal, caustic metal weapons. Somewhere, a brazier overturned, and embers scattered towards the sky. Several huts caught fire, and the blaze grew rapidly.

The sounds and scents of battle spread everywhere. Chaos took hold as the churning cloud of hungry carrion birds sewed confusion.

Before anyone could remember to check on Chief Krogga, a hooded figure mounted upon a stolen horse galloped through the churning streets. The figure originated from Krogga's home in the stronghold's inner circle.

Aderyn Corff flew past on the charger. Almost as quickly as he'd been spotted was he gone, leaving the Severed Foot clan encampment in the throes of flames, pain, and raw anarchy.

Chapter Six

Remy took his time riding back toward Rhylfelour's fortress. News traveled faster than horseback, anyway, and he assumed that word of Krogga's death might reach his master ahead of him.

He had little desire to return with haste. Something about the way Krogga had died weighed on Remy's heart and mind.

For all his faults—Krogga was no hero. None of the orc tribes could be considered bastions of charity or goodwill—yet, despite the problems Severed Foot Clan caused the powries and so many others, Krogga had met his end with a kind of noble grace. Remy had not seen that before, and he'd never expected to find anything admirable in an orc.

By the time Remy had returned to the Broken Hand territory, Corax had rejoined him at a distance, lazily pacing him in the sky. His two companions had gone elsewhere. Remy could not even guess where. It seemed like crows understood his words, but Remy did not speak crow.

The corpse bird arrived at Rhylfelour's inner sanctum, but the warlord was not there. Genesta met Remy there, but reported that

Rhylfelour had gone on to Arctig Maen to spend some time in the company of the spider queen. Shadarkith had been dragged along to continue his training at the hands of the orc.

"He wanted you to head for Rhagathena's castle and report once the deed was done," she said.

Remy raised an eyebrow. "He did not take you?"

She shook her head very subtly. "Just because Rhagathena is his ticket to the throne, that does not mean he trusts her."

He nodded. Rhylfelour kept strange company with his collection of non-orcish—and even seelie—vassals. But keeping his pet aes sidhe secret in the heart of the Winter Court would be too difficult a prospect.

Remy asked, "Did you foresee my task's successful outcome?"

Genesta shrugged. "I did not bother attempting to scry it, even."

He gave her a cockeyed look.

"Rhylfelour had left for Hulda Thorne well before it would have been possible to have concluded your business. But I believed you would succeed. And so did the warlord, for what it's worth." She gave him a far and away look. "You should leave immediately for Rhagathena's citadel."

"Why?" he asked. "What did you see?"

"Unclear," Genesta said, with a voice that indicated she was not fully present; she was still half dreaming. "But you should leave now. It may lead to… freedom."

He made her look at her. "Freedom?" he asked, looking for a clear answer.

"That's maybe an imperfect word…" She trailed off, looking for a better one, and then gave up. "But hurry."

Remy stared at her for a moment that grew ever more tense the longer he waited. He knew that pressing her for more information would be useless… Her future sight did not work like that.

Finally, he nodded, mounted the stolen horse, and then galloped away with his mount pointed for Arctig Maen.

Remy's horse drew ever nearer the massive city of Hulda Thorne. Its towering bastion walls made the wooden spiked palisade surrounding Rhylfelour's look like a child's plaything by comparison.

Hulda Thorne was surrounded by a frost sheened ring of massive white stones. Builders in King Wulflock's day had filled the spans between them with polished stonework that stretched to the sky. In the shadow of that mighty unseelie city, Remy stopped his horse.

Presently, he rode through the inconspicuous parts of the wilderness that led to the main road. The tangential trail had cut through a forest road, which provided Remy enough privacy to travel unmolested. But he was not so foolish as to think that the rest of his journey would be quite so easy.

Hooded as he was, he might be mistaken for any random sidhe male, albeit perhaps more muscular, especially in the chest. This close to the spider queen's lair, however, he expected to be outed as a human, and soon. Some members of the tuatha—especially the unseelie ones—might not care about his affiliations. If Rhylfelour had taught him anything, it was to always be prepared.

The human dragged his feet around the dirt of the trail until he found a few larger stones. Using the ones with flat sides, he dug a small trench and put the rocks inside to create a kind of box. He laid a spare dagger within it and then covered the hole with sticks, then leaves, and then a thin layer of scree and soil. He marked it with the stone and then returned to his horse. Remy had stashed several caches similar to these in places he frequented.

Remy looked up and spotted Corax hovering lazily in the clouds, and then he mounted his horse and then headed for the city.

After passing through its main gates and into the outer courts where the markets were, Remy pulled his hood tighter over his head to keep his rounded ears concealed. As he did so, he spotted a shop with a few runes engraved on the posts at the threshold.

Dismounting, he lashed his horse to a hitching post. Traffic bustled outside the small shop which, according to the engravings, traded in both information and in arcana. Despite travelers passing by, few went inside.

Remy wasn't sure what drew him in, but Corax had flown down and perched upon a signpost and pecked at its shingle. Sometimes Remy could have sworn that the bird was more than he appeared. Other times, he was convinced that the bird was merely a greedy little thing that knew Remy was his meal ticket.

The human looked down at a halfling child who loitered nearby. "Hey, kid. Watch my horse," he said, producing a silver coin and showing it to him. "Keep it safe and I'll give you this when I come out."

The child's eyes widened. They sparkled as they fixated on the coin.

Remy ducked inside and spotted an older sidhe. He had silver-streaked hair and knowing eyes that had a hunger for knowledge and a certain curiosity that conflicted with his apparent older age.

"I saw your symbols at the door," Remy said. "You trade in arcana?"

"Yes, yes," the elf said. "I am Fremenor, formerly of the aes sidhe."

Remy raised a brow. "You are seelie, then?"

Fremenor shrugged. "Yes, and no. I have renounced Summer and left a good post at the Radiant Tower." He seemed to catch Remy's inquisitive look and explained, "The Summer Court is not that much different from the unseelie, my friend. They are just as dangerous as any person trading lives for a position in the Spider queen's court."

"So, you were betrayed by Suíochán Naséan?" Remy asked, using the name of the wizard's tower commoners referred to as the Radiant Tower.

Fremenor nodded gently. "I was never a high-ranking maven, but I was talented in distilling the akasha. In fact, I helped design much of the systems that provided magic to the masses, at a price."

"Akasha?" Remy asked.

The elf wizard held up a small vial of glowing stuff and shook it. Remy couldn't ascertain if it was a fine powder or a liquid, but it seemed to radiate an aura of power.

As his eyes met Fremenor's. He got the distinct impression the old sidhe was only sharing this knowledge because Remy was human—not unseelie—the folk of Winter would never accept a human. That made Remy as much an outsider as Fremenor... And everybody needed allies.

"Most folk lack the ability to draw magic from its source—from Arcadeax. But magic is potent stuff, and offering it to the masses creates so many opportunities, and this allows any common folk access to magic. Usually, it's just to power low level mystic abilities. Minor prestidigitations and the like."

Remy raised an eyebrow as he looked at the stuff. "Like the magic woven into a scroll?"

Fremenor's eyes brightened. "Exactly like it. But rather than a scroll designed to cast a specific spell, the energy woven into the words that would power can be distilled into raw energy and used for various minor functions, like creating a light in the darkness or chilling a vat of wine." The elf picked up a tiny mechanical device half the size if his thumb. "Or like this gadget."

"What is it?" Remy asked.

Fremenor shrugged. "Just a bauble, really. The queen had me produce many of them. I guess they're used to light the torches in the royal citadel." He touched a thumb to a striker so that it linked to him, and then demonstrated. After dipping his index finger and thumb in the akasha, he set the thing down and snapped his fingers. It sparked like a striker.

The elf then clipped the device to a candle wick and repeated the operation. It lit the candle with barely any effort. "As I said, just a bauble. A toy for the rich, but it was a payday for me. I have half a dozen left over if you'd like to purchase one."

Remy's eyes narrowed shrewdly. He could see it coming in handy someday. "I'll take them all." He handed over some coin and placing the small bundle into his pouch. He wrapped them for safety along with a vial of akasha to power the minor spell.

A horse squealed outside, and Remy dashed out and into the street. He found the tiny child fighting against a pair of larger sidhe children who tried stealing Remy's horse. The halfling child, barely half the height of either of his opponents, charged and attacked them. Being rebuffed each time, the elves tried to snatch the horse's reins and abscond with it.

Remy chased the delinquent children off. They knew the game was lost as soon as they saw Remy and guessed that he owned the mare.

"You have that coin for me, mister?" the child panted. He dusted himself off as he stood and wiped away a trickle of blood from his nose and lip.

Remy nodded and tossed him the piece of silver. Then he mounted his ride and tossed the child two more identical coins.

The halfling scurried off happily as the human pointed his horse for the pathways leading deeper through Hulda Thorne. And then Remy spurred his mount ahead.

It was not long after passing through the tall white arches of Hulda Thorne's second wall that he was identified as a son of Adam.

"Ddiymadferth," a guard called. He drew a blade and stomped over to Remy, ripping the reins out of the man's hand.

"Don't you know humans are forbidden?"

Remy looked down his nose at the elf. "Forbidden from what?" He kept his voice neutral, even though he wanted to stab the cocky sidhe in the face.

Even if Remy didn't put any malice into his voice, the elf took issue with him, nonetheless. He signaled three of his fellows and they dragged Remy to the ground. They were not gentle with it.

"Ddiymadferth are not allowed to carry weapons within the city wall," the first of the guards snarled. "*Or* ride horses."

"Ha," quipped the second. "If he's not careful, we might just throw him in with the others of the Lightstarved."

Remy stared. He didn't know what the Lightstarved were, and he didn't have any time to ponder it.

The guards stripped him of his weapons, including both dúshláns and his sword. One of them yanked off his jacket and cloak. The others searched his flesh for marks of ownership; a brand or tattoo would indicate his slave status and who owned him. None of the elves had listened when he tried to explain that he was there at his master's behest and about the warlord's business.

Finally, when they were done abusing him and ready to listen, the first of the guards shook Remy and demanded, "Why is there no slaver's mark upon you, ddiymadferth?"

Remy bristled at the comment. "If you had listened to me," he did his best to keep his words even, "you would know to who I belong and what my businesses is."

The elf sneered and then sucker punched him. His trio of friends snickered and watched, clearly enjoying the show.

Remy stood stiffly. His nostrils flared, and he bared his teeth. He spoke again with carefully chosen words and an implacable calm. "Listen to me... you son of an elvish whore and a dvergr bastard. You will not attack me again or I shall see your blood and feed it to my crows." He hissed in the olde tongue, [I so swear it.]

The elf lost his composure. "How dare you, ddiymadferth!" He lunged for Remy. The human easily disarmed him, stealing the elf's weapon and then pressing the blade's edge to its owner's throat.

Startled, the other three guards readied their blades and postured as if to attack.

"Take one step and your friend is dead," Remy hissed. "I gave you a chance to listen. I am here on the business of Warlord Rhylfelour, who is a confidant of Queen Rhagathena and a friend of the unseelie court."

They still barely paid him any mind, and so Remy dragged the blade across his prisoner's neck ever so slightly. Blood trickled out in a thin stream. The elf screamed for his friends to stop.

"I am Aderyn Corff and I am here to report to Rhylfelour, a guest of Queen Rhagathena."

The elves all swallowed hard. They apparently recognized the name. *I guess Rhylfelour has been bragging me up,* Remy realized.

One of the guards ran off to dispatch the message. He returned a few minutes later with a royal servant from the castle at Hulda Thorne's center.

"Apologies," the sidhe servant said. "I shall escort you to the Queen herself."

Remy, still held his blade to the prisoner's neck. He replied, "I am here for Warlord Rhylfelour. If possible, and if the Queen permits it, I would very much like to report to Rhylfelour on my most recent mission. This was the last order given to me, and I must comply."

The elf fixed him with a narrow gaze and then nodded curtly. "Please follow me."

Remy thanked him. And then he remembered the promise he had just made. Here, he was not a mere human. He was Aderyn Corff. By invoking a connection to the orc warlord, he represented the empire of the violent orc chieftain. That role carried a certain weight and obligation to act on Rhylfelour's interests, just as the orc would.

As an emissary of Rhylfelour and the Broken Hand clan, he had to uphold the warlord's image. He cut the throat of the elf who had sighted him. Blood sprayed skyward as the guard shrieked and then collapsed.

The vassal from the castle tilted his head and merely stared as the elven sentry crumpled in a gurgling heap of shaking limbs and made a mess in the growing pool of blood.

"Was that necessary?" the servant asked.

Remy glared at the three elves, who gave the human a fearful look. "It was. An insult upon the warlord's messenger is an insult upon him," Remy said. His words resonated like shifting ice. He was in the heart of the beast, and he knew the seriousness of social games that played out in the halls of the sidhe courts.

The queen's envoy bobbed his head in recognition. Remy's words were true, and he might have been taken less seriously had he not insisted on defending his master's honor.

"You have my property." Remy glared at two of the three remaining elves.

Remy held his arms out at his side, forcing the guards to dress him as if they were his valets. They replaced his belt, and the two stolen dúshláns, affixing one to each side before stepping back quickly. The human was well within his right to revisit upon them the abuses they'd offered him.

Instead, he merely sneered at them, cowing the arrogant guards, who now averted their eyes.

"Right this way, then," the royal servant said. He turned to one of the frightened sidhe sentries and muttered quietly, "Clean that mess up."

"No." Remy overruled him. "I made a promise. You may dispose of them after the crows have had their fill."

"Crows?" the queen's servant asked.

Remy nodded. After taking a few steps away from the body, Corax descended and took a few hopping steps towards the corpse. Bouncing forward until he landed atop the dead elf, he let out a loud caw, and then a swell of carrion birds thickened overhead. The murder dissented and joined Corax in the feast.

The three remaining guards blanched. Their gazes swept over Remy with a kind of dread awe of the human.

Remy assumed if he feigned an attack towards them, the trio would have pissed themselves. And then he turned and followed the elf into the inner walls and towards the towering fortress of Arctig Maen.

After a short wait, Queen Rhagathena's attendant led Remy into the main hall of her castle. The hair stood up on the back of his neck and he felt every sense in his body warning him of danger.

Remy scanned left and right as he walked. Try as he might, he could not spot any of the igniter artifacts Fremenor had crafted for the queen upon any of the candles or torches in the fortress. He shrugged, assuming they were hidden elsewhere, perhaps in the private residence chambers.

They entered the main reception hall. The massive space was empty, and his footsteps echoed. Whatever dangers his senses warned him of, they were not physical in nature. Far ahead, at the end of the meeting hall, loomed a raised dais and a white throne.

Rhagathena's seat of power was made of some unknown mineral, but it looked as if it had been carved out of pure ice. The Rime

Throne glittered as if covered in frost, and upon it sat the spider queen, Rhagathena.

Her deep black eyes fixed upon the human with recognition. They'd seen each other once prior at Rhylfelour's home. Standing next to her was that same elf servant who Remy had noticed as he heralded her arrival. He was her majordomo—the queen's personal attendant.

"High servant of Warlord Rhylfelour, Chief of the Broken Hand clan," announced the elf servant who Remy had followed. He offered the queen a stiff bow, and then departed.

Rhagathena smiled at Remy. She wore even more immodest clothing than the last time they'd met. Here, she wore no scaled covers for her breasts and opted for sheer fabric instead.

Remy's chest tightened. He was careful not to let his eyes wander. Something in the queen's gaze felt distinctly predatory.

Her bulbous thorax rested upon the seat of the Rime Throne, and she rose to her full height when meeting her guest. "Leave us, Chokorum."

The majordomo bowed, giving Remy a stern look the whole way down, and then Chokorum departed.

"If it pleases the Queen, I am here to see my master and report that his task is completed."

"Yes," she purred.

Remy remained rooted in place as the spider queen walked a slow circle around him. She looked him over, as if tasting him with her eyes. "Rhylfelour said you were perhaps his greatest student... and his most deadly asset. He had no doubt that you would succeed. In fact, he was so confident that he has already returned home in order to meet you and claim his prize."

The human swallowed as the somehow sultry female rested her body near his feet, bending those long spider legs that carried her. In effect, she was kneeling before him, and she pawed at his pocket with her distinctly sidhe hands. They rested upon a hard lump there. "I want to see it," she said.

Remy withdrew Chief Krogga's ring. *Genesta... You could have just told me.* Remy bit his lip, realizing his seer friend had sent him to chase some potential future by standing before the queen instead of meeting Rhylfelour at the fortress.

The queen's smile quirked playfully upon her face. "So, the orc was right about you... Even if you are a son of Adam."

Remy bowed slightly.

Rhagathena noticed something on his face and tilted her head. "Tell me, human, are you loyal to Rhylfelour?"

"I am bound by an oath in the old tongue," Remy responded.

"Yes. He said as much." The queen stared at him. "Speak your oath. I want to hear it."

Remy said, [I swear my allegiance to Rhylfelour, son of Jarlok and warlord chief of the Broken Hand orcs.]

Rhagathena grinned. "And you are aware that your master is attempting to court my hand... *and my throne?*" she asked.

Remy nodded.

She watched him for a few more moments. And then the intrigue lessened.

"It seems to me that your oath is overly broad. Tell me this, child of Adam, is your oath to Rhylfelour more powerful than obedience to your queen?"

Remy cocked his head. "Pardon? I'm afraid I do not understand the question."

Rhagathena's smile was impishly innocent, but also devilishly calculated. "If I ordered you to murder the warlord and bind yourself to me, would you do it?"

The human stared at her for a few long minutes. "If this is a test of my loyalty, I'm afraid it's a poor one. If you gave such an order, it would be impossible for me to carry it out. The answer is moot."

She crossed her arms beneath her breasts, propping them up to punctuate her annoyance. "Is it now? Perhaps that is impossible, perhaps not. Maybe the point is to draw out an answer rather than to bind you to a course of action."

Remy recognized the game. He chose not to play. "My Queen, I believe the best person to ask would be my master."

She traded a conspiratorial smile with him, and then she returned to her seat. "I suspect you will not inform him of this question." Rhagathena made a hand motion to release him from her company.

Remy returned the ring to his pocket and bowed before heading for the doors and back to the road which would lead him home. *Rhagathena was already laying plans for Rhylfelour's Allied orc armies—armies which she might attempt to use for her own means as soon as she secured the warlord's compliance.* Remy knew manipulation when he saw it.

"I assume we shall see more of each other in the future," Queen Rhagathena called as he departed.

Remy's stomach turned as he walked away. He was certain she was right, and he felt sure that she just strung the first line of her web around him.

Chapter Seven

More than six months had passed since Remy returned to his home with Corax gliding in his wake. He had delivered Krogga's ring to Rhylfelour, giving him ancestral control over all the orcish tribes and making him the Grand Warlord and High Chief of the Demonsbreak clans.

Remy had hoped those months would have brought better times. Rhylfelour had gotten exactly what he wanted: a place of honor and a title within the Winter Court.

Instead, it offered a fresher dose of the same hell he'd endured for the last dozen years. This time, instead of falling under the lash of the orc instructor, Remy had to stand by and watch as Rhylfelour trained Shadarkith.

Remy thought watching it from the outside was worse than enduring it firsthand. He spent many nights binding up the boy's injuries. Remy tried to show the boy a few techniques that might help him advance, or at least block the worst of Rhylfelour's brutality, but Shadarkith was not particularly adept at fighting—and he was even worse at enduring his instructors' blows.

Luckily, Shadarkith was twice allowed to heal marginally when Rhylfelour headed for Arctig Maen to present himself at the court with the other high-class tuathans. Remy had been instructed to continue the lad's education while the warlord was away. As long as he'd be able to show some improvement after the orc's absence, Shadarkith would not be beaten when Rhylfelour returned. Shadarkith hadn't, and Rhylfelour's threats proved good.

After the second trip to call at court, the orc returned in exceptionally high spirits. His ambitions had finally gotten him noticed and his bid for the Rime Throne was being entertained.

The queen decided she should wed soon. Past rulers, each anointed king at her side, had met with unfortunate and suspicious ends—a challenge which Rhylfelour thought was either evidence of his predecessor's weaknesses or that it was his fate to rise where they had failed.

On his last trip, Rhylfelour had made the formal overture for her to join with him and make Rhylfelour king. Those sorts of unions were formal arrangements amongst royalty. There was little love in them, and they were common in upper-casted houses—especially among the sidhe.

Rhagathena thought the alliance favorable, but required some time before she would provide an answer. In the meantime, she had provided Rhylfelour with a list of names. Each name on the list represented someone who had either wronged her or had somehow bothered her. Rhagathena had a long memory, and Rhylfelour desperately wanted to provide value to her, thereby currying favor.

There were multiple offers seeking the hand of the spider queen, and though Rhylfelour did not have the largest wealth, likely it was the least. What he *did have* was a like mind and command over a brutal fighting force. He was the newest member of the winter court, but he had the corpse bird.

Whether Aderyn Corff was as deadly as the rumors which the orc spread did not matter. He had created a folk legend, one corroborated by those few who had seen him before, and belief was a potent power.

Remy had spent the last several weeks focusing on the queen's list.

As much as Remy loathed being sent on clandestine assassination missions, any argument from him meant Rhylfelour would beat Shadarkith ever harder. Since the warlord's return from his last call on court, Remy had eliminated two names from the list already.

Remy stood in the courtyard and stared at Corax. *I think the bird is getting a little fat. Do birds even get fat?*

The warrior watched Shadarkith train as he prepared to leave soon, chasing down a new name from the spider queen's list. Using a wooden sword, Shadarkith squared off against the tutor Rhylfelour had hired... mostly it just added to the number of people abusing the boy.

Remy scowled, about to offer some advice to the young student when a horn pealed upon the distant lookout tower. Several minutes later, a trio of sidhe riders arrived from Arctig Maen.

Chokorum, Rhagathena's majordomo, dismounted as Rhylfelour descended the steps. The orc offered as much of a formal greeting as was possible.

The queen's attendant handed him a scroll stamped with a wax seal of the signet representing the Rime Throne. As Rhylfelour broke it and scanned the document, Chokorum summarized.

"Rhagathena has narrowed down her selections to two potential suitors. You are among them," Chokorum said.

"In the other?" Rhylfelour asked.

"Myvarath of Gaeafdale," said the elf.

Rhylfelour cursed. Not only was Myvarath wealthy, but he was equally ambitious as the orc. They'd already puffed up their chests and measured cocks at court, according to whispers which reached even back to the rumor mill in the warlord's stronghold. While the orc had a great deal of physical might at his disposal, Myvarath traded in secrets, knowledge, and the arcane. The spider queen greatly valued assets provided by both suitors.

Chokorum explained, "She has decided upon the contest. Bandits from the faewylds have been harassing her unseelie forces for quite some time now. Diplomatic negotiations with their queen, Mab, have yielded little. Rhagathena's future ambitions rely on taking care of this problem."

The way he stressed the words *taking care* implied the Rime Throne would be equally pleased with murder as a solution to their present difficulty.

"Certainly, Myvarath is sending his own envoy to provide a remedy," Chokorum said. He turned his eye to Remy and added,

"Queen Rhagathena has also stipulated that neither Rhylfelour nor Myvarath nor any of their forces may harm either those two named parties. Doing so will result in forfeiting this contest."

Remy's expression remained neutral. Rhylfelour, however, openly wore disappointment on his face. Two suitors testing the strength of their assassins versus their opponent's defenses was not the game the Queen desired.

"To be clear," Rhylfelour asked, "whichever party can satisfactorily stop the invasions by these faewyld bandits will earn Rhagathena's hand and the unseelie crown?"

Chokorum nodded.

Rhylfelour grinned and rubbed his hands together greedily.

Remy could already tell he would pursue that third name later. The orc would likely dispatch him tonight for a task that might take months, or even longer.

But Remy noticed what had gone unaddressed by either Chokorum or Rhylfelour: assassinating the elf noble, Myvarath, or the orc warlord, Rhylfelour, were both prohibited.

There was no rule given against targeting their servants.

The game was to stop the bandits. But *the game within the game* was a duel between the suitors' best warriors.

Remy rode hard for the borders where the reaches of the unseelie petered out and those of the faewylds began. Rhylfelour had given

Remy the last known location of Tylwyth Teg city of Capitus Ianthe.

Mab ruled her domain from the city of Wildfell, but Capitus Ianthe was the closest source of quality information. And he would need lots of it to pull off such a high-profile job. Mab's reluctance to intervene seemed to implicate her in the ordeal, and Capitus Ianthe was ruled by the wild queen's political rival, her niece, Princess Maeve.

Maeve's city was more likely to offer intelligence against Mab than any other place. If it turned out that the queen of the Tylwyth Teg was indeed behind the bandits that harried Rhagathena's forces, Rhylfelour's assassin would be tasked with nothing short of executing a fairy queen.

Remy certainly hoped that was not the case. In addition to his distaste for murdering, he had no idea how such a task was even possible. Killing tuathan nobles and warlords already proved complicated... *But a queen?*

Rhylfelour had made it clear that nothing short of taking the head of whomever was responsible for these bandits was his task. "I did not create Aderyn Corff to simply cast aspersions and manipulate myself into the correct position to take the Rime Throne. My empire—the name I am making for myself as the new unseelie king—will be one of strength. It is the ferocity of orcs which has earned me my rank, not our skills for guile."

Remy knew that only one outcome would please the warlord: a bloody one.

The ruler of the faewylds was currently embroiled in a cold war with the next in line for her title, and control of the Briar Throne. Queen Mab's successor, Princess Maeve, had waited patiently in the wings for centuries. Rumor was that she grew impatient.

If they were to be believed, and rumors almost always had some shred of truth, Maeve was positioning herself to overthrow her aunt and take the crown. Maeve traveled with the mobile tent city of Capitus Ianthe as it wound a circuit through the faewylds.

There, Remy hoped to find the information that he sought. If it proved a greater conspiracy, perhaps the caravans would supply allies against the queen of the Tylwyth Teg and ruler of the wildfey.

Remy rode many days before he came to the edge of the unseelie lands. Both the seelie and unseelie realms were surrounded by vast stretches of wilderness in which the wildfey roamed. These faewylds possibly bordered other, different areas, but little was known about them. Whatever lay beyond the reaches of the faewylds was of little concern to either the Winter and Summer courts.

Those two courts, perpetually at war, grew extremely close on only one side. A thin strip of wilderness, split by an immensely deep chasm, separated the two kingdoms where the Selvages provided a buffer. Long bridges crossed the deep Solstox Cliffs, and both sides stationed garrisons to enforce their borders. Keeping enemies out was much as important as keeping their own kind in.

Here on the outskirts, the borders were marked by tall guide stones positioned along the major roads. There was little need to bother with the borders of the faewylds. The human kept his hood up to ward against both the elements and also allay the gaze of other travelers. There were few of them, and none bothered to do more than trade pleasantries.

Border markers aside, the lands closest to the wilds and the unseelie lines were a kind of gray area when it came to the allegiances of the regular folk. Few conversations brought about schisms and murderous intent like political ones. In this part of the world, it was wiser to keep your head down and pass through quickly than engage too long and become trapped in debate and invite murder.

Remy was fine with silence. He enjoyed his own company, and keeping a tight lip meant his cover would remain intact. Above all else, he needed stealth, especially if circumstances forced his hand against Queen Mab.

"Of course, I'm not alone." He looked to the sky and spotted his ever-present feathered friend. Corax's companions had returned to flank him. "Spreading my infamy to the other flocks, no doubt," Remy mused.

A few days' ride into the faewylds he noticed that the other two crows would occasionally slip into the distance further behind him. Another day and night of it developed a pattern.

"There's something back there... or *someone*," Remy noted. Somebody was following him, and the crows kept dropping back to check it out.

That his present pace and heading, Remy would have arrived at Capitus Ianthe with another day's travel. But something about the crows' warning convinced the human to deviate course. If it was just another traveler headed for Maeve's city, he could let him or her pass and his suspicions could dissipate. *But if they did not pass...*

Remy urged his horse left, and they took a seldom used road along less desirable terrain. He set his jaw and continued unabated. No traveler would choose this path without specific intent.

Giving enough distance between a new location and the main road where his potential follower was, Remy dismounted earlier than he normally would have and pitched his camp. Thick trees populated the region and scrubby bracken tangled with snarls of thorn and vine on either side of the trail.

He made a fire, erected a small tent, prepared his meal, and then waited. As his small pot of stew heated upon the coals, Remy used his shovel to begin digging a shallow grave.

Three crows swooped down to roost in the branches overhead, watching over the area with great interest, like judges presiding over a hearing. That was how Remy knew the attack was imminent... Or at the very least, whatever creature had been tailing him neared its arrival.

A tall sidhe sat atop a horse. The beast ambled at a leisurely pace. Horse and rider strolled along the rugged trail, which circumnavigated several fens and cut through the lowland wastes.

The elf wore a tall hat and a cloak that obscured whatever items the sidhe kept on his person. His face took a flinty edge, and the jaded light in his eyes informed Remy that he was a fellow player in the queen's game.

Like Aderyn Corff, this person was a fellow assassin—and neither did it for pleasure. Both pawns murdered for the sake of their masters.

Remy walked out onto the road and stood there. He squared up, facing the newcomer.

"I've been expecting you," Remy called. "You work for Myvarath?"

The other assassin tugged slightly on his reins and brought his horse to a stop. He scanned Remy with narrowed eyes. Finally, he responded, "I am Frer Harten. And you have guessed correctly, for what it's worth."

Remy grinned at the elf. He knew it was important not to show any indicators of trepidation. He bobbed his head towards the hole which he'd dug. It was clearly a grave. "I prepared a place for you," he told Frer Harten.

The elf tilted his head and said nothing. He'd obviously read the same rulebook about showing emotion to your enemy.

"How do you want to do this?" Remy asked.

Frer Harten raised an eyebrow. "How do you mean?"

"You and I have been set on the same path, I am certain. I have been tasked by Warlord Rhylfelour, and you've been given the same job by Myvarath, the sidhe noble of Geafdale," Remy told him. "We have the same prohibition against harming opposing patrons, and we are both well aware of agents sent by the other party. Unless Myvarath is shortsighted, then you've been tasked with first eliminating me." Remy spoke frankly and Frer Harten only acknowledged his peers' words with the shrug.

"If what you say is true, it seems like you are well prepared for whomever this agent of Myvarath is," Frer Harten said noncommittally.

Remy never took his gaze off the elf. If anything, he hardened it. "I certainly hope I am not mistaken in your identity, Frer Harten," he said. "My master's mission is such that I cannot let you pass. If you are not the envoy from Rhylfelour's opponent, it only means you will be that much easier to put into that grave. But you're going in it, one way or another."

Frer Harten grimaced. He finally nodded from atop his mount. "It is true what they say about you, corpse bird. You may be ddiymadferth, but you are no fool."

Remy stood on the road with his sword drawn. He could feel the enemy's eyes as they roamed, looking over both him and his encampment.

"How then do you wish to proceed?" Frer Harten asked.

"I'll not let you leave, not while I have you here. The last thing I want is to constantly watch over my shoulder and wonder where you'll strike from," Remy insisted.

"Likewise," Frer Harten said.

"I suggest we duel now have it over with," Remy said.

Frer Harten set his jaw. "And what is to stop you from attacking me as I dismount?"

Remy grinned. "If you are vulnerable doing something as simple as getting off your horse, then you deserve to die before you set foot on the ground. If Myvarath promotes warriors who are so inept to your present rank, then he deserves ridicule rather than an option for Rhagathena's hand."

Frer Harten nodded, but then the he-elf practically chuckled.

"However, I will extend you a professional courtesy of allowing you to dismount and prepare with no ill intent," Remy said.

"Professional courtesy, eh?" Frer Harten stroked his jaw and then nodded.

Remy could tell that he'd not expected chivalry from a human.

"Then I accept," Frer Harten informed him. "I shall inform you before our battle commences."

The enemy took his time and made a show of preparing blade and shield.

Remy had a sneaking suspicion that Frer Harten made too big a deal about what items were in his possession.

The elf gave him a salute while gripping his sword in his hand. "I am ready to begin. Our duel shall commence after the count expires." Frer Harten gave Remy a smug look. "To the death?"

"Our masters would have it no other way."

Frer Harten nodded. "Then we begin in three. Two. One." Immediately after the count ended, the sidhe surged forward with blade drawn high. He muttered some word of power and disappeared just before Remy closed the gap.

Taken by surprise, but only barely, Remy's sword sliced through the air. He gasped when an invisible blade drew blood on his side.

Remy knew exactly what Frer Harten had done. "Fucking aes sidhe," the human growled. He realized suddenly that Myvarath's assassin was a spellcaster. The unseelie baron was something of an arcanist, and Remy chastised himself for not expecting it.

Before Frer Harten could strike again, Remy scooped up a handful of dirt in one whirling motion and thrust it into the air near the enemy's last position. Gravel bounced off the unseeable Enemy and Remy thrust out with his sword and returned blood for blood.

Frer Harten had likely never missed with that maneuver before, but Rhylfelour had trained Remy to fight blind and on instinct. Once the human had been able to defend himself with a wooden practice sword, Rhylfelour would amuse himself by blindfolding the boy and attacking.

Remy was far from perfect, however, his senses were attuned for locating invisible dangers. He refused to ever thank the orc, but Remy acknowledged he would be dead but for the warlord's painful lessons.

Before Frer Harten could put any distance between them, which would have let him capitalize on the invisibility spell, Remy press his attack. He could see neither sword nor shield of his enemy, but keeping the sidhe assassin on the defensive was the only way to control the encounter.

Remy hacked and chopped and swung combinations of blows, which he knew were generally effective against even the most skilled warriors. After a few blows, Remy succeeded in knocking the elf's shield and sword out of his hands. Once free from the elf's grip, they became visible again and they clattered against the packed earth of the trail. The tall meadow grass nearby swooshed with the sounds of unseeable feet as Frer Harten dashed to safety.

Remy stood with a foot over either side of the stripped weapons. He opened his senses and listened. The human tilted his ear and used his eyes to search for clues. Moving grass. A snapping twig. Anything.

From the corner of his eye, he caught the light, brilliant like the sun and crackling like lightning. Remy whirled to find the elf visible again. A jolt of pure energy flung from Frer Harten's hands.

The elf was more than some mere low-level spell slinger with a few tricks up his sleeves. Pulling energy enough to form raw and destructive energy was something that took either an immeasurable amount of talent or a great deal of specific training—the aes sidhe had devoted whole schools to working their craft, and much like with the talents of a warrior, dedicated training made all the difference in battle.

Luckily, Remy's instincts were good, and he dropped to one side just in time to avoid the burning shaft of power. It lanced through the air as the human scrambled to his feet, snatching up Frer Harten's lost shield.

As quickly as Remy moved, talented spellcasters could unleash gouts of fire at the speed of sound. Uttering another word of power, Frer Harten hurled another spear of crackling magic at him.

The black bolt of eldritch energy shot at Remy like a crossbow quarrel. Frer Harten had him dead to rights, and both warriors knew it. Time seemed to stop as their gazes met and acknowledged that fact.

And then something happened which neither could explain. The bolt of deadly energy caromed off the human and bounced harmlessly away, fading into the sky.

Rather than pausing to ask the gods if they'd intervened or checking himself to see if his eyes had lied and the sidhe had simply missed, Remy flung the shield at his enemy.

Frer Harten ducked the thing, and it sailed barely over the spellcaster's head. But turning back, he found Remy charging forward.

This time it was Remy's turn to deliver a speedy, unavoidable blow. The human swung his sword and, with one swift stroke, separated the elf's head from his body. A look of surprise remained frozen on the assassin's face as it thumped upon the soil. The body, barely realizing it was dead, didn't collapse until Frer Harten's head came to a rest.

Remy stomped over to the corpse, checking to make sure this was not some magician's trick, and then threw the head into the grave he'd dug.

He waved Corax away. This deep in the faewylds, he did not want to announce himself or give away his position, or the fact that he'd killed Myvarath's agent. With any luck, it would be weeks before Myvarath deduced his agent was eliminated.

Hastily, Remy dragged the body over to the shallow grave and reunited it with its head before shoveling the soil back overtop. He glanced up as soon as he was done and spotted a group of long-eared elves watching him.

They had a look of wildness to them and a feral light in their eyes. *Tylwyth Teg*, he realized.

Remy dropped the shovel, and before he could address them, the whole group of them began applauding.

Chapter Eight

"It's not every day we see someone capable of outsmarting a spellcaster," said the leader of the ragtag group. The elf stood at the front of those who had watched Remy defeat the aes sidhe.

The group included several Tylwyth Teg elves, one faun, a few of the little folk, and a troll who towered chest and shoulders above the others. Remy cocked his head at the behemoth.

Apparently, the troll was not the lumbering oaf he appeared to be. He recognized Remy's body language.

"You are wondering how I can stand in the daylight?" the troll asked.

Remy nodded.

"Queen Mab, of course," the troll said. "You are obviously from the unseelie... even if you are a child of Adam. Mab's magic has done something to the faewylds. Here, the sun is... different."

Remy squinted and surveyed his surroundings. He glanced skyward at his crow and realized that the troll was right. The air felt somehow *other*. There were not words to describe it. Though he'd experienced both day and night, daylight was accompanied by a palpable feeling of dusk—even at noon.

Remembering his manners, Remy offered them a bow, although he did not take his eyes off them. "My name is Remy Keaton," he said.

The elf leader of the Tylwyth Teg gave him a nod in response. "I am Thurfin." He nodded to the troll and one of the short folk, a stout, bearded looking fellow barely taller than Remy's knee. He offered names in turn, "Zulkuzz and Wildbean... and then the rest." He waved a hand at the group.

"Greetings," Remy said. "I was on my way to Capitus Ianthe when I noticed I was being followed," he explained.

Thurfin narrowed his gaze quizzically. "Truly? A man of your skill... and on your way to Maeve's city?"

Remy thought he inferred derision in Thurfin's voice.

I need information. I suppose it doesn't matter where it comes from, Remy thought. He decided to take a gamble, hoping he would not need to dig more graves for it. Especially for the troll. Not only were they notoriously hard to kill, but digging a hole that size was a lot of work.

"I came this way looking for work," Remy said.

"Work as a bladesman?" Thurfin asked, weighing every word and twitch of the human's body language.

Remy tilted his head measuredly. "You have seen my work."

Thurfin stared a bit longer. And then his face cracked into a big grin. "I may know where a human could find such work," Thurfin offered with a chuckle.

The tylwyth teg relaxed his posture, but Remy could feel the elf remained suspicious.

"You are from the unseelie," Thurfin said, "so tell me why you have come to the faewylds? There must be some reason more than employment. Certainly, your skills are equally valuable there?"

Remy gulped. Thurfin was smart. *If he doesn't believe I'm running towards something, it may make more sense that I'm running from something... something they would be familiar with and that would make sense for a human.*

"I am done with the unseelie. I... I had family... or at least something like it." Remy imagined how Shadarkith must have felt when he lost his mother and his brother. Hot pain involuntarily squeezed Remy's neck; it made his voice warble and flushed his cheeks. Remy hissed one infamous name, "Syrmerware Kathwesion."

Thurfin averted his eyes and nodded. The orc slaver's reputation had made it even to the faewylds.

The short fellow, Wildbean, asked, "Yeah, yeah... But there's a question we all care about far more than that." His bedraggled beard bobbed and waved as the diminutive creature eyed up the human killer. "Are you for Maeve or for Mab?"

Remy responded with a look of confusion. He'd heard there was much discord between the two leaders, the current queen and the heir, but he hadn't realized exactly how deep the politicking went.

Blinking, Remy ran down what details he knew. Thurfin's group looked too ragged to be a living in Capitus Ianthe—Maeve's nearby town. They were outsiders. And the troll had spoken appreciatively of Mab's gift.

He sighed and decided to take another calculated gamble. "Queen Mab, of course," Remy declared for her side.

That elicited many smiles. This time, Thurfin seemed to genuinely relax.

Remy took it one step further. *Perhaps these fellows can point me in the right direction or even make an introduction for me.* "Now that you know what I can do and why I so hate the unseelie, perhaps you can help me? There are rumors of wildfey that have been raiding and pillaging the spider queen's convoys."

The troll raised his eyebrows and stood slightly taller. It looked more like a gesture of pride than anything else.

"I don't think I could ever join an army against Rhagathena. Open warfare would be crushed swiftly and effectively, I think... But a little banditry? That is more my style," Remy said.

Thurfin tried to play ball and keep a neutral expression. But Wildbean, who Remy guessed was a cluricaun—a kind of diminutive fey humanoid—was all grins.

The cluricaun spoke before Thurfin could slow him down. "You've never been more in the right place at the right time, my friend."

Remy traveled many days with the crew of wildfey. They left the regions surrounding Capitus Ianthe and headed west, towards the Selvages.

Wildbean's initial excitement, Remy learned, was largely due to Remy's humanity. The little trickster thought it would be amusing to include such a wickedly talented human in some of their plots, but he would not say why any son of Adam would be useful.

"That bitch, the spider queen, has something in mind. I just don't know what it is, yet," the clurichaun said, riding on the back of Thurfin's horse. He balanced there with unnatural agility.

Thurfin scowled as he spoke. "I think I know. Rhagathena has been hoarding slaves and using them as miners."

Zulkuzz shrugged. He spoke with stunted verbiage, "That don't sound worse than normal."

"Have you ever heard of the Lightstarved?" Thurfin asked.

None of the others had. But Remy nodded slightly. "I heard it referenced once," he said. "I was being abused by guards at the time and did not know what they were talking about. And I didn't stick around to find out—but I assume it's some group of humans, then?"

"Yes," Thurfin acknowledged. "It's a new bit of information we've discovered. And Wildbean might be right. You might represent our best hope of stopping whatever Rhagathena has planned for the Lightstarved."

Wildbean practically glowed. "It's not often Thurfin says I'm right," he smiled. "Pardon me while I celebrate." The clurichaun did a strange little happy dance upon the rump of the horse, seeming to defy gravity as he did so.

Thurfin explained what he knew. "The group we are bringing you to are called the Reavers." The sidhe fixed Remy with a sidelong glance and admitted, "We are all Reavers."

Remy nodded. "That much I'd discerned within thirty seconds of meeting you."

"In some of our raids upon Rhagathena's supply caravans, many of our people were burned," Thurfin said. "Cold iron."

Thurfin had the attention of all members of their party. It was all news to them.

"That *bitch*," Wildbean hissed.

Thurfin nodded. "Nothing is sacred for the unseelie. They're apparently willing to use iron weapons, even. But getting enough of the stuff requires a force of miners who can touch the metal. There are so few capable amongst the fey, but human slave labor is cheap."

"There's the redcaps," Zulkuzz noted.

Thurfin shrugged. "Sure, but they have always used an affinity for iron to their advantage. But they're too hard to capture and no redcap has ever set eyes upon the Rime Throne. In fact, a powrie has never held any office in the Winter Court."

Remy rubbed his jaw, following the logic chain. "This sets a new precedent."

"And it may be a sign of further evils yet to come."

The sidhe's words cast a pall over the reavers. In silence, they continued onward towards their hidden base of operations.

Remy did not mind traveling in silence. It allowed him to best take in sight of the expansive country sides of the faewylds. Within a few days, he had seen just about every sort of terrain imaginable.

As they made camp for an evening, Wildbean sidled up alongside Remy as they sat near the fire. He shook out his dreadlocked mane and beard and then dug in his satchel for a bag of pungent fungus. He also produced a few vials of other herbal remedies and concoctions.

Remy asked him about them. The other travelers rolled their eyes as if the human had committed some grave sin.

"Great, now we'll have to listen to this all night." Zulkuzz sighed.

Wildbean shot him an angry look. "Don't worry about them. They're all just jealous." And then the clurichaun launched into a whole tangent about herbal remedies listing which plants had certain properties that could be harnessed. He had encyclopedic knowledge, and he enjoyed showing it off.

"Like this one," Wildbean said. "It's called fool's foil. If you apply it to your eyelids, it's vapors allow you to see through glamors… it might have come in handy when you fought that aes sidhe a few days back."

Remy held up a vial of the stuff and examined it.

"You can keep it. I have plenty of the stuff." Wildbean pulled out a few dried mushrooms and brandished them. "But *this* is the stuff."

Remy cocked an eyebrow. The spongy mycelium had a very pungent odor and looked like porous, natural fibers. "What is it?"

The small creature grinned. "Egwyl meddwl." He popped a bite of the fungus into his mouth and begin chewing. He offered it to the human who did as demonstrated.

The other Reavers chuckled and watched the human with rapt interest.

"What?" Remy asked. A dread sense of foreboding lodged in his gut, and he realized he may have just done something a wiser person would not have.

Thurfin watched him from across the fire. "You're about to embark on a wild journey, my friend."

Remy cocked his head. "What do you mean?"

"Have you heard of the aither?" Thurfin asked.

"Only a little. It's kind of like a dream realm?" Remy asked.

Wildbean chuckled. "Kind of. It's kind of like the spirit realm some talented aes sidhe can enter by using astral projection. It's a realm of pure thought and will. Similar to very lucid dreams. But it's the kind when you know you're having a dream and can assert your will, making things happen, or building scenes out of pure intention."

"I've heard of it," Remy said. "Sounds like mind magic to me."

Wildbean shrugged. "It's all those things... and none of them. Well," the clurichaun grinned, "you'll see."

Remy stared at the leaping flames, and his eyes fluttered with a sensation of drugged drowsiness. He drifted as if into sleep—but it felt decidedly different. Something carried him off, voyaging away with both soul and mind.

The human felt conscious leave his body, as if this physical form somehow tethered him to reality, but that layers of reality somehow overlapped with each other. Each layer was somehow more real to Remy while in this state.

He saw Wildbean there, standing amid a stack of trophies. These were his memories of shenanigans he'd pulled: plaques and engraved crystals for his accomplishments. There was also a trio of paintings, folk who looked like they could have been Wildbean's siblings.

Remy realized he was in Wildbean's home in the aither... something the clurichaun had built. He waved a hand in front of his own face, making sure his body still worked as he was used to. "I feel like my soul has left its body."

The small fey chuckled. "It's something like that... I call it an untethering. You're still connected, but more as if by a rope instead of glued like wallpaper. It'd take something very nasty to cut *that* cord."

"Like death?" Remy asked with a hint of trepidation.

Wildbean conceded the point but waved away his friend's concerns. He stood near the human a moment. The imp winked at him. "Have fun out there... and be careful."

"You sound as if you're abandoning me?" Remy asked.

Wildbean shrugged and pointed. "I'm going over there."

Try as he might, Remy could not see what or where Wildbean was pointing. The aither was not laid out with any coherent sense of geography like the physical plane was.

"This is a realm of thought and intention," Wildbean said. "'Over there' could mean anything. The aither is not limited by any kind of map like you're used to. Things here resemble daydreams more than they do reality." He winked. "So be careful... Mind your thoughts and you'll do fine. I'm heading that way, towards the light."

Remy watched the clurichaun go. Wildbean seemed to shrink out of existence entirely, leaving him alone.

"Mind my thoughts... things aren't real here—so what could possibly go wrong?" Remy scoffed. His thinking rolled over Wildbean's last word, *light*, over and over.

Remy's mind latched onto it, and he remembered the term *Lightstarved*.

He tumbled down a hole, and into darkness as his undisciplined mind wandered. Taken by the wild imaginings, Remy could barely see, but he could feel the cold, hard earth and feel the heavy cupronickel chains at his ankles. A voice barked a promise that he'd get no food or water until he returned with his quota of ore.

A whip cracked somewhere in the cave, and a woman cried out. And then Remy felt rough hands grab him and drag him away to an area illuminated by dim torchlight. It was enough that Remy could identify his assailants as they beat him: the faces belonged to men and women he'd killed at Rhylfelour's insistence. Guilt overwhelmed Remy and he felt every blow of the violent assault.

Remy growled and tried to argue with them. He told them they weren't real, but in this place, they were. Finally, afraid of what might happen if he fought back against them, or worse, surrendered to their onslaught, Remy pushed past them.

He hurried into the black labyrinth of the caves where the pickaxes of the hopeless Lightstarved toiled in darkness. He ran and hid, keeping on the move to evade any pursuit and telling himself he'd done what he had to in order to survive.

Finally, Remy awakened with a gasp. The other Reavers chuckled. Zulkuzz offered him a bladder filled with water. Remy drank greedily and then looked over at Wildbean, who reclined peacefully, still enjoying his trip through the psychedelic aithersphere. He had a smile on his face.

The human felt a little jealous, but he was glad to be back... And he had no intention of returning to learn more.

The following days passed uneventfully. Remy was grateful that they'd quickened their pace. The riders moved just fast enough to shorten their transit time, but not enough to draw undue attention.

What had eased Remy's nerves the most was that the new pace also made it too difficult to have conversations. While banter helped take his mind off the dark thoughts inspired by his wild trip through the aither, it had cast a pall over his spirits.

Certainly, there must've been a trick to controlling the experience, Remy knew, otherwise there's no reason Wildbean would willingly go there. Until he knew more, Remy had no desire to play with aither again. If he saw egwyl meddwl in the wild, he was more likely to burn it than harvest it.

Evenings spent around the fire had not provided many more details pertinent to Remy's mission. He only learned that Thurfin and his crew were returning from Maeve's city after meeting with one of Queen Mab's spies there; they had stumbled upon the human's duel with Frer Harten quite by accident.

Thurfin learned that Princess Maeve had entertained a second group of emissaries from Queen Rhagathena only recently. The first team of diplomats had made overtures to the heir to the Briar Throne after visits with the Tylwyth Teg queen proved unfruitful.

Maeve had sent the first ones away and refused them. But her attitude had shifted and become increasingly oppositional since then. The new emissaries sent by Rhagathena stayed for many days in her company. The reaver's moles believed that Maeve had come to an understanding with Rhagathena... It was likely that she would soon move against her aunt, Queen Mab.

All the political doublespeak and swirling conspiracies made Remy's head swim. He had hoped that Mab would not be his target. But it became increasingly evident that, in order to fulfill his Master's orders, he would have to assassinate the Queen of the faewylds.

Remy felt bad about it. However, his mission was clear—probably clearer to him than whatever chain of events Thurfin and his company understood about political gambits among Briar Court.

Still, Remy did not want to kill the queen, even if he was exceptionally good at such tasks.

Bits and pieces of his aither trip still haunted him each night as he drifted off to sleep. Adding more faces and to that dark cave built by his guilt was Remy's least desirable outcome.

Perhaps I can use Maeve's ambitions to my advantage, he thought.

Remy glanced sidelong at Thurfin and the others. Heat lodged in his gut. The sting of betraying those who had so easily befriended him weighed on his mind. *If there was any other way, I would pursue it,* Remy told himself, but he could see no other.

Thurfin's mount slowed as they arrived at the edge of a forest. The trail here was less straight. The road flowed and wended, bending around large stony outcroppings and massive trees that were nearly as old as Arcadeax.

Eventually, the travelers split off the main road and onto a well-used but narrow forest trail. Remy had spotted several others like it, and Remy assumed that it led to the reaver's main hideout. He had gleaned from conversations that there were many small roads; there would have to be in order for them to accomplish the jobs they'd pulled so far. Arctig Maen's supply caravans were not left unguarded, and the reavers needed a sizable force to contend with unseelie defenses.

Remy assumed that the different paths let them split up their numbers so as not to pack down such a trail. They might otherwise give away the size and location of their encampment.

Finally, the woods thinned, and they arrived.

"Welcome to Brakkholme," Thurfin said.

Brakkholme was no mere encampment. It was a full-blown, hidden city. The stockade's walls stretched a number of directions and incorporated the old-growth into it. Camouflaged lookout posts hung from massive limbs, and swinging bridges stretched from tower to tower. It was an impressive, organic design.

Thurfin led the procession towards the front of the main palisade. A Tylwyth Teg scout stood on an old tree limb the size of a bridge. He waved back at Thurfin and gave a signal to the guards operating the door.

"You'll find that many of us reavers came from the unseelie," Thurfin said. "Those disgruntled with the spider queen often find a new home amongst the Tylwyth Teg and creatures of the faewylds. Similarly, we also have a few displaced tuatha from the seelie that have found their way here as well. Brakkholme is a place for outsiders." Thurfin halted his horse a short distance away as the gates opened.

The large door opened outward from the main entrance to Brakkholme. Behind the palisade door, Remy spotted posts driven deep into the ground. They prevented the door from being battered inward by invaders. Remy raised a brow; he realized the reavers were a more intelligent and organized group than he'd given them credit for. These were not some random group of brigands after a fat purse and an easy score.

As the horses passed the outer wall, Remy spotted a large pool fed by natural springs. Not only did that solve a freshwater problem and help prevent a blockade trying to wait them out, but it also provided defenses against being firebombed.

Thurfin guided them towards the Brakkholme pool so they could water their horses after the long journey. Both Remy and Thurfin looked up as an orc stormed their way. He wore a terse look and had fixed both of them with a fierce glower.

The orc spoke to Thurfin, but leveled a finger at the human. "Thurfin, don't you know who this is? You have led an agent of Warlord Rhylfelour, an agent of the Rime Throne, directly into the heart of the resistance. This is Aderyn Corff!"

Before Remy could react, every person within the forest stronghold had drawn either blade or bow and leveled them at him.

Somewhere in the foliage overhead, Corax cawed.

Chapter Nine

Remy knew he was good with a blade, and he was fairly certain there were a number of other talented warriors in this camp. He would have taken them all on individually, but now?

He flashed an apologetic look to Thurfin, who scowled in response. The Tylwyth Teg Had been willing to sponsor him into the gang of reavers.

"So, it is true, then?" asked Thurfin.

Remy said nothing, hoping the accusation had some possibility for error.

The orc told him, "I was there when he killed Chief Krogga. The powries attacked us with their iron boots. I was in the thick of the fighting when Aderyn Corff, the corpse bird, rode through the camp after killing Krogga."

Remy opened his mouth to argue that it could have been anybody… There were many lies he could have crafted, but then the orc pointed to Remy's waist.

"See? There at his waist? The assassin carries two dúshláns. The one on the left belonged to Krogga," the orc said.

The human set his jaw. It was hard to argue with the evidence.

"He speaks truly," Remy told Thurfin.

Thurfin narrowed his gaze at the human. "And you are prepared to fight your way out of here, I suppose?"

"Only if need be." Remy was grateful for a diplomatic solution.

"Are you here to kill someone in particular?" Thurfin asked.

"Not here," Remy said.

"But you *are* on a mission to kill someone?"

Remy gave him a stiff bob of his head in agreement.

"I don't suppose you can offer up a name?" Thurfin kept his questions polite. Neither party wanted the situation to devolve into bloodshed.

"I am afraid not."

Thurfin nodded. "Then we shall confine you here, within the walls of Brakkholme until we know what to do with you." He looked on his nose at the human. "Will you surrender your weapons to us?"

Remy shook his head. "I don't think I will."

"Will you force us to use violence to disarm you?"

"If you think you could take them from me, you would've had someone attempt it already." Remy and the wildfey sized each other up. "You've got a good sense of me by now, and apparently my reputation precedes me. If I wanted to leave, I probably could... but I'd prefer not to."

Thurfin squinted at him. "But you are exactly where you want to be?"

Remy inclined his head. "I would very much like an audience with your master."

The tylwyth teg's eyes widened a moment when he recalled he'd given up that person's identity. "You are here to kill the Queen?"

Every member of the encampment bristled at the declaration.

"No." Remy tried to dispel any absolutes, even if the revelation was more or less accurate. "I have a certain amount of levity in my orders."

Thurfin's jaw set. He had a difficult decision to make: risk exposing his queen to a skilled assassin, or try to stop the man now. The elf barked at the clurichaun, "Wildbean. I need to send a message to Wildfell—and require an answer straight away. Inform Queen Mab of the situation."

Wildbean gulped and then rummaged in his satchel for the fungus he'd taken previously. He wandered a safe distance away as he munched on the egwyl meddwl and then he leaned against a post and slid to his rump.

The tiny creature's eyes glossed over, and a few moments later, he slumped as he dozed off.

Remy understood the logic. Neither party wanted to sleep without an answer… and Wildbean hadn't gone to sleep, not truly. He'd slipped into the aithersphere where his mind could contact one of Mab's advisers. She likely kept one in that ethereal space for just such occasions as this, Remy assumed.

They only had to wait for a few tense hours until Wildbean gasped awake, then he yawned. He fixed both Remy and Thurfin with a placid look. "Queen Mab will entertain Aderyn Corff."

Thurfin did not appear pleased by the report.

The clurichaun tried to calm him. "She's always been one step ahead of the game, Thurfin." And then he turned to address Remy. "Mab believes she can find a mutually beneficial solution to your errand."

Remy crossed his arms and asked, "When do we leave?" He made no mention of what his true orders were. Mab might not have been so hasty had she known them.

Wildbean pointed at the gates. "Now. You and I will leave post haste. Mab gave me a location to deliver you to, and she guarantees your safety and free passage. We'll travel alone by horseback, if you agree."

Remy nodded.

Thurfin stared at the clurichaun. "You are sure of this?"

"Yeah," Wildbean said. "I'll be safe. If the big one wanted to hurt me, he'd a done it already. Mab knows what she's doing." Wildbean gulped as he glanced up at the greedy crow crouching in the branches overhead. "I hope."

Midway through the second day since Brakkholme Remy realized they were not headed to Wildfell. Mab's capitol lay by a more northern route. Ever present, Corax followed, dodging between the clouds, and following the assassin.

"Are we headed back to Capitus Ianthe?" Remy asked him.

Wildbean shrugged. "Something like that," he finally admitted.

The human's brows knit. Suspicions brewed like distant storm clouds. "Are you a traitor, Wildbean? Are you secretly in league with Maeve and trying to play the other side?"

The clurichaun spat a raspberry. "No. You've got it quite wrong." Wildbean stood atop their mount's head and bobbed up and down, perched comfortably, practically weightless and like a hat upon the horse. "But your suspicions may be well founded. There are no fewer than eight of Maeve's spies in Brakkholme. Thurfin is entirely too trusting. Perhaps your discovery will help us remedy that."

Remy scowled at him. But the little folk had a point.

Wildbean continued, "Mab wants to meet, but your arrival speeds up several of her plans, which were already in motion long before we found you dueling on that road. As soon as Maeve receives word of you, the entire game could change, so we must be hasty."

"And it hasn't changed already?" Remy wondered. "There's no way Mab could have foreseen my arrival unless... by the fey! She's got a seer?"

"No." Wildbean chuckled. "Nothing so exotic. No... The game *has* changed. *But if Maeve doesn't yet know,* Mab can position herself for victory before her niece yet learns the rules."

Remy stared at the clurichaun.

"You're Mab's wild card... provided you're willing to play along."

The human set his jaw. "I dunno. It makes sense, if we can come to terms—but I don't see how that's possible. My master demands blood. I am no diplomat. Aderyn Corff is dispatched to visit violence and the blade upon the condemned... not to barter for boons."

Wildbean tapped his lips thoughtfully. "You said something days ago. Something about having a certain degree of levity in how you handled this particular job."

Before Remy could argue his position, Wildbean held up a hand to stay further conversation. "Just remember that," he insisted, and then they said no more about the mission of either person. Instead, they spent the next few days talking about completely unrelated topics.

Remy learned that Wildbean had several siblings who he hadn't seen in ages. The little fellow missed them greatly.

He learned that the reason so few trolls remained in the unseelie was their unyielding devotion to the true king and rightful lord of the Rime Throne: King Wulflock, Oberon's brother. Both were powerful sidhe lords. Wulflock had gone missing many centuries ago. Trolls despised Rhagathena, and Mab's magic made the faewylds an easy choice for them to take refuge in.

He learned there were at least five kinds of tylwyth teg, though the near-sidhe type of elf was the most recognizable. The sidhe's longer eared, slightly feral cousins were called the Ellyllon, and they had become practically synonymous with the term tylwyth teg, probably because Mab was among their number.

In addition to the ellyllon, there were also the subterranean Coblynau, the diminutive Bwbachod, the Gwragedd Annwn who lived in the aquatic environs, and the Gwyllion who resided upon the craggy mountains.

Wildbean was a fount of data. He spouted information whether Remy wanted it or not, but it served to pass the time as they rode for Capitus Ianthe. Nearing the midpoint, the navigator indicated Remy should turn his horse and cut cross-country, aiming them towards a distant landmark.

After another day's ride, they arrived at a waypoint. An elaborate, gilded tent was erected in a field. It flew the flags of Wildfell above it. Nearby, the finest carriage Remy had ever seen was parked. The tongue, which would normally have connected to a pair of yoked beasts, seemed to hover in mid-air.

Once they'd arrived and dismounted, Remy noted a shimmering glow at the carriage. Wildbean split off towards the pavilion as the human checked it out. Instead of horses, the yoke was held aloft by a glimmering cloud of atomies. The tiny fairies were lashed to the yoke by tiny filaments. Atomies were the smallest fey Remy had ever seen, resembling winged sidhe so small that their voices sounded like tinkling bells at their loudest.

Remy was not fooled. He'd never seen an atomie, but he knew they were incredibly strong—and *fast*. How Mab had bound them to her service, he did not know.

Wildbean cleared his throat a short distance away. He stood near the opened tent flap and motioned for Remy to follow.

"Right this way, Aderyn Corff. Queen Mab awaits."

Queen Mab reclined on a comfortable-looking lounge chair in the center of the tent. Wildbean ushered Remy within and formally presented him.

Remy looked around, unsure how all of this got here given that he'd only seen her chariot outside and no others. The interior of the pavilion tent was comfortably outfitted and boasted a complement of personal guards, attendants, and even a chef.

His eyes fell upon faewyld queen. She was beautiful: as gorgeous as any she-elf he'd ever seen, with smooth skin with high cheekbones and a kind of feline grace. Like others of the ellyllon tylwyth teg she had longer ears than the sidhe and they angled back like a long-eared cat as they framed her delicate face. Remy knew her beauty was a trap. *The beautiful ones are always dangerous.*

Members of the high faerie courts aged differently than others. Remy didn't know why, but Mab looked only a few years older than he, and she was as old as Oberon.

Mab welcomed them in and instructed her staff to make them comfortable. "They are our guests, and we shall offer them all the hospitality of Wildfell."

Servants brought food and drink and laid them out on nearby tables. Remy watched carefully to make sure Mab and Wildbean had sampled from tray and cup first. *Maybe I should reconsider everything and become a diplomat after all,* Remy thought after tasting it.

"And now, let us get down to business," Mab said. She fixed him with a detached sort of gaze, slipping into a mechanical, pragmatic voice. "You are here to kill me, I am told. I'm certain you can understand how I feel that this is not in my best interest."

Remy inclined her head to her. "I can both understand and appreciate the sentiment."

"So it is your mission, in truth?" Mab asked. "Wildbean had indicated you might have some leeway in your orders."

Remy set his jaw. "Yes... but also no."

"Out with it, then." Mab gestured for more wine. One of her servants poured. "Perhaps if you can share a little more, we can find an amicable solution." The tylwyth teg queen offered him a wink. "Orders of this nature do tend to be inflexible. But if you know where the rigid lines of your orders are, or the exact words of binding, such as oaths, it is often possible to circumvent them. Oaths are like a cage with no roof."

Remy gave her a shrewd look. He appreciated her sentiment. Both parties stood to profit from an amicable outcome.

Telling her as much as he felt comfortable, Remy explained the orc warlord's ambition for the Rime Throne. "I'm certain that you already know all this. I'm telling you as a means of context more than anything else."

Mab nodded. "You are correct. But first-hand knowledge is more desirable when weighing decisions of life and death."

When Remy explained the duel against the spell casting assassin sent by Myvarath of Gaeafdale, Wildbean nodded as if finally connecting some dots in his mind.

Mab summarized. "So, you are oath bound to Rhylfelour. The spider queen will take him as consort and unite with him, making him the unseelie king if you can stop the bandit raids plaguing the convoys, which are running on Rhagathena's orders. We know that she is mustering for a conflict against the forces of Summer. That will potentially reignite the ancient wars between the seelie and unseelie realms."

"We don't know that last part," Remy said. "Not for sure."

"But we do," insisted Mab. "Perhaps Rhylfelour does not know it, and Rhagathena does not know to what extent you are aware of it, but it is information I am bringing to the table. Further, you should know that if this conflict is ignited, it will have far-reaching consequences. Not only will countless tuathans die painful deaths in battle, but the misery of war will plague everyone in *all the kingdoms*. And the worst suffering will be upon the humans."

Remy raked a finger through his hair. "I don't see how that's possible. Besides conscripting a few of those who know how to fight, humanity is scattered and unaligned."

Mab tilted her head at him like a gentle schoolteacher. The look caught him off guard.

"Rhagathena is using forbidden weapons, and she's using human forces to mine the toxic minerals. Certainly, she must be using them for other things as well. There are very few creatures who can handle the stuff. Oberon's reaction to iron on the battlefield will be extreme. He will order that every man, woman, and child of Adam's line be executed. It will start in the seelie realm; he'll put a bounty on the rest. No place will be safe for a human."

Remy gritted his teeth. He knew she was right. "But I cannot refuse my orders."

Mab grinned at him. "No. Of course you can't. But there is a lesson that I must teach you: *the words matter.*"

He gave her a skeptical look.

"Say it. Speak the lesson so that I know you heard me." Her words were somehow not condescending.

"Words matter."

"Good. I'm convinced you heard it, but not that you have learned it. However, you may learn it in time," she said.

"You speak in riddles," Remy accused.

"Perhaps. But if I told you outright, you would have only knowledge instead of wisdom."

Remy rolled his eyes. *She's doing it again, even.*

Mab said, "Speak your oath. Repeated exactly as if I am Rhylfelour."

Using the high tongue, he said, [I swear my allegiance to Rhylfelour, son of Jarlok and warlord chief of the Broken Hand orcs.] "Not a lot of wiggle room in the oath."

"It is a very broad oath," Mab said. "Just remember. *Words matter.*"

And then she stood as if their business was concluded.

Remy furrowed his brow, and the queen insisted, "You will keep your oath and fulfill your orders. I can promise that the attacks will cease for five years, and then the faewylds will resume holding the spider queen in check at the borders."

"But Rhylfelour demands blood. He wants the head of Queen Mab as a present for his bride."

Mab winked at him. "And he shall have it," she said.

The human crossed his arms. "It cannot be an illusion or some product of magic. If Rhylfelour demands the head of Queen Mab and the cessation of the raids, then I must make that a reality."

She grinned deviously. "And so shall it be, and with no guile put on him and with no resistance from me. Just give me some time to put my affairs in order."

Remy, thoroughly confused, said, "I've no wish to take your head, Queen Mab."

She held up a hand. "In three nights, you shall have your prize, and you will be able to swear by all the powers of Arcadeax that you have done so in earnest." She winked. "And you will have learned a valuable lesson, Corpse Bird. Three nights hence," she promised.

"And until then?" Remy asked.

Mab smiled and called for her tailor as she refilled her cup. "Until then, enjoy the hospitality of the faewylds."

Chapter Ten

Remy and Wildbean traveled with the Queen's caravan. They were secreted away among the military forces after they met up with them on the following day. The army, mostly made of ellyllon, neared Capitus Ianthe.

On the morn of the third day, the tent city came into view. It was a sprawling collection of canvas huts and teepees, dwellings made of skins and cloth. Despite it being a caravan city, it looked well apportioned. Roads in and out of Capitus Ianthe had been packed down with frequent travel. Traders and merchants had come and gone for enough time to make trade at Maeve's city a frequent occurrence.

Queen Mab's procession brandished banners and moved with enough fanfare to signal the arrival of the town's patroness. There was no mistaking exactly who they were. Mab had brought a good chunk of the military with as a show of force meant to quell any of Maeve's wayward aspirations for the Briar Throne.

As they neared the city, Wildbean grew increasingly agitated.

"I... uh... I am not welcome in Princess Maeve's city."

Remy gave the small creature an inquisitive look.

"Maeve harbors grudges for ages. I pulled the prank on her once. It was maybe a decade ago, but it impinged her honor."

"Wildbean, really?" Remy said, judgmentally.

"You'll know what to do when the time comes. But I... I cannot stay," Wildbean said. He shrugged off the satchel he carried and gave it to Remy. It was barely the size of a small bag and fit neatly into the palm of the human's hand, much like a coin purse.

"What's this?"

"Take it," Wildbean insisted. "It's my parting gift to you. You might have hated the aither, but you never know. This might come in handy for you at some future date."

Before Remy could protest, the clurichaun hopped down and scurried away into the tall grass beyond Remy's vision. The human set his jaw and remained on his horse, where Queen Mab had neatly inserted him among her royal guards.

The elves that made up her most trusted soldiers each wore a matching helmet, and they were dressed mostly the same. Remy was well hidden and could step forward at a moment's notice to act when called upon.

However, the crow that flew overhead seemed to know exactly which one he was, and as they entered the tent city, Corax cawed loudly. Other crows answered loudly and soon, a gathering had flocked to the trees. Oaks sparsely populated Capitus Ianthe, but their leafy canopies had darkened with murders.

How fitting, Remy thought, recognizing what it meant. The crows knew why he was here—even if the average tylwyth teg wouldn't realize it until after the fact. *A gathering for murder.*

Trumpets blew in Capitus Ianthe and criers shouted announcements.

"A royal visitation! Queen Mab is present! Report for her address in the eve!"

By midday, all inhabitants of the city would have received the summons.

Mab entered the main tent which served many purposes. Primarily, it was the primary hub of local government and the seat of Maeve's power.

Four of Mab's guards closely flanked her.

Maeve sat reclining indignantly upon her large and comfortable chair. She'd obviously been waiting for this visit from her aunt, queen of the faewylds, ever since the announcement came of the approaching army.

Like her aunt, Maeve had the same long ears and cat-like eyes of the ellyllon. So similar in appearance were Mab and Maeve that had a stranger met them he or she might have suspected them sisters. Maeve even wore her hair in a similar manner.

The difference was only in their eyes. Maeve's harbored a hard glint of bitterness and a brilliant streak of jealousy.

The queen and her heir traded tepid pleasantries. Once the small talk had petered out, Maeve asked, "What are you doing here, Queen Mab?"

Mab stared at her quizzically without responding.

The younger elf somehow both bristled and wilted beneath Mab's gaze.

"I wanted to tell you that I am fully aware of the sedition you are planning," Mab said.

Maeve clenched her jaw and refused to look her queen in the eye. Keeping her voice even, she said, "All lies. You may be certain of it."

"No, dear child. These are not mere rumors. These are facts." Mab remained in her chair. She balanced a goblet of wine between two fingers and sat as demure as ever. "I understand you are ambitious, and you desire more power and control than you've wielded thus far."

Maeve remained silent, though she did at least meet her aunt's eyes.

Mab continued, "I also know that the spider queen has called on you and offered you this very thing. Understand that I do not blame you for thinking it is possible to usurp me. But it is not wise."

The younger elf finally snapped, "What you know of wisdom?"

Mab stiffened in her seat and set the drink down.

Maeve ranted, "You have held the Briar Throne for centuries, since inheriting your name and title. It is time for new thinking. There is wisdom in allowing younger blood and fresh ideas to gain and exercise power."

After her outburst, Maeve slumped in her chair. She had all but admitted treason, and no elf of her status would be so bold unless she had enough military muscle to guard herself.

Both she-elves knew it.

"Is that it, then? You have marshaled your forces and are prepared to plunge the faewylds into a civil war, with control of Wildfell as the prize?" Mab asked.

Maeve glared at her. The sharpness of her eyes was enough to admit as much.

Mab asked, "Do you not see how the spider is playing you, child? I assume she has pledged troops to your cause… Rhagathena knows that Capitus Ianthe is the key to her current supply problems. Division between Capitus Ianthe and Wildfell splits our attention and disrupts involvement with the reavers. She suspects their orders come out of Wildfell, but if those orders come from Capitus Ianthe, then she has offered the Briar Throne in exchange for their cessation."

"And what does it matter?" Maeve asked. "In either outcome I will emerge having gained the throne—something which has been long held from me." She glared daggers at her aunt. "Have you prepared to battle your rival—an ellyllon who is more than your equal? Auntie, you taught me everything I know," she hissed. "You have made me a perfect, unstoppable enemy."

Mab bowed her head. "Indeed, I have. And that is why I came here today. I'm here to offer you the throne. No coups are necessary; there's no demand that blood be shed."

Maeve's stare did not soften. She clearly harbored animosity which she'd pent up over centuries. "And what if I *want* blood?"

Mab's demeanor caught her niece off guard, disarming her. She offered a gentle smile instead of responding with a barb. "You will learn in time that we do not always get the things that we want. You have a choice to make now. If you wish for blood, then so be it. Simply speak your desire. But if you want the throne, I will willingly abdicate... The criers have already made the announcement to assemble an audience," Mab said. "I have only a few conditions for the succession... But the crown could be yours this very night."

Maeve gritted her teeth together and stared at the floor. Her anger clearly boiled beneath the surface. Given enough time, it might eventually simmer to a more manageable level, but Maeve was not well known for her patience... or her forgiving nature.

"Fine," Maeve finally spat. "Let us discuss the transfer of power. Explain your conditions."

With attention brought back to manageable levels, Mab retrieved her cup and sipped some wine. "There are none that are out of the ordinary. The requirements are the same as what I took when my mother stepped aside for my rule, plus one other—a simple one. I shall not take up the mantle of Mother Wild and displace the dowager's role as adviser in Wildfell. I shall take *your* role as princess-lady of Capitus Ianthe. In case you should meet an untimely end or decide you wish to yield power back, I shall remain your heir until such a time as you produce your own bloodline, and then I shall step aside and assume the role of Mother Wild."

The room grew cold and tense for a few moments as the younger elf thought it over.

"Then let us make the arrangements," Maeve said, nodding. But never hid her vengeful, sharp eyes.

Mab snapped her fingers and a collection of scribes and scholars entered the tent and got to work on the chain of succession.

Taller members of the wildfey carried braziers as they wandered through the crowd, racing against sunset. Small pyres lit upon stands and provided illumination for the assembly.

Artisans had hastily erected a stage at the center of Capitus Ianthe's main square. Upon the platform they'd mounted scaffolds and hung upon it bioluminescent plants that glowed more brightly than the lapping flames used throughout the city paths.

Gongs rang out as darkness crept closer, enhancing the lamps efficacy. And then Maeve took the stage, followed by a gwyllion, one of the tylwyth teg from the mountains; her age was impossible to tell as all gwyllions looked like old haggard versions of the more populous ellyllon.

The gwyllion's long ears were bound up with her hair which had been tied back. Bent and withered, she was known in the city as a potent spellcaster and Maeve employed her often.

She employed her craft and cast a spell which shimmered around the platform, barely visible. Her bubble of energy supernaturally amplified the sounds on the stage. Once cast, the gwyllion moved off to the edge, clearing the way but maintaining the mystic effect.

Maeve took the center of the stage, and Mab joined at her side. Together they represented the pinnacle of political power in the faewylds.

[Hear me, folk of Capitus Ianthe. Yield your ears and minds to our Queen, Mab, daughter of Mab, ruler of the Briar Throne and the faewylds.] Maeve spoke in the high tongue, as was the tradition for royal proclamations and edicts.

As Mab stepped forward, every creature, except for those on the stage, bowed and lowered to one knee.

[Peace to you all, my loyal subjects. I am here to encourage you, give you hope, and to protect the Briar Throne from disruptions as much as staleness.] She cast her gaze across the sea of faces. Every one of them gave her their rapt attention.

[Princess Maeve has brought to my attention that my reign has extended over long. In all of Arcadeax, only Oberon's rule has proved longer, and with such longevity, it is possible that I have overstayed my duty to crown and throne. I am loath to let our glorious faewylds stagnate and Maeve has long waited patiently in the wings for this day.]

A murmur of excitement rippled through the crowd. The crowd of Capitus Ianthe was very much pro-Maeve, so far as the political discourse leaned.

Four of the Queen's Royal guard walked onto the stage. There was not so much room on the platform to allow them much distance, but they created a sort of backdrop to frame the procession... And also provide a reasonable amount of security, in case Maeve's violent streak took over and interrupted the proceedings.

They faded into the background and were more like furniture than anything else.

[I am here to abdicate both throne and title. Having no children of my own, I shall willingly yield these to my niece and heir, Maeve, under the same conditions as the title was passed to me by the Dowager Queen Mab, the Mother Wild, and with only one added contingency.]

Mab continued, [Mother Wild, the first Mab, told me once, "There must always be a Queen Mab. *Words matter*—they are important—and that name is a constant among the wildfey."] She turned to her niece and heir. [We shall, at the moment of transferring this authority, take each other's name in perpetuity, as Mother Wild had intended. From that moment until you die, your name shall be Mab and I shall take up yours. I shall be Maeve.]

The she-elf curtsied before her queen. [So shall it be.]

[Then I crown you the ruler of the faewyld,] Mab said. She walked over to one of the guards and knelt. The guard withdrew a dagger and made cuts through her hair.

Mab's crown was a twisted thing made of vine and branch and antler and bone. It was a wild symbol of the wild folk. The crown had become such a part of her that it was difficult to distinguish that crown from her dreadlocked mane.

After it was freed, Queen Mab shook out her hair. Long locks fell as clumps and strands of gossamer, piling upon the stage. She cleared the tangled symbol of her authority until it was free of any vestige of its former owner.

Mab held the thing aloft. The sheer act of it seemed to steal the breath from the crowd which hung on every word and action that occurred on the stage.

Maeve faced the audience and bent to her knees, waiting to take her vows and for her predecessor to set the crown upon her brow.

[Do you swear to protect the integrity of the faewyld and its inhabitants as its Queen, to the best of your ability?] Mab asked.

Maeve answered, [I swear it by the power of the Dagda.]

[Do you promise to uphold the power of Wildfell, keeping with our traditions and the power of Arcadeax?]

Maeve answered, [I swear it by the power of the Dagda.]

[And do you promise to name an heir and keep alive the chain of succession when you take your crown and assume the mantle of Queen?] Mab stared hard at her.

Maeve answered, [I swear it by the power of the Dagda. Until I produce an heir of my own, my successor shall be Maeve, aunt of Queen Mab and daughter of the Mother Wild.]

Mab nodded solemnly. She slowly lowered the crown upon her niece's head. [Then I pronounce you, Mab, Queen of the wildfey and Lady of Wildfell. All duty, power, honor, and authority due to that position now belong to you. Rise and be recognized by your subjects.] The former queen stepped back and faded towards the edge of the stage.

Maeve, who was now Mab, rose to her feet and basked in the applause of the assembly.

"I have much to say," the new queen said. "You have my promise that I will never again return to the ways of old. Too long did we stew in our resentment of the previous regime. Too long did the voices outside of Wildfell's walls go unheard and unheeded."

There was fire in the younger elf's eyes, and she looked at her aunt. There was a murderous glint in them. It ran so deep and violent that the former queen should have been aware of the danger inherent any bargains with the mad ellyllon. Giving absolute power to a foe whose hated consumed them could result in nothing but an untimely death.

The murderous queen practically shrieked, "Words matter, aunt! I am now queen—and I have the authority to make such judgments as execution! By morning I will have your head on a pike and..."

A crow flapped down from a tree branch and landed upon the she-elf's shoulder. At first, a ripple of amusement snaked through the crowd. But it quickly turned with shades of awe and concern.

The queen tried to shake it off, but the bird merely flapped its wings to hold on. It stared directly at the royal she-elf.

The crow focused only on the former Maeve—newly named as Mab—and it cawed. The unexpected hammer call echoed so loudly, it hurt the ears of those fey nearest the bird. The gwyllion maintaining the amplification quit the spell, dropping a kind of muting effect over all in the gathering.

Fey twitched their ears, rubbed inside them with fingers, and tried yawning to reset their hearing. Three of the four soldiers standing sentry on the stage removed their helmets and shook out their ears, trying to regain their senses.

And then the one of the queen's guards who did not remove his helmet stepped forward briskly and seized the young Mab by the hair. Unlike the rest of the guards present, this one carried a sword at his side but also a dagger on each hip.

She gasped and straightened almost to her toes as the soldier stretched her tall and then drew one of the daggers. Clearly disturbed less by the excessive volume than the elves, the creature clutched his dagger and shook off the helmet, revealing human ears.

Only those nearest could hear him above the ringing in their ears. "The orc Warlord Rhylfelour sends his regards."

"Aderyn Corf!" howled several in the crowd. "The Corpse Bird is here to take the queen!"

Remy gritted his teeth and slashed. One vicious stroke of violence sliced cleanly through the tylwyth teg queen's neck. He whirled on one foot, still clutching the lifeless head of the ambitious elf.

Every eye was on him, but he especially felt those of the previous ruler of the Briar Throne. Her face was plastered with shock and indignation... but her eyes—they were smiling.

She had used him to get exactly what she wanted: the removal of her chief political rival. Furthermore, Remy's words before rendering the killing blow would unify the faewylds and bolster them against the unseelie. They gave the wildfey a common enemy and united them under the new queen, Maeve, formerly Mab.

Her strength was only reinvigorated by giving the orc exactly what he'd asked for. She had upheld her end of the bargain and surrendered the head of Queen Mab, as well as stopped the reavers.

Words matter, Remy reminded himself of Mab's lesson as he sprinted away. He launched off the back of the stage and into the darkness before the other remaining guards could apprehend him.

Chapter Eleven

Remy fled through the night, aiming for the edge of Capitus Ianthe. He had a few steps on the other three guards already, and they would be hard pressed to catch him.

The human sprinted past a few tents and then down a narrow lane between rows of tent homes, trying to lose them in the maze-like layout. He didn't know how the royal guards were able to maintain such a dogged pursuit; Remy normally excelled at evasion.

No others milled about the city. They'd all been at the assembly, and so there were no crowds to hide among and little to slow down those sword wielding elves sworn to protect a queen who he'd just murdered.

And then Remy looked down. He still clutched the severed head, holding it by the hair. Blood leaked from the wound, drawing a trail directly to him.

Remy snatched a burlap sack from a cart, spilling its contents, and dropped Rhylfelour's prize inside. He tied the bag to his waist and hurried around another row of homes. A few minutes after staunching the bloody head, sounds of the pursuit tapered off.

Near the edge of Capitus Ianthe, Remy spotted the carriage which he'd ridden in with Mab, now named Maeve. He hurried for it even as alarm horns echoed nearer the center of the city.

The soldiers have called for help, he realized. Nearby, but still out of sight, several horns signaled a response. He had only minutes to escape. *They are coming for me... all of them.*

Remy hurried to the carriage and clambered onto the driver's bench on the flat perch at the front of the vehicle. He picked up the reins and tried to spur the atomies into action.

The cart did not move.

Remy cracked the reins. *Nothing.*

"Come on, you guys," Remy yelled at the miniscule fey. "It's me. You saw me with the queen only a day ago. I need you to move—and now."

The winged atomies seemed to glow as they tinkled a response like tiny bells. The tone took a decidedly minor note. If a chord could have sounded indignant, this one would have.

"I'll make you a deal," Remy said. "One last ride and then I'll set you free."

The atomies tinkled again, but not negative... interrogative, maybe? *They need more information... probably took an oath, too.*

"What was it that Mab kept saying... words matter?" Remy asked, "Are you guys bound to Queen Mab's service?"

The chimes sounded affirmative.

"Then your master is gone," Remy told them. "There *is no more Queen Mab*. She was murdered by the assassin, Aderyn Corff."

Another quizzical chime.

"How do I know?" Remy reached into his bag and pulled out the head. "*Because I am Aderyn Corff* and this is your queen's head. Now do what I say, or I'll pinch each one of you between my fingers and make jelly out of you."

The chimes shifted to a mournful yet terrified note.

Remy replaced the head and picked up the reins even as the sounds of hooves grew louder behind him. The soldiers had guessed at his location and were rapidly approaching.

"Last ride," Remy said. "Get me home and I'll set you all free when we get there." He shifted to the high tongue, [So do I swear it.]

He snapped the reins, and the carriage took off like a shot. The glow of the atomies formed into a streak of light as they pulled the royal chariot. It accelerated so fast, Remy nearly rolled off the back of the carriage.

It rolled over the terrain on fine springs, riding smoothly as a finger across silk. He'd never moved this fast in his entire life. Remy pointed the vehicle where he wanted it to go and let the tiny fey do the rest.

There's no way those soldiers will catch me now!

The atomie driven carriage came to an abrupt stop a short distance from the gates of the Broken Hand orcs' palisade walls. Remy, still holding the reins, blinked dumbly. He could scarcely believe that he'd arrived.

It had been barely more than a few hours since escaping the gathering at Capitus Ianthe. Mab's carriage had made the journey in a single night.

Remy expected the journey to take several days just to reach the border of the faewylds. The atomies tinkled their expectant cries from their position at the cart's yoke.

"Eager little things," Remy said.

They chimed again. Their indecipherable words were clear by their tone. *Do as you promised... Free us.*

Remy stared at them for a moment with a grimace locked upon his face. *Such speed... A carriage like this could come in handy in so many circumstances.*

He shook away the dark thoughts that temped him to break his promise and keep the little fey imprisoned. Remy knew how bleakly his life had turned after the warlord had bound him. He refused to partake in similar actions. Remy was everything Rhylfelour was not.

Hopping down from the driver's seat, he smelled the aroma of smoldering greenery. The carriage's wheels, rimmed in some kind of metal, turned dark as the orange glow from the friction heat cooled. The wheels had produced so much friction that they'd turned sunset orange by the time the trip had finished and the super-heated wheels scorched the vegetation where they rested.

Remy approached the atomies, who pulsed brilliantly with anticipation. They wore tiny filigree lanyards as thin as fishing wire which tethered them to the yoke. He cut the lines and then released the creatures.

They swirled around him in a tornado of light and movement, and then dissipated in a cloud of brilliant particles that exploded into the sky. Each one rushed off to wherever they'd come from before being bound to Mab's service.

Remy looked up and spotted the orc sentries eying him from their observation posts. The human picked up his sack, which held the grisly trophy for his master, and then began the trek through the tribe's outer edges and headed for Rhylfelour's fortress.

Remy strode into Rhylfelour's main courtyard. He wore a smugly victorious look on his face as he walked for the stairs to the main fortress. Remy carried the stained and bulging sack.

His steps faltered as he spotted Genesta standing nearby. Her face was despondent.

When she saw him, she tried to hide the overwhelming look of sorrow. She wiped her face and tried to smooth away the redness at her cheeks.

Remy paused, but she waved him away before he could ask what was wrong. A foul odor drifted from somewhere nearby.

Suddenly self-aware, Remy asked, "Where is Shadarkith?"

"He is here," Genesta promised. "You will see him soon enough. Your mission was a success?" She nodded toward his bag.

"It was." Much of the bravado had gone out of his voice as he spoke with the sidhe seer. They both knew that this victory had bolstered Rhylfelour's claim on the spider queen's hand.

Glancing aside, Remy spotted Rhagathena's carriage parked nearby. He also recognized a few of the horses, specifically the one belonging to the queen's majordomo, Chokorum.

"The queen is here?"

Genesta nodded. "It's been a few days now. This race for her hand, and for the Rime Throne, is a serious matter," she said. "Rhagathena has already been to visit Gaeafdale. One of the sidhe nobles there, Myvarath, has dispatched his own agent. He's supposed to be some kind of specialist. It sounded like he might be a sorcerer, in fact." She eyed her friend with concern. "Whether you are successful or not, Myvarath is a vengeful elf. You should be on your guard. This spellcaster may try to kill you regardless... just to hurt Rhylfelour."

Remy gave her a kind of shrug. "I already met him." He wanted to make a joke about Genesta's gifts not being able to predict everything, but he knew better than to make even the slightest inference about her abilities when there could be others listening. "He won't be a threat to anyone ever again."

She gave him a satisfied look.

The human held up the bag as if to excuse his departure. Genesta nodded and beckoned that he leave.

Remy strode confidently up the stairs and pushed his way through the doors, which led to an interior gallery. He stood straight, surprised to find Rhagathena resting there.

She smiled with a hungry, sharp-toothed mouth, and then instructed Chokorum to retrieve the warlord. The spider looked the assassin over with appreciative eyes.

The serious-looking elf bowed stiffly and hurried away.

"You have accomplished your master's task? And so soon?" Rhagathena asked him.

Remy said, "I have." He stood there at attention, waiting for Rhylfelour's arrival.

Rhagathena licked her lips, not bothering to disguise her desire for the human.

He felt certain that yearning had less to do with sexual lust and more to do with her desire for control of such an efficient and expedient agent. She *wanted* him—wanted to bend him to her will and use him up.

"When last we met in private, I told you we would likely see more of each other, Aderyn Corff. And now here we are," she said.

Remy offered only a stiff bow and refused to engage her. He knew that even conversation could prove deadly. Thankfully, Chokorum and Rhylfelour entered a few moments later.

"You have finished your mission so soon?" Rhylfelour asked. "I anticipated this would take months or even a year, not mere weeks."

"The bandits are dealt with. It should be several years before they're able to rebuild. Those who guessed the orders were coming from Wildfell were correct. The unseelie's borders are secure and the raiders, a group calling themselves the Reavers, have been scattered," Remy reported.

"And the wild queen?" Rhylfelour asked.

"Dead." Remy tossed his sack to the orc.

Rhylfelour shook out the burlap and the battered head of the tylwyth teg queen tumbled out, losing her crown of branches and antlers.

The orc picked up the macabre trophy and dangled it before him like a bauble.

"Maeve, the queen's successor, may prove more pliable if my emissaries are to be believed," Rhagathena said. She poked at the severed head with one finger. "Rigor mortis has not been kind to poor Mab."

Misshapen lumps and dents had formed where the face had bounced repeatedly against the carriage seat during Remy's flight.

Rhagathena asked, "You are certain this is the offending queen? She appears somewhat... *different* than I recall."

Remy swore in the old tongue, [As surely as I live, this is the head of Queen Mab, Ruler of the Briar Throne, and Lady of Wildfell: Queen of the Faewylds.]

Both Rhagathena and Rhylfelour nodded. Arcadeaxn magic would have prohibited his ability to speak falsely.

"Then it must be as you say," Rhagathena said, turning to Rhylfelour. "It appears that Myvarath has been eliminated as a suitor. We shall retire soon to discuss how we might proceed."

The queen glanced back at the human assassin. "Your agent has certainly proved to be a terrifying force... one that will make a welcome addition to my court."

Remy made sure not to look the spider in the eyes, but he did not much disguise his dark tone when he said, "The corpse bird *is* a terrifying thing. Death comes for all in its time. Even kings and queens."

"Surely." Rhagathena chuckled, missing the point entirely, "As Queen Mab could certainly attest… if only the bitch could speak."

The queen took her leave and followed Chokorum as they went further into the fortress.

Rhylfelour shot his pet human a look of approval and then accompanied him toward the courtyard.

Remy said, "If there is no other business, then I should take my leave for some breakfast. I want to visit with Shadarkith. I'd like to see how his training has progressed," he lied. Remy was more concerned about the boy himself. He didn't give a damn how well Shadarkith could fight—he wanted to see the boy truly live, and that was not always the same as surviving.

"About that," Rhylfelour said, pointing the way. "There's a simple task you should see to beforehand."

Remy glanced sidelong at the orc who accompanied him towards the steps. It was uncharacteristic of him, unless the warlord was gloating.

Together they walked, but a dark seed of dread lodged in Remy's gut. Every step made it bloom a little more.

The stench in the courtyard grew stronger the closer they got to the hovel where the orc had housed Shadarkith. That dread seed in Remy's gut felt heavier with every step he took to the shack.

Remy opened the door and found the boy sprawled out on the floor. Dead.

Shadarkith's skin had turned gray, except for where the bruises on his arms and face had discolored. He lay face down and must have been that way for several days, judging by the stink.

Remy settled on one knee and rolled the boy onto his back. Livor mortis had made the blood settle on his front side, forcing a blotchy rouge into his skin.

He looked up at Rhylfelour and growled. "What happened?" He added an accusatory tone, "What did you do?"

The orc shrugged nonchalantly from where he stood in the door.

Genesta watched the proceedings from across the courtyard.

Rhylfelour looked pleased with himself. "You will want to bury him, I'm sure. He succumbed to his wounds during training." He tsked, "The boy simply refused to learn."

Remy snarled and narrowed his gaze. He bit his lip so hard it bled, and then he roared profanities at the orc warlord.

Rhylfelour laughed them off as playful banter; it was common treatment amongst orcs. But then Remy wagged a finger in Rhylfelour's face and hissed, "*You* are ddiymadferth."

The orc stiffened, and his eyes grew wild with ragged red fringes of rage. He bared his teeth. "If you were not such a valuable asset, I would throttle the life from you like I did this whelp."

Remy curled his lip and spat in response, "And you will *never* know what I know."

Rhylfelour stiffened with surprise. He could have understood the human firing back threat for a threat. But this was different. He did not understand.

"Explain yourself," the orc demanded.

Remy sneered. He knew that physical threats were meaningless. They carried no weight since he could not defy his oath or the Arcadeaxn magic that bound him. He could only withhold knowledge as a form of revenge.

"You will never know."

The orc repeated, "Know *what*?"

Remy glared at him. Hate burned inside of him. Rage strong enough to burn down this orc's house with him inside. Remy would laugh as he watched the flames. Rage that made him less of the human he was and more of the Death Bird this wicked creature had made him into… if only his oath could be dispelled, then Remy would kill Rhylfelour for his crimes. This one, and every other evil the orc had visited upon him.

"I know that you cannot beat me if we fought." Remy balled his fists and stared up into the eyes Of the massive orc warrior. "Not truly. I have surpassed you in talent."

Rhylfelour had made his name as a mighty warrior in his younger days. He was unbeatable. Unstoppable. Surpassing in skill and in strength and more intelligent or scheming than any of his kind. He was the best.

Remy, dwarfed by the size of the orc, did not take into account sheer muscle size, nor height, nor the years of experience that Rhylfelour had on him. "You were once the best. *Were,*" the human hissed.

Rhylfelour stared down at him. Shock took over his face. It mixed with those yellow eyes as he examined Remy. The comment had taken the orc aback. Further, Remy could tell that of all the things he might have told Rhylfelour, this was the one thing they genuinely hurt him.

Remy pressed his advantage. "You will never know—*but I will.* I will always know. If we were to fight. I would kill you. And I would not think twice about it."

Unable to cope with the thought, and unsure of how to respond, Rhylfelour snapped, "Repeat your oath."

Remy crossed his arms, feigning as if to refuse.

Rhylfelour screamed, "Speak your oath, damn it!"

Begrudgingly, Remy slowly and cautiously articulated his words. But his eyes remained fixed and as hard as iron. Iron that was malignant to the fey. [I swear my allegiance to Rhylfelour, son of Jarlok and warlord chief of the Broken Hand orcs.]

The big orc's nostrils flared, and he flexed and relaxed his hands in quick succession. And then he whirled on his heel and headed back towards his stronghold.

Remy spoke just loud enough to make sure the warlord heard him. "You will never know because you are too scared to learn the truth of it."

He knew his master had caught those words by the way he bristled as he moved.

Remy turned his gaze up and saw the spider queen's majordomo spying from the edge of one window. Rhagathena would soon learn how the altercation unfolded, and the human knew she would likely approach him again, perhaps with some clever way to weasel out of the orc's bondage if he pledged to her. But he would deny her. He would refuse her with every ounce of his being. Remy had already planned his way out of the mess that was his life.

The human stood there for a few long minutes. When the scene was finally safe and the courtyard had cleared, Genesta walked across and gave him a hug.

"I'm sorry I didn't tell you," Genesta said. "The warlord would not allow it. He prevented anyone else from handling the body."

Remy's brows pinched inquisitively.

"I... I think he meant it as a compliment to you," she said. "In some strange way, he meant it as a gift."

The assassin growled several choice words. "Some gift. Maybe his next act of kindness will be to pluck out my eyes."

Genesta said nothing until Remy calmed. Then she explained, "I am not defending him, but knowing how he thinks is the key to beating him."

Remy kicked a stone across the yard and crossed his arms.

"Shadarkith could not survive even one year of the same instruction he inflicted upon you," Genesta said. "If anything, Rhylfelour took it easier on that boy. You... you *endured*. In his foolish orc brain, he meant for that to be a compliment. He meant to express how special you are to him."

"That doesn't change anything," Remy growled, grabbing a shovel to bury his friend. "Rhylfelour must die."

Genesta bowed her head and whispered, "I agree. He has to die."

Chapter Twelve

Remy killed again.

One year had passed since Shadarkith's murder at the hands of the orc warlord. Rather than push his grudge openly, the human found an altogether new way to subvert Rhylfelour's plans. He disassociated.

Remy barely spoke to the cruel taskmaster who held his reins. He kept his own company, and chatted with Corax and Genesta, but he was through talking to orcs.

Whenever Rhylfelour had orders, Remy remained silent except to answer direct questions from the warlord. He kept his face neutral when he disagreed, which was nearly always, but he carried out Rhylfelour's wishes with swift and unyielding ferocity.

Remy knew what he was doing; he had a plan. Remy was waiting. The death of Queen Mab had taught him everything he needed to know about dealing with the fey… and before Remy had killed her, Princess Maeve's biggest mistake was overplaying her hand and alerting the Briar Throne to her rebellion.

Remy would not make that mistake.

After a year of seeming compliance, Rhylfelour seemed to think Remy had become his most loyal supporter, maybe even a friend. Or perhaps the orc assumed he'd finally broken the human's will. Whichever it was, Remy did not care. Rhylfelour gave Aderyn Corff a target, and Remy acted.

Everything else was just a matter of biding his time.

"Rhylfelour's going to get everything he wants. And then, so will I," Remy said, his thoughts snapping back to reality.

The human, in his role as Aderyn Corff, was covered fingertip to forearm in blood. Five elves lay dead on the trail where he'd ambushed them. Three lay with arrows sticking from their bodies. The other two he'd beaten in combat. Four were guards, and the last was some unseelie elf who had offended Rhagathena in some way.

Remy used the victim's clothing and wiped the blood from his hands. He'd felt reasonably certain that the elf wasn't even aware he'd offended the mad queen. Remy only knew that the elf's name was on the list and Rhylfelour's wedding gift to Rhagathena was the completion of it.

Somewhere in the trees overhead, Corax cawed to summon the carrion eaters. The human bit back the twinges of guilt that nibbled at his gut as he sheathed his blade. His fingertips brushed the dúshlán at his side... Krogga's blade.

Memories surfaced, feelings resurfaced: he recalled how the chief's honorable death had made him feel. Remy wanted that. *I will have it soon enough,* he thought. *The queen's list is finally complete.*

The last year, ever since Rhagathena accepted Rhylfelour's proposal, had crawled by in one seemingly endless mélange. One day seemed to flow into the next; it all blurred in barely discernible shades of gray... Just an endless loop of violence and murder.

No, thought Remy. *It's not exactly murder, is it?* He knew that no names on that list were innocent, not that it made his job any more palatable. Each person named, with the additions of Rhagathena and Rhylfelour, was guilty of great atrocities. But Remy refused to consider his part an act of pure justice, either. The stains of their guilt stretched to Remy, even if he had no desire for the death of these victims. Remy resented each assassination. But he was still complicit, albeit unwillingly.

Remy returned a few days later to Rhylfelour's stronghold and reported that the task had been accomplished.

The orc smiled as he dipped a stylus in his inkwell and crossed the final name off his betrothed's list. And then he dismissed Remy.

Rhylfelour dispatched orders to his riders to make announcements and proclamations. Messengers would call on each of the orc chieftans, demanding their presence at the coming wedding. Another messenger he sent to Arctig Maen, alerting the spider queen that the time had arrived.

Genesta joined Remy in the courtyard outside Rhylfelour's home. The human sank to his knees, feeling hollowed out.

"It is finished?" Genesta asked.

Remy nodded. "Rhylfelour just sent riders out to make his announcements." He looked at her. "Are you ready?"

"Ready for what?" Genesta asked.

"Within a month, I am certain we'll all be relocated to Hulda Thorne, probably the fortress of Arctig Maen."

She kept her expression reserved, but Remy could tell that the prospect bothered her. She had become reasonably comfortable here. The orcs were terrible, but Rhylfelour kept her insulated from the rest of the unseelie.

Genesta sighed. "I am as ready as I think I could ever be."

Together, they watched the dozen orcs on horseback leave through the main gate of Broken Hand. And then they dispersed, each going different directions.

Corax flew over the sprawling rooftops of Hulda Thorne, keeping a keen focus on his human companion.

Remy walked the streets of the large city, keeping a wary eye out for his safety and also exploring as much as he could. The move to the city had come quicker than expected, and he'd already been quartered in Arctig Maen.

The main fortress was at the city's center and the human had free rein to explore it—even if soldiers frowned on an unbranded human roaming the streets. But only those who did not recognize him voiced their opinion on the matter.

Arctig Maen, by itself, was larger than the entirety of the Broken Hand orcs' home. While the unseelie capitol may have dwarfed Rhylfelour's stronghold in comparison, the warlord ruled more than just his tribe. The twelve rings he wore gave him claim to lead all the unseelie orcs... And the ferocity of orcs was nothing to sniff at. After all, it had been the strength of their kind which had finally brought down the berserk infernal prince who'd attacked when the unseelie king, Wulflock, had refused the demon's offers of an alliance.

Remy kept his hood up. By now, the persona of Aderyn Corff had been well established throughout the unseelie. His skills had been tested, and he was hardened by experience. Remy thought it better to avoid confrontation rather than seek it out.

Best if no one realizes a free human walks the city streets, he told himself. And then he frowned. *Free being a relative manner of speaking.*

Remy visited a local vendor to buy a few sundries and wares. The palace provided for all his needs, but they also monitored everything very closely. Most of the things Remy shopped for were common and would give no cause for alarm. But Remy hated being spied on. It was just one more form of control he endured from folks who desired authority over him.

The disguised human put a little bread, meat, and cheese in his pockets, along with an apple that he purchased. He also managed to procure a tiny set of lock picks which he secreted away between seams where the leather of his boot met the footgear's sole.

Remy knew what he had planned. Aderyn Corff greatly desired the murder of his master, and he learned that people with ill intentions typically often got into trouble along the way. The least he could do would be prepared for it, hence the lock picks. Remy was in danger here, more so than ever before... even more than when he'd murdered a wildfey queen at the heart of her power.

After walking some distance, Remy found the more rundown sectors of Hulda Thorne. He did not want the tourist's version of the city. Black as it was, he wanted to see the true heart of Hulda Thorne.

Standing in the margins between the forgotten parts of the city and the more prestigious sections, Remy noticed the stark difference.

One side had been blackened and decayed as a clear sign of urban blight. Sallow faces of forgotten citizens peeked from windows and stared at him from entrances to derelict buildings. Foundations crumbled where the regular frost heaves chewed away the bases of those structures, cracking and pitting them.

Opposite the withered zone towered square and plumb structures, white like teeth and protruding proudly from the ground like monuments. Discoloration ran from only the ground to waist height, where the regular frosts marred the otherwise smooth finish of the buildings. Frostclouds moved through Hulda Thorne each morning like a mist.

Remy turned back to the disenfranchised hovels and strolled through the streets. He walked for some distance, stopping only after something buzzed at the edge of his senses. He was not specifically looking for trouble. Mostly, he was just looking to stretch his legs, learn more about the city, and clear his mind so he could more carefully prepare for the coming wedding of Warlord Rhylfelour and that spider Rhagathena.

Nonetheless, trouble always seemed to find him.

As he paused, he studied everything his eyes revealed. Remy realized that the scene was *somehow* indescribably wrong. He passed several ragged denizens in this quarter. They included sidhe, faun, little folk, a few displaced wildfey and goblins, and they all had a certain look of dejection. It was on both their faces and expressed in how they dressed.

Ahead, Remy spotted a mostly collapsed building. Examining that area proved that sense of *wrongness* to him.

The structure might have once been a warehouse of some sort. The few beggars and residents nearby did not belong. They camped within sight of that building and glanced back at it far too often. Their clothes were wrong, too. Remy spotted belts at the waists of several of them. They were *too perfect in their rugged appearance,* as if they'd been tailored made by some high-quality playwright to play the part of denizens belonging to a slum.

They were pretenders.

Remy chided himself as he walked past that zone and circled back from behind, sneaking through an alley and cutting through an adjacent abandoned building to get a better look at the discreetly guarded structure. After creeping through the dark, disintegrating sister building, Remy found a gap in the boards through which he could spy the warehouse's interior.

Inside, more guards were posted. Metal wheeled carts were mounted on rails that formed a system leading down a steep ramp and below ground level.

The facility looked like some sort of processing center. A large gate on one wall could be opened to the city streets, where all the watchers waited; wheel marks had cut grooves through the dirt near that large door.

They must receive shipments on the regular. Those secret guards on the street are likely meant to chase off any traffic before any deliveries are made—that would prevent witnesses to their operation, Remy thought. They could minimize any sight of their deliveries. There wouldn't even be witnesses of questionable integrity.

"But why would they bother going to such lengths to keep this hidden?" Remy whispered to himself.

Of those guards posted inside, Remy could identify a few key markings and styles of their weaponry. These were members of the royal guard: Rhagathena's special security forces.

Remy took a few steps back and skulked through the building. A familiar smell beckoned his nose, and he followed it. The tang of smoke hovered nearby, though he could not quite isolate its origin. He sniffed some more and detected odors of oxidation. Someone heated and melted metals nearby.

Lowering to one knee, Remy sniffed near the spongy, ancient floorboards. "The entire operation is underground. And someone is smelting metals down there."

Remy drew himself back up and walked cautiously through the dark, searching for more clues when the floor beneath him gave way entirely. He fell into a heap but found himself in a storage room. Luckily, it was unoccupied but for container after container of tiny metal pellets and jagged shards of black ore.

He knew what they were at once. *Iron ore.*

This entire place was toxic to the fey. Whatever this operation was about, the queen was building something out of a forbidden metal that burned worse than fire and whose pain could not be assuaged.

Remy could think of only one target the unseelie queen had in mind—especially since Remy had already personally killed so many of the individuals who she hated; there were too few left for them to be unseelie. *Mab was right. She's planning to reignite the war between the Winter and Summer Courts and is building some weapon to win the war!*

To harvest and work this sort of metal, the elves had to have a workforce of human slaves, that or powries. *Probably both.* Remy grabbed a large fistful of iron pellets and stuffed them in a leather bag, pocketing it.

There was not much else in the room. He spotted a massive metal shape that looked like a horse-sized seed pod. Remy recognized Fremenor's sparking lighter device affixed to it and assumed the thing was some kind of cauldron. Its primary interest was that it was tall enough that Remy thought he could use it to climb up and escape back to the ground level.

Instead, he crept out from the storage building and further explored the underground halls.

He stole through the shadows and peaked through doorways. Sidhe taskmasters, each wearing padded armor and other protective gear to keep them from touching the toxic stuff, presided over multiple small chain gangs of slaves.

In addition to the humans who'd been tasked with working the deadly metals, there were a few of the dwarven dvergr. They were likely pressed into service because of their expertise in the craft. Also present were a few coblynau, the wildfey who looked like ellyllon except their eyes were deep violet and their skin as black as pitch. They lived their entire lives below ground and could see perfectly in the dark, which made them excellent miners.

All the slaves were emaciated. They looked as if their taskmasters worked them to death, using them up like chattel, and then discarding them. As if to support that suspicion, Remy spotted a pile of human corpses. They still wore chains and been carted off to the side and abandoned.

I have found the Lightstarved, Remy realized.

Anger kindled in his gut. But it quickly turned to panic as he recognized footsteps directly behind him. He whirled on his heel, but there was no place to hide.

The chain gang consisted of four humans. They'd come around a corner, likely reporting for some duty. A man about Remy's age stopped in his tracks, disrupting the rest of the line. He recognized Remy for what he was.

"You—you are human?"

Remy realized his hood had dropped when he'd fallen through the floor earlier.

"I am," he whispered.

The gang leader looked around to see if they had been spotted. Terror was written across his face. "You must get out of here. Leave while you still can," he insisted.

Remy felt an immediate kinship to him. This man tried to save them for no other reason but that they had humanity in common. But Remy could do nothing for him.

Reaching into his pocket, Remy produced the meager foodstuffs he'd placed there and handed over to the slaves. They nearly wept with joy and quickly shared it amongst themselves.

Remy put a finger to his lips as a universal sign for quiet.

The gang leader nodded vigorously. "We never saw you. You were never here. Flee while you're still able."

Remy pulled up his hood, sprinted through the dark, and escaped back the way he'd come. All the while, he recalled the tortures of his youth. He wondered if he'd had a comparative life of ease.

Remy flitted through the hall, passing from shadow to shadow like a wraith. And then he went back up and through the busted floor he'd fallen through. He emerged at ground level and skulked through the abandoned warehouse.

A guard's voice cried out, "You! Stop right there."

Remy instinctively reached for a dagger at his hip. Then he thought better of it. He turned and fled, drawing his hood tight to keep his face and ears concealed. He had never been an overly lucky man, but with any amount at all, he would appear like any one of the homeless drifters he'd seen in this part of the town.

The guard's footsteps stomped in pursuit, but Remy was faster, and they faded behind him. He burst out through the door and into the alley. A few moments later, he was well beyond his pursuer's reach. Seconds after he rounded a corner, he found a cluster of vagrants and fell into step with them as they ambled aimlessly through the ramshackle sections of Hulda Thorne.

Once he believed the coast had cleared and his fiercely beating heart calmed, he turned and headed back toward the city's innermost section. The truly dangerous part of the unseelie capitol: the royal fortress of Arctig Maen.

Chapter Thirteen

Remy bound up the stairs in the citadel where Rhylfelour's closest personnel were housed within a block of apartments. A spacious common area interconnected many of the rooms on that floor. It was an efficient design, Remy noted, especially if the spider queen wanted to keep eyes on a large group of people.

A single spy watching that central atrium could keep tabs on the comings and goings of every resident on any given floor.

Remy had a small apartment on that level. Its door was opposite Genesta's, and the elf waited for him in the lobby.

The other doors led to appointments for different trusted lieutenants from the Broken Hand clan. At any given time, one of them was appointed as the chaperon for the elf seer.

Over the last year, Rhylfelour had come to trust Remy more closely in many things, but not those concerning the aes sidhe. He and Genesta had been close ever since the day they'd met beneath the Aphay tree in the Grinning Wood. Genesta had not been a mother to the child, but perhaps something like an aunt or an interested patroness.

Remy closed the distance and whispered to the elf. Genesta's chaperon barely looked up at them. So long as they didn't openly plot rebellion or attempt to escape, the orcs didn't particularly care what the two outsiders did.

"I found the Lightstarved," Remy said, explaining his previous interest in them. "It's a whole force of mostly human slaves who have been forced into terrible service." He explained everything that he'd seen, but he'd already secured the stolen sack of iron filings in his room. He would not risk injuring his friend with them. Many believed that even remote exposure to ferrous ore had an effect on a fey creature's health.

"The warlord already knows of it," Genesta said.

"What? Rhylfelour is aware that Rhagathena is using iron?" Remy asked incredulously.

She nodded and used hand signs to bring his volume to a more discreet level.

"It gets even worse," she said. "I'm not sure if the queen is using him, or if his passion for violence has rubbed off on her, but between the two of them, they've agreed to send the full orc army to the Selvages. They've concocted some plan to expand the unseelie realm's borders and take the crags and bridges separating the lands, giving them unfettered passage over the Solstox Ravine. Rhylfelour's exact words were, 'We can send those seelie bastards all the way back to Faery Cairn with any luck.'"

Remy grimaced as he rubbed his chin. "That only makes my plans to finally eliminate the warlord that much more pressing," he growled.

Both looked up, each catching subtle movement at the fringes of their vision. Chokorum, Rhagathena's majordomo, moved toward them.

Remy was not sure how long he'd been there, but he suspected that the sidhe servant had overheard at least part of the conversation. And that meant that the spider would know it as well.

The human tried to smooth any worry out of his face. When he'd last privately met with the Queen, she'd seemed to signal that Rhylfelour was a means to an end and that his death would not terribly bother her, provided Remy would pledge his service to her. Of course, that was before they had agreed to their betrothal. But Remy suspected there was no true love in their arrangement.

Neither Remy nor Genesta had said anything against the *queen*, and so he wasn't significantly worried. Any resident of Arctig Maen with any reputation or standing was caught up in the grand pursuit of power—it was the queen's game.

Should Chokorum have overheard the conversation in its entirety, it might change nothing besides renewing Rhagathena's overtures for his loyalty. If Remy had entered the game, she would redouble her attempts to tempt him into her service and watch him more closely as she did all the legitimate pawns in her power contests.

Chokorum bowed deeply once he'd stepped between Remy and Genesta. "The queen has sent me to invite Aderyn Corff for a private audience."

Remy returned the bow stiffly and formally. He knew he could not deny her a simple meeting. He'd been expecting her to call on him ever since they arrived in the city a few days ago.

The human accepted the invitation and then watched the queen's servant depart.

Rhagathena sat waiting for Remy. The royal hall had been cleared out, and she rested casually upon the Rime Throne.

Remy approach the throne again, much as he had before.

Her eyes washed over him appreciatively. There was a certain glimmer of lusty greed in them. Still not sexual, but he had denied her access to him previously—and that made her want him even more.

In one hand she tightly clutched the completed list of names which have been delivered by Rhylfelour. "It appears my betrothed has offered me a gift, which he has barely paid for." Her eyes skimmed the collection of blotted out names. "I believe you had more to do with this offering than he did."

Remy gave her a bow appropriate to her station. He said nothing. Just as before, he felt a knot of warning tighten in his gut. Saying the wrong thing or even saying the right thing in the wrong way to the treacherous unseelie spider queen could have fatal repercussions.

His cautious silence allowed him to determine the best response... which was often more silence.

Rhagathena recognized his hesitation. She leaned forward and waved away any notion that Remy should have suspicions. The queen chuckled and made some small talk, which Remy ignored. None of it was relevant, and he felt keenly aware of how his life could hang in the balance.

"My, you are a serious human, aren't you?" she asked, pouting slightly when he would not engage.

"I take my duties seriously, my Queen. Life has not dealt a hand that allows me to take any situation lightheartedly," Remy said.

She nodded measurably, and with a hint of recognition touching her features. Rhagathena knew his tale.

"When last we parted, I had given you some words to think about. I should hope you've considered them. Your queen would make a far more generous master than Rhylfelour has ever been," she spoke in a tone that asked for a response.

Remy nodded grimly. "I am bound by the oath to which Rhylfelour has ensnared me by."

"Oaths are often superseded by a greater power... Provided that power has the strength to eliminate the holder of any present commitment." Rhagathena raised her eyebrows.

Remy remained standing at attention but gave the web weaver no footing with which to crawl into his life. He stared dumbly and feigned ignorance as to her intentions.

"A pity," she said. "I will control you whether you like it or not. The only question is of who directly holds your leash, human.

Your refusal merely requires me to keep the warlord around longer so that he may yank your chain and direct your paths."

Remy did not react.

Rhagathena rose from the throne and walked closer to him. She raised up to her full, impressive height. Rhagathena was head and shoulders taller than Rhylfelour, even though not nearly as thickly muscled as the orc.

"I am aware that you've discovered my operations in Hulda Thorne. You have discovered the Lightstarved." She traced a finger around the edge of his face, touching him seductively. "Apparently, I have been found out, and you now see now why I need humans. Only they can work the mines and craft what I need."

She finally had Remy's attention, and he turned to look at her. "What are you making with the iron?"

Rhagathena grinned. "That, my dear son of Adam, is a secret reserved for only my most trusted generals."

Remy asked, "Is that what you are offering? A position as one of your generals?"

"If that is the cost to which you will rise, then yes. I find myself in need of a strong general to lead my humans. Someone who understands them… but also who understands the paths of violence. A man intimate with suffering." Rhagathena eyed him greedily again. "The unseelie could benefit from the sons of Adam in the coming war."

In that moment, Remy knew what this whole marriage was about. The blood thirsty unseelie queen was marshaling forces, but she needed more pieces on the board. And both orcs and humans made excellent, expendable grunts.

Rhagathena clicked her sharp talons upon the tile floor. She begged the question in the oldest tongue, [I assume you will swear secrecy of our conversation?]

[I shall not tell Rhylfelour or any of those loyal to him of it, as directed my queen,] Remy responded.

"Excellent," the queen said. "I have given you much to think on, but I shall require an answer soon."

Remy nodded. It was all he was willing to give her for the moment. She seemed to sense as much and accepted it... for now.

She waved her hand to dismiss him, and Remy turned and departed. He was careful to keep his speed and check, but as eager as ever to exit the treacherous queen's presence.

Remy departed the spider's lair and walked through the halls, heading back towards the Citadel where his apartment was located. Rhylfelour spotted him. The warlord was there giving a tour to a cluster of orcs.

He waved him over, demanding Remy's presence with a motion of one hand. His fingers sparkled where his rings of authority rested.

The human approached and realized that together these twelve creatures made up all the tribal leaders of the Demonsbreak orcs.

Remy recognized many faces from the Enclave, though he'd not made a memorable appearance at that gathering—he hadn't become *truly* notorious until his actions afterward.

One of them commented, "So this is the corpse bird?"

"Aderyn Corff," said another.

"He doesn't look like much."

Rhylfelour made a low growl in his throat, barely perceptible to the human's ears, but he felt the rumbling note of warning in it. The Broken Hand warlord had *made* Aederyn Corff—flippant dismissal of the Corpse Bird was an insult to Rhylfelour.

"Careful there," Rhylfelour said. "I trained this one myself. If I give the word, he could easily kill any of you... possibly all of you at once."

Remy had often misunderstood the orc's compliments. But he understood this one.

The human bowed but purposefully remained silent. It was the same approach one took with the queen.

Rhylfelour asked Remy, "Have you secured a gift to present at the wedding?"

None noticed Remy's scowl. It took him great effort to keep his face neutral. Rhagathena was right: Remy had already gone to great lengths to secure the first gift, the one that Rhylfelour had passed off as his grand gesture.

"I have spent a great deal of energy preparing gifts for both you and the queen," Remy promised.

Rhylfelour grinned broadly. The orcs behind him stiffened; their ears perked up, as if impressed with their leader's pet assassin.

Remy could see a few of them whisper to each other. His comments had sown a little discord between them. None of the other orc warlords wanted to be outdone by a mere human.

"It is a grand gift indeed," Remy embellished.

Rhylfelour leaned closer, intrigued. "Now I am curious."

"The anticipation will make it that much more worthwhile," Remy said. "I can assure you that I've prepared the only thing worthy of a creature of your reputation and honor."

And then Remy turned, dismissed himself, and headed for his quarters.

The following day, Genesta met Remy outside on the lawn.

He was due to leave shortly for the royal wedding ceremony. The wedding would occur at an immaculately maintained park lay within the walls of Arctig Maen, near its gates, which led to the greater city of Hulda Thorne.

Remy could see it from the balcony of his apartment. The garden was the crown jewel of beautiful locations nestled inside the capitol of the Winter Court. There were many several such gardens in Rhagathena's private sanctuary, and only those with clearance to her interior borders were allowed to access them.

Few folk actually used the green-spaces, though. Members of the court were generally too busy plotting and scheming their games of shadow and dagger. Little time was left to appreciate the wonders of nature.

The human met his longest friend in one of the smaller parks nearest the castle entrance. Remy spotted Genesta within a gazebo. Her handler, one of Rhylfelour's lieutenants, watched from a distance. He looked bored and resentful of pulling this duty today, of all days, when the revelry would reach peak hedonism.

"The wedding hour will be here soon," Genesta said, as if she'd foreseen how the day's events would play out.

"What do you know? What did you see?" Remy asked, hoping that everything unfolded exactly as planned.

She shook her head, expression dour. "Only that today marks many endings and new beginnings."

"I cannot see your path amid all the tangling and unraveling of threads." Genesta locked eyes with the human. "When I search for your part in what comes next, all I see is raw chaos. I can see nothing much past this wedding, and I fear that today, right now, is the last time we may speak like this."

Remy swallowed. *If I'm surrounded by chaos and she cannot see my fate, perhaps I fail utterly and catastrophically?*

"Then tell me what you see for yourself," Remy said. "I've heard that seers can always see *their* fate in things."

The elf squeezed Remy's hands as if to say, *I wish that were true.* Genesta gave a melancholy smile. "I can see that. For me, at least, today's actions will result in my freedom."

Hope sparked in Remy. *Then my actions today will earn a net positive, at least... even if I burn out in utter and total catastrophe. Maybe that provides her the opportunity to escape to a better life.*

Remy embraced her momentarily. "Then this is goodbye, my friend."

She squeezed him harder for a moment. "Indeed, it is, Remington Keaton. We have had many moments of conversation and shared much truth over the years. Remember, whenever you hear my words, heed them," Genesta said. And then she pulled away and headed back for her chaperon.

Remy watched her go, wondering why her parting advice had been phrased cryptically. He wanted to unravel the riddle of it, but he could barely spare the focus. He had a wedding to attend, an unbreakable oath to destroy, and a monster to kill.

Chapter Fourteen

As a matter of preparation for the ceremony, Rhylfelour drank several flagons of strong liquor with his companions. All were other chiefs of different orcish tribes. Around their necks they wore a lanyard by which they dangled their macabre trophies. Each denoted their clan name and position as chief: Fractured Skull, Severed Foot, Busted Horn, and more.

Rhylfelour wore his own lanyard, the infernal Broken Hand. The grim motif was apparently what passed among orcs for formal wear.

Attire styles aside, Remy knew that he did not fit in among them. Instead of joining them, he had been invited to provide security for the wedding party.

Opposite of the revelers below, he remained sober and vigilant. He walked the archways that spanned from column to column; the standing pillars marking the edges of the garden grounds where the wedding would soon occur. Corax flew in lazy loops overhead and regularly popped down on whichever archway Remy was headed towards as the human stalked back-and-forth, keeping a watchful eye on Rhylfelour's activities.

Slowly, more and more members of the Winter Court trickled in and formed their own cliques. Knots of elvish sidhe formed; they were aligned together in the various schemes and plots of the uppermost castes. Many clusters that formed were in opposition to other groups with opposing viewpoints.

Remy watched it all. They sifted each other like oil and water. But nobles from each of the factions glared hatefully at the orc groom—his elevation had ended the hopes of many others who contended for the throne.

No harm would come to Remy's master. Rhylfelour was about to be wed, and Remy was committed to ensuring that dream was unspoiled. It was crucial to Remy's plan.

Only by ensuring Rhylfelour ascended to the Rime Throne could Aderyn Corff finally fly free.

The Bard arrived.

Not only would the Bard entertain guests and regale them with famous tales, but he was appointed to officiate the royal wedding. He meandered between the different clusters of noble tuatha with seeming indifference to the many cliques. Either he was allied with none of those individual sects, or with all of them. Remy could not tell. The only thing Remy was certain of was that he was the only human in the garden.

Rhylfelour was already drunk and feeling free with compliments and praise. He raised his cup and shouted at Remy. "Corpse Bird! Aderyn Corff, my pet Adam. Come down from your perch."

Remy looked sidelong at Corax. The bird tilted his head and blinked with strange sideways eyelids.

Sighing at the bird, Remy descended the stairs and met the orc.

"We cannot have a human running around the interior of Arctig Maen," Rhylfelour said. "But you've proved you're so much more than a mere man... But still, we've got to cover those unsightly, stunted ears."

Rhylfelour produced a strange cap that had been crafted out of bird feathers. A hard, chitinous material made a kind of bill and shaded his eyes. It was shaped into the form of a beak. The orcs placed it upon Remy's head. It did hide the distinct appearance of his humanity, and it marked him as the figure that haunted unseelie dreams: *The Corpse Bird. Aderyn Corff. Friend of the carrion eaters.*

The orcs all had a good laugh. Remy used a reflective surface to catch sight of his image. He approved. Whomever the craftsperson had been, they did a good job of constructing the crow-like mantle.

Remy left it in place and wondered how Corax would react to the sight.

When he turned back, Rhylfelour begun instructing his accomplices as to how the ceremony would go. It sounded typical as far as the order of service went.

"You orcs are my warlords. Warrior chiefs gathered under one banner: the Rime Throne of the unseelie kingdom and its Winter Court. You are co-equal Warlords of the twelve clans..."

"Eleven clans," a voice piped up.

Rhylfelour cocked his head quizzically. Then he shook his head. "No. There are twelve clans, not eleven," he argued.

Remy leaned closer. "You still lead the Broken Hand clan," he whispered an accentuated honorific, "*Warlord.*"

The orc nodded and then waved his servant off. "Right, right," he noted the numeric change and turned the rings on his fingers one by one. "You have each sworn loyalty and fealty to me, giving me your allegiance. Today, I tell you to give that same allegiance and devotion to Rhagathena once our union is finalized. Give her the same deference that you owe to me."

Rhylfelour raised his cup and tried to fix each of them with a short but appreciative look. They appreciated the attempt, but barely any of them had eyes that could focus much beyond their cups at this point. "To Rhagathena, the spider queen, Lady of the Realm."

They each shouted their agreements and accolades. About that time, Rhagathena entered through a large stone archway. She seemed to blush as she overheard their cheers for her.

Remy thought it all a load of crap. He suspected the queen had staged the entrance, timing it perfectly. But her arrival had the desired effect upon the revelers. One by one, the eleven gathered orcish chiefs bent their knees and swore allegiance is to her in the old tongue, with the caveat that her marriage to the orc champion was fulfilled by rite and ceremony.

The human returned to his perch, where he could watch over the pre-nuptial gathering. Remy could see the entire game unfold before his eyes. Rhylfelour was on track to take the throne. Rhagathena had just earned the promise of a mighty orc army filled with violent, muscular warriors. And Remy had sown seeds, tiny and minuscule things—the most deeply planted one was in the ear and mind of the monster who had tormented him for so many years.

Remy smiled. So far, everything went exactly according to plan.

"Can you imagine what the unified army of orcs can do when open war breaks out against our seelie enemies?" Rhagathena asked.

"We are at war?" asked the chief of the Bleeding Femur clan.

Those around him perked up optimistically. All eyes turned to the queen, and it was evident that the orcs were eager for battle.

She gave them a slight bow. "We have never been *not* at war. That tension that simmers between Winter and Summer is not a true peace, and the first party to admit that the conflicts of old still endure shall be the one to win."

Rhagathena offered a kind of feminine shrug, switching back into a posture more appropriate for a bride on her wedding day. "But we can talk more of that later. For now, I should leave you to decide how best to pay tribute for making your leader into king of the unseelie and Lord of the Winter Court."

Sharp, toothy grins spread from ear to ear across the eleven chieftains.

"The strength and ferocity of the twelve orc tribes is what made this union come to pass. It is the strength of their warlords that will make it prosper and by their strength, we shall conquer all of Arcadeax." The Sspider queen glanced aside at Rhylfelour. And then her eyes drew up to the corpse bird where he perched in his roost atop the marker stones. "As their king, you should not be their equal, my dear," she told Rhylfelour.

Rhylfelour's volume shrunk to a level others could not hear, but Remy could ascertain the argument. He had never considered them his equal; Rhylfelour had never been a mere warlord. He'd seized control of the Broken Hand clan twenty-five years ago through brute force and cunning. Since the start, he'd been their superior.

The human's gaze narrowed as he watched with rapt interest. The royal couple did not exactly bicker... Although, given a few years of marriage, it would likely develop into that.

Rhagathena placed a hand on Rhylfelour's shoulder and tilted her head as she whispered something. *A fake apology? An explanation for words misspoken?*

Rhylfelour seemed to bottle up his indignation and let her comments slide. After all, there would be no mistaking the chain of authority amongst orcs once he took the throne.

Remy was not overly familiar with Rhagathena. But he could clearly see that she was manipulating him. Using tiny, verbal prods to move the belligerent orc with uncanny ease.

The queen offered her guests a mildly apologetic bow. She turned and then departed.

Rhylfelour roared a suggestion that they decide upon the queen's reward and a gift befitting their king. Half drunk, overly muscled warrior chiefs argued amongst themselves for a few moments. A fight broke out between Busted Horn and Hacktail clan leaders. It ended in blood, but true to orc fashion, it settled the quarrel.

The collection of orcs banded together and then the head of the Weakened Clavicle tribe informed the almost-king, "We have decided on the gift. We shall present it to her at the coming feast."

Rhylfelour's eyes bulged as he recognized what they had planned. He hissed, "A most excellent gift," and then they showed it to him.

At the Bard's call, all the gathered members of the court move towards the center of the gardens where the wedding would occur. Remy moved with the assembly, meandering through clusters of sidhe lords, tuathan barons, foreign nobles, and the like.

The innermost section of the expansive gardens was ringed by standing stones like the ones upon which he'd just been perched. These ones, however, were less organic and had been chiseled into an artistic façade, making a sort of gallery. The upper balcony was not in use this day; the queen's guards had closed it down in order to focus on the smaller crowd in attendance.

As Remy walked among the gathering crowd, he spotted a familiar face and traded knowing glances and nods with a foreign queen who was present as a dignitary guest and witness to the event.

Queen Maeve inclined her head at Remy and offered him a wink before finding her seat. Her wildfey entourage stayed close to her, though Queen Rhagathena given promises of proper hospitality and assurances in the old tongue.

There was only one guest from the realm of the Summer Court. Remy overheard another attendee identify him as a member of Oberon's court: the High Maven, Calithilon the White, Lord of Suíochán Naséan—The Radiant Tower. He was the second most powerful aes sidhe, in terms of magic ability, superseded only by Oberon himself. Despite that, and the logical assurances of fey hospitality, Calithilon frequently glanced aside as if nervous for his safety.

At the front of the assembly, the Bard began chanting as his officiating duties began. The parties quickly found their seats and settled in for the union ceremony.

Silent as a gentle breeze, Remy stalked through the outskirts of the gathering. He barely paid any mind to the proceedings. The assassin was on high alert against trouble. He'd laid precise plans for this day, and the moments leading up to the Bard's pronouncement, unifying husband and wife as king and queen, was the last closing window for any outside intervention.

The Bard, dressed in his most regal finery, had the attention of all. But Remy noticed one head in the audience kept turning aside and glancing towards one of the lookout posts on the upper gallery.

Remy recognized Myvarath, the sidhe noble from Gaeafdale. He was the same elf who'd sent an assassin to kill Remy to prevent Rhylfelour from securing the queen's hand. Remy's nostrils flared. If any creature would disrupt the proceedings, he was the most likely suspect.

With all due haste, Remy hurried up the stair and prowled through the upper gallery.

Rhagathena's security had placed a sentry on the upper landing. The soldier lay dead in a pool of blood. Someone had cut his throat.

Remy hurried forward, creeping stealthily until he spotted the lithe form of an elf stringing his bow. He was hidden well enough in the shadows, and Remy watched him work.

The assassin handled the arrow he was preparing. It was a *bleeding arrow*, a type similar to the regular kind, except that it had three razor-sharp blades at the tip. There were more fragile than the mass-produced broad heads used by military forces or by hunters of exceptionally dangerous game.

Rhylfelour was not wearing armor, and these arrows were designed to open wounds that could not be closed. Victims of these missiles typically bled out within mere moments.

Myvarath's killer nocked his arrow and took one step towards the open edge of the gallery when he stiffened against the touch of Remy's blade at his throat. The assassin froze, suddenly realizing another killer had come in behind him.

"Who hired you?" Remy demanded.

The sidhe bowman chuckled. "You should know that I would never divulge that... you are Aderyn Corff—the Corpse Bird, yes?"

Remy said, "It matters not. I can hear the Geafdale accent on your words, as I suspected I would."

The killer hissed. He'd obviously not meant to give anything away. "The orc must die. Surely you see that?"

"You have no argument from me, assassin," Remy told him. "But neither do you have the right to kill him."

"Myvarath has been trying to prevent a conflict that will claim countless lives."

Remy could hear the worry in the elf's voice.

"My Lord has no desire for the throne—not truly. But the orc and the spider queen want to ignite the old wars between Summer and Winter. For the sake of our people, you must see how that must not come to pass?"

"You are right," Remy said. But he did not relax his knife. "The flames of war must not rekindle—but I cannot afford for you to take a shot which you might miss."

The assassin scoffed. "And will you take it, oath-bound?"

"I will not allow you this opportunity. But neither will Rhylfelour and his orcs go to war," Remy insisted.

"Am I to trust that some human, a ddiymadferth son of Adam, can keep the queen's madness at bay? You are no protector of the realm, Aderyn Corff." He spat on the floor. "You are one man... not some long-lost dragon of Arcadeax."

"Perhaps. But you will not take what belongs to me."

"The orc's life is yours?" He sneered his question. "By what claim?"

"I lay no claim upon Warlord Rhylfelour's life. But I lay a claim to King Rhylfelour's death by the weapon in my hands," Remy growled with adamant rage in his voice.

The assassin looked down and noticed the blade in Remy's grip was a dúshlán: Krogga's dúshlán. Unsheathed and in the presence of the orc champion, the runes inscribed along the supernaturally sharp dagger burned with azure light.

There, in the light of the mystic dagger, the assassin knew the depths of the human's claims.

The Bard spread both of his hands wide to signal that the big moment had finally arrived. Both Rhagathena and Rhylfelour had their wrists clasped together. With cord, the officiant binding their hands together, wrapping the ties in a knot symbolic of tying them together in union.

And then an elf howled in the audience, standing straight up as he did so.

A tall, gaunt elf noble named Myvarath rocketed to his feet. An arrow stuck out from his back. Its tri-bladed head protruded from his front and blood gushed from the wound on both sides. And then Myvarath pitched headlong to the ground, dead.

All eyes turned to the upper gallery and locked on Aderyn Corff, just in time to see him release the body of the Geafdalean assassin. A broad crimson stain spread out from the bowman's neck. His body fell to the ground with a sickening crunch. A gasp rippled through the ceremony guests as if they were its echo.

Rhylfelour's eyes met Remy's.

"All is safe," Remy called. "Your rival had planned one final wrinkle. I have smoothed it."

Rhylfelour motioned towards the gallery. "Aderyn Corff, the Corpse Bird," he introduced the assembly to his pet assassin.

The guests murmured, and Remy bowed. Dipping his feather adorned head to show off its crow like features.

He cut the assassin's bowstring and threw it from the gallery like so much trash. "And no," Remy said, "that was not your gift. It is still to come." He nodded his head and faded back into the shadows.

Once silence had returned and attention fell back to the Bard, the officiant made the proclamation that the two parties were wed. "Folk of the unseelie and guests from abroad, I present to you, Queen Rhagathena, Lady of the Arctig Maen, ruler of the Rime Throne and the Unseelie Lands, and her husband King Rhylfelour, Lord of the Demonsbreak, and ruler of the Rime Throne and the Unseelie Lands."

The two raised their fastened hands to the applause of their guests, and then the true celebrations began in their honor.

Chapter Fifteen

It took some time for the servants to direct all the guests to the outdoor feast hall. Rows and rows of tables had been laid out for the guests. Attendants passed small plates of snacks to tide the assembly over until the meal was served. Entertainers walked through the aisles to placate the gathering until the grand feast was served.

Knowing that it would take some time to prepare the feast, the wedded couple retired to a tent for an hour to consummate their union. Remy made sure to stay as far from it as possible. He had no curiosity about the mechanics of intimacy between an orc and the spider queen.

To Remy's left, the head table sat upon a raised stage where it was visible by all. The front several rows were designated for the orc chieftains of the Demonsbreak.

Remy walked down the aisle, pushing a wheeled cart with six centerpieces that he'd made. Each one was an ornate pot topped with a special trophy: one of the decomposing heads that had been collected by Aderyn Corff in order to secure Rhylfelour's ascension to the throne.

He placed them on the tables, spaced out equally. The worst of the rot on the cadaverous skulls was on those at the orcs' tables. He knew they would not mind the stink. In fact, they found the gifts amusing, and at least one orc poked at a dead face with macabre humor.

Spotting an empty seat where Queen Maeve of the faewylds should have sat. A servant informed him that the tylwyth teg ruler had opted to leave after the ceremony. Apparently, Oberon's White Maven had also done the same.

Remy looked over the empty place settings with shrewd eyes. If they had not opted for a diplomatic exit after Remy dropped a corpse from the gallery, the human might have questioned whatever rationale kept them here.

The human turned and headed for the kitchen. Remy ate some food there and remained in the scullery until the marriage party arrived at the raised platform. They took their seats at the head table as Remy watched from the distance.

Rhylfelour raised a glass in salute to his bride and clinked a knife against the goblet until he had everyone's attention. The feast hall quieted, and he made his announcement.

"It seems good to me that I, King of the unseelie, appoint a new warlord to the orcish Demonsbreak. Krillig," he called to one of the orcs providing security. Remy recognized the creature as another of Rhylfelour's lieutenants. "Krillig, get your hairy ass up here."

The announcement had come as a surprise to Krillig. But not to Remy. Krillig had always been a suck up. Historically, what he'd lacked in talent as a warrior, Krillig made up for with flattery.

Rhylfelour held up his hands and brandished all twelve rings. "These I am keeping. They look pretty on me. But they are mere symbols of my authority over all the clans. But it is now time that I relinquish my title as warlord and chief. I have loftier aims now that I am king."

Krillig knelt and Rhylfelour tossed him the rope around his neck, upon which hung the severed hand of a demon, the namesake for the Broken Hand clan.

[Do you accept responsibility and leadership of the Broken Hand clan which I freely relinquish and give to you?] Rhylfelour asked in the old tongue.

[I do, my King,] Krillig said, accepting the transfer of title and power.

[Then rise as Warlord and Chieftain,] said the king.

Behind him, at the head table, Queen Rhagathena took her seat and smiled at the proceedings. Looking around and taking note that all foreign guests had departed early, she cooed, "The unseelie is more unified than ever. Soon, we shall show the rest of Arcadeax exactly what the Winter Court is capable of!"

That brought cheers from the twelve orc warlords and more subtle applause from sidhe nobles and the various tuatha of rank and title.

The chief of clan Busted Horn took his demonic trophy off his body and held it high. He said, "In response to this glorious news, let the Demonshead give you the gift we have prepared for the royal couple." He approached the queen and laid before her the broken horn of the fallen infernal prince, which his tribe had preserved throughout the centuries.

One by one, the orc leaders brought to her their dismembered demonic body parts, making a pile of them.

Her eyebrows rose. "This is quite a gift," she said. "The prince of hell can never die, you know. He is still alive in there. The fiend's mind and soul are fractured into these twelve pieces… fully alive, fully conscious, but trapped in his dismembered pieces." She grinned wickedly. "Trapped, and yet still subject to the torments of decay. Thank you. I shall cherish this gift above all others."

Queen Rhagathena's elven majordomo had only finished carting off the desiccated body parts of the ancient demonic prince when Rhylfelour signaled for Remy's presence at the stage.

"This human saved my life today," Rhylfelour said, publicly thanking him. The king signaled for one of the servants to add a place setting at the king's left hand. "Today you dine with me, Aderyn Corff. You have earned your seat. And you will continue to earn it as we take the seelie realm by force."

Remy gulped, but accepted the orc's request. A few minutes later, Rhylfelour mingled through the crowd, especially amongst his warlords, now neatly arrayed beneath his absolute rule as the unseelie king.

Somewhere near the kitchens, a bell rang to signal that the food was ready for serving. Attendants emerged with great rolling carts stocked with wines and plates of delicacies available only to members of Rhagathena's Winter Court.

According to tradition, none could begin eating until the King and Queen were seated with their meal before them. Scullions and bussers set flatware as fast as they could be laid out.

A more regal spread was arranged on the head table and one waiter stationed a serving tray between the king's and queen's seats. Rhagathena wrinkled her nose and pushed it to the left. She would let the orc have the food.

"Apologies, my Queen. Would you prefer something else?" the server asked.

Remy glanced down at her and overheard her speak to her majordomo, who'd just returned. "No. My appetite is for something... else."

The queen caught Remy's surreptitious look. She gave him a strange expression and then raised her brows towards the orc. With Rhylfelour's back turned, she was attempting to signal him that the time was right.

So, she does desire the death of her husband—provided I pledge to her and lead the Lightstarved...

Remy frowned and pretended not to understand. But deep down he knew... *She's already secured the orc army simply by marrying Rhylfelour and making him king. Once I pledge my alle-*

giance, she would have everything she desired from this bargain well in hand.

He raised his eyebrows and then nodded at her, signaling that he understood her intentions. But then he frowned and shook his head as if rejecting her offer. The whole exchange took place within a fraction of a second, and the queen pouted.

She had already promised that if she could not have him, Rhagathena would keep Rhylfelour alive just to control the orc's pet assassin.

The final carts emerged from the kitchen. Galley staff had prepared a delicacy more fitting for the orc pallet. Remy had come to know which meals were traditionally orcs preferred for formal gatherings through his years of experience among the Broken Hand.

Eagerness overwhelmed the orcs, and they shifted in their seats. Rhylfelour hurried back to his place at the head table so that all could begin dining once his closest companions had been served.

Rhylfelour claimed his goblet and again clinked it with his knife and then took his seat. All down the rows and rows of guests, people began feasting. Raucous music and myriad conversations ensued—the most raucous of the noise was centered on the front tables.

Orcs were not known as polite diners. They scooped into their gullets, heaping loads of stuffing and tore great mouthfuls of flesh free from bone.

Remy leaned over the table to appear as if eagerly partaking. But he did not touch his food. He'd eaten already and made all his preparations.

It is about to begin. The perfect moment will arrive in seconds...

Rhylfelour picked up a giant leg of roasted beast and was about to tear into it when he looked across at his new wife. She cast a sidelong look in his direction, and he set down the food. Picking up a knife and fork, he began using the tools to carve into it like a proper gentleman.

The king looked at his pet human. "So, tell me about this wedding present?"

A kind of madness had overtaken Remy. He saw his goal with such intense focus that everything else seemed clouded.

"It should arrive here in moments," he told the king.

Rhylfelour's brows stitched together as he tried to figure out what the human could have gotten him. And then, just before taking a bite of the same meat that his warlords were voraciously tearing into, those same orcs of the Demonsbreak clutched at their stomachs, throats, and mouths. They screamed in pain.

Shrieking like burned children, they caterwauled, carrying on with such noises as had never been heard in that court. Blood and fluids leaked from noses and mouths and several orcs spat out the food they were chewing. Mucus, food mash, and teeth clinked with a metallic chime as they were vomited onto plates in bloodied wads.

One of the orcs picked up an iron pellet that had been jammed into the flesh of the cooked boar. He stared at it momentarily and then shook his hand with pain, dropping the ferrous ore. His eyes widened with betrayal.

At least two of them tipped over dead, foaming at the mouth. They'd succumbed to the deep internal pains unlike any fey had been subjected to in modern times.

Chaos erupted within that court. Sidhe nobles stood erect, dropping food, but feeling unaffected. They searched around for answers.

Rhylfelour looked down the rows of his champions and then felt a blade at his neck. He stiffened and kept his head still. The orc king located his wife from the corner of his eyes and saw her hedging back from the head table.

"So, this is my gift?" Rhylfelour asked.

Standing behind him, Remy held a blade to his throat. "You're damn right. And you've earned this."

The human leaned forward and stabbed Chief Krogga's glowing dúshlán into the table for all to see. The vengeance blade glowed at the edges with an azure light. They burned much the brighter with such close proximity to its intended target.

"I've spent a long time preparing this gift for you," Remy, Aderyn Corff, growled at his former master, "and only just now have you allowed me to finally deliver it!"

Chapter Sixteen

Rhylfelour stood there with Remy's blade pressed to his throat.

Guests sat stiff and at attention. The guards did likewise. None of them moved to intervene—the assassin was tensed like a hair trigger, and none wanted the blame of setting him off. None could understand why the feather-hooded human would suddenly do this. It did not make sense to them. Aderyn Corff had just saved the king from an assassin. By what logic did he now threaten Rhylfelour's life?

The tension broke as Rhylfelour burst out laughing. The details still did not make sense with orc chieftains lying on the ground writhing and coughing up blood. But it bordered on what passed for humor amongst orcs.

"A jape? This must be a jest," Rhylfelour cackled.

The warlord from clan Fallen Leg roared, "It is no joke, Rhylfelour!" Blood and saliva drooled from both sides of the creature's mouth. He spat, wincing as he did so. A fang and two metal pellets clacked upon the plate when they landed. "It is cold iron! Your traitorous ddiymadferth put iron in our food!"

Fear finally widened at the edges of Rhylfelour's eyes.

The guards finally understood what was happening and reached for their weapons.

Remy tightened his grip on the king and insisted, "Tell them to back off."

Rhylfelour held his hand up to stay the soldiers. But then he insisted to Remy, "You cannot kill me, human."

"I assure you, I can," Remy hissed defiantly. His words brimmed with such confidence that the orc's certainty vanished.

Rhylfelour's gaze tracked down to the glowing dúshlán. "That blade does not belong to you."

"I assure you that it does. It may not have come to me in the same manner as when you found me in the Grinning Wood, but it came to me, nonetheless." Remy snatched the vengeance blade and pressed it against Rhylfelour's neck, sheathing his personal dúshlán. Remy had needed the orc to see the instrument of his undoing.

"That blade belonged to Chief Krogga. Yours does not glow because it is linked to the one who has done you the most wrong in your life," Rhylfelour sneered.

"That certainly sounds like you from where I stand," Remy insisted.

Rhylfelour laughed. "Only so far as you know. You remember nothing from before the Grinning Wood. You only think I am the greatest monster of your life... but there are far worse than I."

The orc continued his line of thoughts, "If you're hoping that some loophole in the ancient fetiche magic will let you kill me, you are wrong. You are still oath-bound. Dúshláns are powerful artifacts, but they cannot circumvent the magic of Arcadeax."

Remy let the orc ramble as he bit off the stopper from a small vial and dumped its contents into an empty goblet at the head table. The raw akasha glimmered as it poured.

"I have learned many things from you," Remy growled. "But I have learned deeper things from others. Would you like to know what I have learned?"

Rhylfelour said nothing.

Remy continued, "*This* is my gift to you. A lesson. Given in the same manner which you delivered lessons to me: *violence*."

Rhylfelour snarled a demand, "Repeat your oath, ddiymad-ferth!"

The tension reached a peak as more and more of the Demonsbreak capitulated, tumbling to the floor with increasing wails.

"Repeat it!" the king insisted.

With perfect annunciation, Remy said in the high tongue, [I swear my allegiance to Rhylfelour, son of Jarlok and warlord chief of the Broken Hand orcs.]

Rhylfelour's eyes went wild. He realized exactly what Remy had meant when he said he *could* kill him. Rhylfelour was no longer the warlord of the Broken Hand tribe—he had abdicated his title to Krillig... And *the oath's integrity relied upon it.*

"The lesson is this..." Remy growled. His eyes flitted to the empty table where Queen Maeve would have sat if she's remained. "Words matter."

Overhead, crows began to call and swirl around the assembly like an ominous, black-feathered vortex.

"No, wait," Rhylfelour bartered. "I shall release you from your oath. I—I will help you find the party linked to your dúshlán! One of the wedding guests knows where you come from—he knows why you possess the blade. Spare me and I will—"

Remy dragged Krogga's dúshlán across the unseelie king's throat with vicious determination. Guests at the head table, including the queen and other sidhe nobles, screamed.

Aderyn Corff took King Rhylfelour's head in a gory torrent of blood. A crimson geyser shot from the grisly stump like a signal flare and the dúshlán's light began to fade.

Guards drew their blades and shouted orders. With no more hostage, their primary objective was to secure the queen and to kill the assassin.

Before Rhylfelour's body hit the ground, Remy discarded the murder weapon and dipped his fingers in the goblet he'd prepared. He snapped his fingers and activated Fremenor's ignition spell.

The centerpieces which he'd placed evenly around the room detonated with deafening fury. They'd been stuffed with explosive powder and the same materials artisans made smoke flares from.

Crows echoed the sharp report and scattered as the thick plumes of sooty vapor erupted in every direction, blinding everyone nearby. Remy used the screen to duck out of the garden and dash for the nearest exit. He'd planned for this; his explorations of Arctig Maen and Hulda Thorne were done as a means to scout his best escape path.

Caws and screams continued echoing behind him. They faded with the distance as Remy sprinted for the gate that led out from the spider's strongest fortress. He dashed into the sprawling city of Hulda Thorne, chest heaving and gasping for clean air, once free of the smoke.

Remy passed through the gate before any trumpet blast or bell could alert posted sentries to shutter the doors or drop the portcullis. He made it past the arches and rounded a corner. Moments later, he plunged into a crowd which provided him a token of anonymity.

The death bird's flight had begun. And Remy was finally, for the first time since he could recall, truly free.

Chapter Seventeen

Bells tolled in the watchtowers of Arctig Maen. A column of smoke arose from within her walls and citizens from the greater area of Hulda Thorne turned to watch and guess at the source of the conflict.

Rhagathena wiped the filmy soot and blood spatters from her face with a rag. She snarled of the captain of her guard, "Find him! Dispatch your best hunters. I'll not have some child of Adam rip such a prize away from my clutches."

The guard nodded. He assured the queen, "We will find him. The murderer is new to our city, and we here are all loyal to you, my Queen. It will take time, but we will close the city gates by nightfall and canvas Hulda Thorne building to building until he is caught." He hurried away to issue orders.

"That insolent ddiymadferth has defied me," she complained hotly. "I would have protected him and allowed him this vengeance extracted upon the orcs if he had but taken a simple vow." The queen was not used to being resisted. Its sting felt the same as treason to her.

"At least we got the true prize," Chokorum said from her side. "The relics of the Demonsbreak."

Rhagathena scowled. She glanced aside at her most trusted servant. He may have been right, but the death bird head impinged her honor with his denial. "That may be so. But one does not slight the Queen of the Unseelie without penalty."

"And the invasion of Summer?" Chokorum asked as he scanned the twelve corpses left after by the human's cruel trick. He shuddered. Iron poisoning was a truly torturous way to die. It had long been forbidden, but it was once the penalty visited upon those unseelie who'd sided with the forces of hell during the Infernal War.

"It continues as planned," Rhagathena said. She plucked the twelve rings from the fingers of her dead husband's headless corpse and placed them on her own digits. "After all, I am now the leader of the unseelie orcs of Demonsbreak."

She eyed her servant. "Dispatch letters to those clans. Give them their orders and have them also supply an emissary from each group so that I can appoint a new local leader… preferably ones I can properly educate regarding the new chain of command."

Chokorum gave her a stiff bow.

"And have some scullions collect Rhylfelour's body and bring it to my chambers," she added as she shuffled towards her castle. "I am wed, and my feast was interrupted. I too must feed." She licked her lips hungrily, wetting the jagged teeth there. "Have them take special care with the hands."

Try as he might, Remy could not outrun the bells. Hulda Thorne was simply too big to flee before the queen's forces blasted signal horns and warning alarms.

Rhagathena also had capable arcanists at her disposal. They could disseminate the word at the speed of thought: *the notorious Aderyn Corff had murdered the King during his own wedding feast.* The city also had a network powered by akasha and aither. All of which were faster methods of spreading Remy's description and announcing news of a bounty.

Remy felt sure that before he would depart Hulda Thorne, every guard in the city would be looking for him, along with bounty hunters and anyone seeking to curry favor with the spider queen.

He pulled his feathered hood down and stuffed it in the pockets of his cloak. Remy knew that he had to do everything he could to conceal his identity. He tore several long strips of cloth and made a bandanna. Tying it around his head to hide his rounded ears behind the fabric.

Remy quickened his pace and pushed through the crowded market. He glanced over his shoulder and spotted an elf whose face felt familiar. That elf had been behind him a few blocks back, despite Remy taking a circuitous route.

His tracker did a double take. Both the elf and the human became aware of each other. The pursuer pushed harder and hurried to catch up, but Remy had already dashed deeper through the crowd.

Shoving folk aside to clear a path, Remy kicked the posts out from under a vendor's awning and caused a little chaos and slow his hunter.

Remy drew his dagger and cut free a horse tethered to a nearby post. He leapt upon the animal's back and spurred it forward.

The creature brayed and sprinted forward at a full gallop. Remy ducked his head and held on.

The crowd parted at the sound of the galloping hooves. As the wild steed charged ahead and for the gates, the horse thief's cape flapped behind him.

Pandemonium erupted behind Remy. The wild horse dragged a wake of anarchy behind it. Screams of panic and shouts of anger filled the air. Remy's ears, despite being muffled by the bandanna, picked up the distinct clopping sounds of a second set of hooves.

He risked a look behind and saw that his tracker had also taken a horse. Remy urged his mount to even greater speeds and soon his stallion raced away from the city's edge.

The pursuer closed the gap, but only slowly.

Remy's horse might have been stronger and faster, but humans were generally heavier than any sidhe. Hooves tore up clods of turf as the riders raced away from the city at a full gallop.

Although the distance between Remy and his hunter shrank, their distance from the unseelie capitol grew by the minute. Remy recognized the area. He had been here before and was familiar with the terrain, at least.

He knew that his only chance at survival was to eliminate any pursuit and remain undiscovered until he could escape into the west. Genesta had always urged him to seek out the lands of the Summer Court. Remy would not be safe in the unseelie, not even in the faewylds. He could not put Aderyn Corff behind him until he reached the seelie realm of Arcadeax.

An arrow streaked past, whistling its warning as it nearly found its mark. *Damn it! The hunter has a bow.*

That would complicate his escape, Remy knew. But he also knew that loosing arrows with any amount of accuracy was difficult from atop a horse, and even harder at speeds like this.

He jabbed his heels into the flank of the animal to goad more speed.

His horse screamed with pain and pitched head over hoof, throwing Remy through the air. An arrow had buried itself up to its fletching in the beast's midsection. Remy may have been the target, but crippling the animal had a similar outcome.

The human tumbled to the air and landed in a painful roll. He skidded to an eventual stop near scrubby copses of brush and thorny bracken. Gravel and hard earth skinned Remy's knees, hands, and face and he groaned with pain as the hunter pressed the knee to his back.

Reaching around his midsection, the elf pulled Remy's dúshlán from its sheath and cast it aside. Before the notorious assassin could get his bearings, the hunter looped a circlet of rope and a pre-tied knot around Remy's feet. He yanked it tight to hobble him. He got one side of his metal manacles locked into place Before Remy was able to shake himself back to attention and resist.

The hunter drew his sword and backed off as Remy flipped to his rump and scrambled backwards. "You're coming in with me," the hunter insisted. "You're worth more alive, but I'll take you in dead if I have to."

Remy kicked his feet, but the bonds held firm. He tried to crawl backward, but could only worm his way a few inches before his free hand sank into the earth and was stuck in a hole.

His tracker stepped forward and held the tip of his blade to the man's throat. "Ah, ah," he cautioned. "None of that. Now, use your other hand and close those manacles on yourself."

Remy winced and set his jaw, but he held up his cuffed hand up to show compliance. In his palm, he held the open end of the metal binders. A length of chain dangled between it and his wrist. He moved slowly to show the hunter that he was obeying.

The human's captor relaxed just enough so that Remy could obey the hunter-elf's commands without accidentally cutting his throat. And then Rhylfelour's training took over and Remy demonstrated why Aderyn Corff's fame had spread so quickly.

He clicked the free end of the manacle around the blade and exploded into motion. Remy rolled forward to his knees and yanked his hand free of the hole. In it, he gripped the handle of the dagger he hid there so long ago. He brought the blade to bear, slicing through his enemy's jugular vein and dropping him to bleed out in the wilderness.

Remy cut his feet free and then dragged the bounty hunter out of sight. He found the key for his cuffs and freed himself, throwing the metal binders away, and then took whatever items of value he could from the hunter.

Moments later, he retrieved his dúshlán, took the dead elf's horse, and rode west as hard as the horse could carry him.

After deciding that heading directly west was too obvious a path, Remy detoured south. Using the stealth that he learned as a young man, he raided small stockpiles to gather provisions and headed into the wilderness.

Stony badlands of blasted earth and scree filled ravines that seemed to stretch endlessly. Frozen dune seas of mounded silica shifted daily as the cutting winds moved them through the region like speeding glaciers that disintegrated and reappeared elsewhere overnight.

Once he'd gotten far enough south, Remy resumed his westward route.

His horse died somewhere in the waterless salt flats one more day's ride from Vale Rhewi. Remy guessed that his horse had died from dehydration. The trip through the wastes had provided only sparse nutrition for the animal, and its muscles had shrunk significantly. Undernourished, the animal's speed and strength had suffered, but Remy could make do with that. But with insufficient water, the beast's health flagged.

With provisions running low, Remy knew he would have to venture into Vale Rhewi to purchase supplies. Luckily, he had the foresight to pack a small stockpile of coin before his flight from the capitol.

Lacking his horse, the journey to Vale Rhewi took three days by foot. It was an oddly situated city and was the last provision point on the way to the Selvages which lay further north, or to the lowest fringes of the feywilds if traveling in the opposite direction.

Along the craggy journey, the human spotted hardy vines that occasionally grew in the shady ravines; the tendrils sprouted tiny fruits. Remy collected the fleshy gourds whenever he could. Cukes had some of the highest moisture content of any edible plants.

The ones he found in the harsh terrain had wilted leaves and withered vines. It did not surprise him to discover the vegetables tasted bitter from the lack of proper hydration. They were almost unbearable, except that Remy's thirst demanded he eat them.

After completing the arduous trek through the wastes, Remy found himself on the outskirts of Vale Rhewi. He knew of the city, but he had never been there before. The one thing he knew of it was that little folk were more populous here. But as far as Remy was concerned, all cities were the same: dangerous and filled with greedy, ambitious folk.

He strolled through the streets for some time, looking for a shop most likely to have all the provisions he hoped to secure. Keeping his points of contact isolated to one store reduced the amount of interactions he would make locally. That would keep the chances of his discovery to a minimum.

None of the buildings were in fine repair. Most of them had serious blemishes or elements of disrepair due to the harsh elements. Regardless, the city looked serviceable as far as its markets went. He squinted and stared at the one recurrent feature from shop to shop. All the storefronts had a bell mounted somewhere on them, usually near the sign shingle if the store had one. He shrugged, assuming that everyplace had its own quirks and traditions.

Remy ducked inside the door to an emporium, which appeared well-stocked. He kept his hood up and his head down as he shopped for whatever travel ready foodstuffs he could find.

Hopefully, he could reach the seelie realm in a few days, though he knew he would have to go north in order to find a crossing, and he wasn't sure exactly how he could get over the Solstox. This far south, though, no bridges reached across the ravine separating the realms of Summer and Winter.

Remy dragged his basket of goods to the shopkeeper. He was a halfling, but tall enough to defy expectations. He took stock of the goods and quoted the traveler a price.

When Remy handed over the coins, the proprietor seized his wrist.

"Sir, unhand me," Remy insisted. His voice was stern, but he kept it low enough to avoid undue attention.

The halfling eyed him suspiciously. "I haven't seen you around here before, traveler."

"I am just passing through." Remy kept his voice calm and firm.

Narrowing his gaze, the halfling said, "That's what they all say… those who pass through Vale Rhewi. You ddiymadferth are all the same. You think you can use our city as some sort of haven and sneak through on your way to hiding." His voice carried an unmistakable hint of disdain.

As Remy shook his wrist free, the shopkeeper yanked a nearby rope. The bell outside rang. Dots connected in Remy's head. *It's a signal device for runaway slaves.*

He grabbed what supplies he could and bolted for the door. Remy did not make it very far.

All manner of folk, various tuatha, sidhe, and orcs flooded the streets on either side of the store and its jangling bell. They formed a wall of bodies hedging in the source of the trouble outside the halfling's emporium.

There was nowhere to go.

And then Remy recognized a familiar face in the crowd: Syrmerware Kathwesion, the notorious orcish slave taker. Slowly, and with crushing force, the two walls moved together and enveloped the human. Only moments later, Syrmerware Kathwesion clapped Remy in restraints. The orc pulled Remy's cloak back to search for any brands or marks of ownership.

Remy had seen the slave taker before on several occasions. He'd recognized the orc, but luckily Syrmerware Kathwesion did not reciprocate.

Syrmerware Kathwesion leaned his face close to Remy's and chuckled. His hot, stinking breath could have curled hairs. "What have we here? An untagged ddiymadferth? Don't worry, little stray. I'll find some value in you."

And then the slave taker dragged Remy off, heading deeper into Vale Rhewi and his livestock pens.

Chapter Eighteen

Syrmerware Kathwesion's orcs threw Remy into a pen constructed of lashed wooden posts. It would not have held him inside except that he was still in chains.

Several other humans occupied the cage. They were all in a similar condition and it was obvious that the slaver was collecting a fresh load of livestock in order to take to market.

Most of the Remy's cellmates were emaciated, unkempt, and severely bedraggled. Neither the wastelands surrounding Vale Rhewi nor the city's occupants had been kind to them. One man sat in the corner, rocking slightly and nearly catatonic. Long, oily locks of hair framed his face; his forehead had been marked with a vicious burn and the puckered skin had only begun to fade from angry pink back to its normal coloration.

The slaver's pens were located at the center of the town. There, the general population sometimes came to visit the miserable sons and daughters of Adam as if they were a traveling freak show.

From the other prisoners, Remy learned that the orc slave trader had been collecting both humans and redcaps in order to meet quotas set by a contract he had set with the Queen Rhagathena.

Syrmerware Kathwesion took his collections to the market and set premium prices. Those humans who did not bring his auction minimums were sent to the queen to become part of her Light-starved; she bought whatever the orc had left over. The redcaps he did not even bother trying to sell. He simply put them in chains and carted them off to Hulda Thorne as soon as he had a full wagon load to justify his trip.

Remy languished within the pen. As day fell to night, the orcs who guarded the prisoners began to tire and wandered away, anticipating the shift change. A pair of lumbering trolls approached under the protective cover of darkness. Without any sun to afflict them and turn them to stone, they were the perfect nocturnal guardians.

One of them wandered off, but the second troll plopped down in the center square of town. Remy called him over.

He and the troll had a short conversation so that Remy could get a sense of his temperament. Like all the other trolls he'd conversed with, the creature was slightly daft... but only a little more so than most humans.

"Where do you stand on the search for King Wulflock?" Remy asked.

The troll cocked his head. "How do you mean?" The troll's voice rumbled low but carried notes of intrigue.

"Of all your kind who I've met, each one has been an ardent supporter of Oberon's long-lost brother. I've always understood it is the hope of the trolls that he should return and restore the unseelie to its former glory," Remy explained. And then he added, "That too is my hope."

The troll's face took a compassionate look. "How was it you came to be imprisoned here, child of Adam?"

"Quite by accident, friend troll."

Other humans walked up near Remy, curious about how he'd gained the goodwill of the massive creature.

An apologetic note rumbled in the beast's enormous belly. "If there was something I could do for you, friend human, I would. For the sake of King Wulflock, I would... But you are young, and you are strong. You will fetch Syrmerware Kathwesion the premium price he desires, I've no doubt of it. There is little I can do to help you."

Remy asked, "And what if there was?"

The troll squinted, willing to hear out the human.

"I think I hear your friend, the other troll," Remy said. "Perhaps you could go check on him? I can handle the rest. You would never be implicated... I am, after all, a fairly capable and noteworthy human. If you were gone for ten or fifteen minutes, completely in the interests of your partner troll, I can handle my own rescue."

The troll looked at him deeply for a few long moments. And then he gave a short head nod before turning. "I think I hear someone calling my name," he said, and then he lumbered away into the distant darkness.

As soon as the coast was clear, Remy tugged the lock picks from where he'd hidden them near the sole of his boots. A few moments later, he had unlocked the binders that restrained him and tossed them aside. Remy handed off the lock picks in case any others cared to use them.

Now freed, he pulled a long string from his clothing. With a finger, he tugged loose some of the bindings at the wooden cage's bars. He pushed the string through the slack and wrapped it around his fingers creating a friction saw.

Pulling the string back and forth rapidly and repeatedly, Remy burned his way through the lashes and freed one of the posts of the cell. Just as he'd finished pushing the bar aside, making barely enough space to slip between, the beaten man who'd sat in the corner all day approached.

"Stranger, do not do this. They will catch you, they will... *burn you*," he insisted. None of the others showed any desire to follow Remy in his escape.

He shrugged. Remy had not come here to free prisoners; his entire life until now had been about freeing himself—a prospect he'd mostly thought impossible.

Remy slipped out of the cell and scooped up his belongings. They'd been dumped just outside the cage where he'd been imprisoned. The orcs had eaten his food, but at least he had recovered a full water bladder and his mystic dagger. The contents of his pockets had remained mostly untouched.

After slipping out of sight, Remy stole through the darkness. He kept to the shadows and flitted from alley to alley.

Finally, he spotted several horses lashed to a post near a local cantina. He crept across the road and began untying the reins of the nearest animal. There was no opportunity to grab any supplies or provisions, but he would be free, and he'd have a horse.

Just as Remy moved to swing his leg up over the horse, blinding pain flashed from the back of his head to the front of his eyes, and he saw bright light. Remy fell to the ground and rubbed the bruise where he had been clubbed. He looked up, too disoriented to react, and stared directly into the face of Syrmerware Kathwesion.

The heinous orc sneered and then used his club to crack the human across the face and incapacitate him. The blow struck with a snap of pain, and then everything faded to black.

Remy awakened to a splitting headache and the sensation of pressure on his hands and chest. He'd been pressed down against a tree stump. Heat made his skin feel stretched; a large fire burned next to him at the center of Vale Rhewi.

The human cursed under his breath. For the life of him, he simply could not get away from this damned city.

He realized that the pressure at his hands was from a pair of orcs. One sat on either side of him and held his arms down, pulling him tight against the stump and forcing him into a position perfect for an executioner's ax.

Really shook his head as he came back to attention.

"Ah. There you are," Syrmerware Kathwesion purred. He turned aside to the fire and withdrew a wicked-looking brand. It glowed red hot from the time spent nestled among the coals.

The orc brought it closer to Remy. The brand glowed with heat, lighting up Remy's face and making him wince.

"I always brand the faces of those human slaves who have proved themselves as difficult as stubborn colts—those needing to be broken. My reputation is important to me. I feel that buyers ought to be aware of which chattel needs a firm and guiding hand," Syrmerware Kathwesion teased.

"So kind of you," Remy growled, wondering how he was going to get out of this. He spotted his cloak rolled up a short distance away. The handle of his dúshlán poked out from the folds of the fabric. *If I could only get to it...*

Remy struggled against his captors, but they were as strong and fit as any of the warriors in Rhylfelour's employ. He remembered that Rhylfelour had been close with Syrmerware Kathwesion.

"Did you know that the warlord is dead? Rhylfelour, chief of the Broken Hand tribe, was murdered only recently in Arctig Maen." Remy hoped the news might distract him and providing opening.

Instead, Syrmerware Kathwesion shrugged. He remained nonchalant. "His time had come. There were few who expected he would live much past a betrothal to the spider queen... If you could name me any mate of Rhagathena who lived a year past their wedding date, I would release you right now," he chuckled.

Panic lodged in Remy's chest. He'd run out of options.

Syrmerware Kathwesion knelt low as the orcs held their prisoner tight. He looked up and into Remy's face. The slaver told his companions, "I like to see the look in their eyes when the brand sears their flesh," he said. His words dripped with masochistic pleasure.

The orc slowly brought the brand closer and closer to Remy's face.

Remy felt the heat of it curling his skin. One of the orcs seized Remy's hair with a massive paw to hold his head still. Closer. *Closer.*

With the brand only a hair away from his exposed flesh, a raspy voice shouted directly behind Remy, "Brand this, motherfucker."

Remy felt pressure upon his back as something crawled right over him and then delivered a mighty boot into Syrmerware Kathwesion's face, knocking the orc all the way backward and dislodging a tooth which fell to the dirt in front of Remy's face. Whatever creature had come to his rescue had leapt atop the human and immediately killed the two creatures who held Remy down.

His rescuer jumped off and allowed Remy to scramble to his feet and identify him. Remy's savior proved to be Redcomb, the powrie hero he'd met almost two years ago when he'd taken Krogga's life.

The mad little warrior screamed and howled as he led his merry band of vicious killers through the town. His iron tipped pikestaff already dripped red with blood and his hat wore a fresh coat of it.

Remy looked forward and spotted Syrmerware Kathwesion lying on his back. The red, puckered flesh formed a perfect mark in the shape of a tiny boot-print. Redcomb's iron treaded footgear gave Syrmerware a permanent mark to remember him by—one that would never heal. Its pain would never cease.

The human lunged himself forward and snatched up his cloak and dagger. He whirled and brought his dúshlán to bear, but the notorious slaver had already fled into the night.

Remy chose not to follow. Instead, he thanked the powrie, but Redcomb merely grinned. "Now it looks as if *you* owe *me* one, if we should ever cross paths again."

The human bowed. "Indeed, I do."

"Have you seen any of my kind on your way here?" Redcomb asked.

Remy shook his head. "No. I've only heard that the orcs recently shipped them off to the capitol as soon as they had enough to make the trip worth it." He shared what he knew of the Lightstarved with the powrie champion.

Redcomb stroked his scraggly beard. "Then revenge it is," he said. Clutching the haft of his weapon, he turned to Remy. "Get out of here while the getting is good. I hear there's a high price on your head and ye best flee before the sun comes up."

Remy grimaced. "But there are other humans here. I can't just leave them."

"We'll smash their cages," Redcomb promised. "After that, it's every man and powrie for themself."

Remy nodded his thanks, offered the redcap a short bow, and then sprinted back to steal one of the horses he'd tried to take previously. He managed to gather a few provisions, stuff them in his pockets, and then clamber up the back of a horse.

Seconds later, the creature's hooves thundered in the darkness, guided only by the moonlight, and Remy was once again free.

Remy's trek to him ever north, and it finished much as it began.

He took many detours to raid small stockpiles and reprovision himself as he headed towards the Selvages. The no-man's-land was technically part of the faewylds, even if Winter and Summer stationed garrisons all along it.

Remy took care to sneak past any areas he suspected of being monitored. As he traveled through, Remy noticed many old signs of where the Reavers had once operated. Those places had been cleared out ever since Queen Mab's murder.

The ground formed a gentle swell and terminated at a tall hill overlooking the road which bisected the Selvages en route for the bridges crossing the Solstox Canyons. Many bridges crisscrossed the jagged ravines, which provided a clear barrier between the courts of unseelie and seelie realms.

Mighty towers stretched skyward, affixed firmly to their anchorage bastions. Past the footings, the long structures provided passages which were seldom used as a crossing. Both parties had to agree that any transit between them was warranted, and such accords were increasingly rare as tensions brewed.

From his vantage, Remy spotted no fewer than six bridges. He knew there were many more, but they lay further up or down the twisting ravine system of the Solstox cliffs.

He was also aware that various bandits, smugglers, and other ne'er-do-wells would often fired harpoons across and created rope bridges in order to make the passage. Military forces from either side often patrolled the Selvages, looking for those. They were quick to dismantle them, and stories were commonly told of mooring points being cut even while folk were trapped between crossing points.

Remy was uncertain he could locate one of those. But even if he could, making the crossing could prove treacherous... And even if it was a safe bet, the owners of illicit bridges typically extracted hefty tolls and Remy was out of money at present. All his coin had been stolen in Vale Rhewi.

The human plopped down upon the hilltop, deciding to wait a full day in order to ferret out the best options to make the crossing. Perhaps one of the bridges was less guarded than the other?

Remy needed to first gather information, and that would take some time. Luckily, he had provisions enough to afford him the days necessary to spy out the safest passage.

Remy had lashed his horse to a tree behind him and well out of sight. It neighed nervously. Remy cocked an ear. He'd learned that the instincts of animals often proved themselves worth listening to.

There came a deep sound on the wind: the hard thrumming sounds of footsteps. Thousands of them. Many thousands of them.

Remy looked east, and he spotted birds regularly taking to the skies from their perches in green canopies. Those treetops covered the wide roads that cut through the Selvages, Remy knew. Something was coming.

Some*one* was coming.

Many someones.

Chapter Nineteen

Finally, the enemy hordes spilled into view. The surrounding woods nearest the Selvages swelled like a termite mound belching forward its angry swarms.

Rhagathena's unseelie hordes had finally reached the approach to the Solstox crossings. Predominantly made up of orcs, there were a few pockets of sidhe soldiers and various conscripts of assorted tuathan species.

This is just the first wave, Remy knew. He'd hoped that his actions at Arctig Maen would prevent, or at least delay the invasion.

Remy's gut sank. There were also many humans in the army's ranks. Lots of them. They had the same sunken eyes and pale skin that he'd seen in the Lightstarved. Rhagathena had evidently emptied those subterranean caverns and bolstered her numbers with slaves.

Exactly as she told me she would, Remy realized. *The forces of Summer have no idea it is coming!*

He looked west towards the Summer realm. Across the broad stone bridge, garrison forces rushed from their guardhouses and Remy heard the ringing of alarms. Certainly, they had already sent to Oberon for aid, but it was unlikely to arrive by the time the Winter soldiers took the bridges.

Something more stirred in Remy's gut.

He'd promised Myvarath's assassin in the gardens of Arctig Maen that he would prevent the orc invasion—something the now dead sidhe noble had been working against. Remy's promise was not a magically binding oath, but still, Remy felt he needed to honor his word if it were at all possible.

A motley collection of malnourished, dead-eyed humans pulled away from the unseelie pack as Winter's army formed a line some distance from the bridge. Ten humans dragged forward a giant metal structure nearly twice their height.

Remy recognized the conical shape. He'd seen it in the room where the iron was stored in the caverns of the Lightstarved. When Remy had escaped back into Hulda Thorne, he'd climbed up one in order to reach the ground level.

The metal thing had the texture of beaten metal and was darkly colored. Metals came in many shades and the tint could always be altered, but Remy knew it had to be iron.

The thing resembled a closed flower, like some massive, ferrous bud. Its human team of drivers dragged it upon a sled where it rested, and they crossed the entrance to the bridge. Each of the human's mouths had binders tied in place to prevent them from speaking.

Sidhe warriors from the Summer garrison bristled at the encroachment. Row after row of elf soldiers stormed the bridge to form a blockade where the arch bottlenecked. The invaders left the other bridges unmolested so that the seelie guards focused their efforts on those making the forbidden crossing.

Still on his knees and a considerable distance away, Remy gripped a chunk of sod in each hand. He leaned forward to watch from his hilltop vantage. Something unnerving wormed through his gut.

Summer's warriors yelled at the Lightstarved, shouting for them to stop. Oberon's troops held their fire, but insisted they would open loose arrows if the humans did not turn back.

One of the Lightstarved managed to rip his gag free. "Get back!" he screamed. "By the fey, get back! This thing is—"

Before he could say another word, a crossbow bolt streaked out from a seelie shooter's aim. The quarrel punctured through the human's neck, and he fell in a convulsing, gurgling puddle of blood. None of the other mules even slowed. Their fallen comrade became one tether dragged behind the sled, bouncing the body gently against the sled and creating a bloody streak.

A Summer sidhe shouted the order. Archers opened fire. In a heartbeat, the human slaves crumpled. Each one had been peppered with more than a dozen arrows.

A disturbing calm fell over the bridge as the fey guessed at the strange item's purpose.

The metal thing lay silent for many minutes. Unseelie forces remained where they'd stopped their initial advance. Many wore displeased expressions.

Remy studied the faces of the orc crowd. Their leaders were not difficult to pick out of the mix. Ranking officers wore specific armor and war-paint, though Remy did not recognize any of the new warlords. Rhagathena had obviously wasted no time in appointing twelve replacements for the ones killed by Aderyn Corff.

In addition to the orc warriors, a cluster of spellcasters huddled near one of the strangely crafted machinations. The one seated upon a sedan chair was obviously in charge of the arcanist corps.

"These guys really came to play," Remy noted.

Then he heard a caw in the skies overhead and turned his eyes up. He could not be positively certain, but he felt sure that it was Corax hovering in the nearby breeze.

Turning his attention back to the bridge, Remy watched as Oberon's forces crept closer and closer to the thing. And then the iron cone announced itself to the world.

It detonated in a furious eruption of flame and ferrous shards. Propelled by explosive force, the device had been packed with iron flechettes that tore through sidhe flesh, eviscerating the tightly packed forces corralled at the choke point.

The flames quickly died down, but smoke still roiled from the wreckage. Despite the distance, Remy could smell the burning flesh. It wasn't the sulfurous odor of caustic chemicals that charred flesh, but an acrid aroma of raw torment as the ferrous barbs tortured its victims with pains that would never cease.

Mature, battle hardened fey wailed like infants as the metal bit them deeply. Unrelentingly.

Remy stared in shock, awed by the wanton destruction. *This was the spider queen's plan all along!*

He felt a deep and foreboding sense that something about this scene was amiss, though he could not put that sense into words. There was something *more* to the situation.

Corax had landed nearby and muttered a kind of rattling groan.

Remy did a double take. He could have sworn he understood the thing. It had not spoken in any tongue he knew or used speech at all. But still... Remy knew what it had said. He felt its meaning in the same way an old crone's joints gave her reliable premonitions. And the message was clear:

There is more at play here than what is visible.

Remy watched, horrified, as the crippled seelie survivors retreated from the poisoned bridge. There were far too few of them, and the crossing had been permanently spoiled. Jagged iron caltrops seeded the bridge from one end to the other, rendering it toxic to the fey.

Once the Summer garrison regrouped, Remy realized that a full sixty percent of their forces had been wiped out with a single ferrobomb. Of those that remained, half of them had been disabled in some way, and with wounds from which they would never fully recover. And the deepest of those wounds was psychological—the seelie had devised a weapon of cataclysmic and deeply disturbing damage... it could instill terror just by its sight.

A forward contingent of orcs pressed ahead, aiming for the crossing. Even a mere fraction of the army, it looked plenty strong to engage the wounded seelie forces, given their present state. It divided and split into three lines. Each one aimed for a different bridge, forcing the Summer soldiers to divide ranks into weak and wounded forces.

Oberon's garrison would not be sufficient to stop even this paltry force of unseelie.

Corax croaked again. *There is more at play here than is visible.*

The bird leapt into the air, and Remy scowled at it. And then a stroke of inspiration hit him.

His hands reached to the pockets of his cloak where he'd kept the herbs that Wildbean had given him so long ago. Syrmerware Kathwesion's agents had left the clurichaun's herbal gifts alone, and Remy had practically forgotten about it in all this time.

The little creature had told him all about herbal concoctions during those weeks spent with him in the faewylds. One of those was a paste made of something he'd called fool's foil.

He chewed up the dried leaves in order to get some moisture back into them. He ground up the foliage into a paste and grimaced at the flavor before spitting it into his hands.

Wildbean had promised it would help him see through glamours, illusionary magic, and the like. It could reveal the truth of things so long as it was applied correctly. Wildbean had been something of a savant when it came to natural medicines.

Remy closed his eyelids and slapped a handful of the glop over each one. He felt a cool tingle, and then wiped his face clean and opened his eyes.

Something augmented his sight. Light seemed somehow… different. Both brighter and more muted. The pain in the wounded elves displayed like ragged, red tentacles of light where the iron burned, and he turned back to the attackers.

A gray haze of battle lust wafted around the air, surrounding Rhagathena's army like a haze. Within that miasma, Remy spotted points of light that glowed with amber hues. *The spell casters.*

The appearance of the world felt familiar to Remy. His first sense of the aither had been of overlapping layers of reality; each of those inter-planar shades intersected differently with the physical one and Remy guessed Wildbean's paste gave him just enough deeper sight to peer into one of those layers.

Tiny shafts of gold snaked through the air and tethered one brightly glowing spellcaster to the ferrobombs. The brightest of the sorcerers was the one seated upon the sedan chair. His body rested against its high back as servants girded it up by its horizontal poles. Remy's paste revealed that it was only the magician's body in the chair... The *real spell caster* hovered in the air above it, and he held in his hand all the tethers that linked to the explosive weapons.

Remy realized what it all meant: the sidhe was using his magic to access the aither, that realm of spirit and will... and he was somehow using his presence there to activate the ferrobombs.

A crow cawed to Corax in the distance. And then another.

Remy growled with an animal-like noise. He looked down at the fungus that Wildbean had also given him as a parting gift, the egwyl meddwl. As much as Remy hated it, he knew he'd have to enter the aither to stop the mad queen's forces.

"Well, shit."

Remy pinched his nose and then threw the clurichaun's dried fungus inside his mouth. He stood on woozy feet, ignoring the rancid flavor, and hurried out of sight where he could drift into a trance-like state and not worry about his body being discovered.

His breathing and pulse quickened, and Remy began to sweat. *Untethering... that was what Wildbean had called it,* Remy reminded himself.

In the nights following his first encounter in the aither, the little druid tried to coax him into returning by explaining it. The clurichaun's overtures had been unsuccessful, but that knowledge might prove useful after all.

Wildbean had explained the aither as a kind of dream world powered by thought and will. It was a place of spirit and untethering the spirit from the body in a conscious manner allowed one to travel to places in the astral planes, to create things, to explore the aither-based creations of others.

The aither overlapped the physical world in many respects, but it was also a much, *much* larger place. It was infinite, in theory, since its only boundary was the limits of the imagination. And imagination was a powerful force—especially when coupled with fear or guilt. Remy had been hijacked previously by a nightmare fueled by his own remorse.

Remy felt his soul begin to unstitch from his body and he chanted a mantra to remind himself that he was in control. He was in control. *I am in control.*

He stomped his feet on the ground, attempting to keep himself grounded; his feet tingled with a sensation like pins and needles. Remy could not afford to let himself be whisked away into some deeper dream state. He had to remain as close to the real world as possible.

Picking himself up off the grass, Remy spotted his body lying behind him and knew he'd made the transition. He tested his feet under him, and then hurried away, feeling confident enough that he was still in that overlap between the physical realm and the astral plane.

Once down the hill, he spotted the unseelie sidhe who sat on the sedan. *He was the key to the ferrobombs,* Remy realized. The orcs and other creatures confined to physical reality could not see him, he knew. He skirted the side of the hill, but kept out of sight as much as possible. The arcanists, using their mystic abilities, *could* locate him if they were watching for intruders. However, the chief mage's avatar was not watching for aither-based threats.

Remy hurried around to the bulk of the army, using it to remain hidden. He knew that they could not see him or touch him... He was a projection of spirit, and not a physical construct.

He needed to stay out of view of the creature on the sedan. He was the only threat to Remy at that moment. None of the orcs could even *touch* him. Wildbean's instructions had been explicit, however. If an astral projection killed Remy's avatar, his physical body would die, too.

Hiding behind the closest ferrobomb, the human skulked up behind the sedan. A glowing node connected to the tether and Remy recognized it: Fremenor's ignition switch was what triggered each device!

Remy's stomach twisted. The massive contraption thing was a giant iron shrapnel bomb, and it was rigged to a command via aithermancy rather than a physical invocation such as the finger snap Remy had used previously. He looked up to the elf, who held the leash to all the deadly weapons. The enemy's back was still turned to him as the sidhe sorcerer watched the forces storming the bridge.

Creeping through the rows of bodies, Remy instinctively tried to avoid touching them, even though he knew it didn't matter. He moved closer and closer to his enemy, walking up and through the sky as if ascending a staircase until he was level with the elf.

Remy twirled a finger around the slack of one of the lines which dragged far into the distance, connected to a trigger on some distant ferrobomb near the rear of the arc's forces. The line was a construct within the aither and as long as Remy willed it to; the thing remained firm in his grip.

Just when the aithermancer twitched with a realization that he was not alone, Remy looped the golden line and swung it around the head and neck of the avatar. He squeezed, drawing it tight like a garrote.

The creature thrashed and struggled, attempting to free himself so he could combat this astral threat. Remy focused on his goal, willing his enemy to die. Strength in this space was not like it was in the real world—just because he was strong in the physical dimension did not mean his avatar had similar strength in the aither.

Remy held on for dear life, knowing he could not let anything distract him. And then he saw her: Genesta.

She stood with the captives and forced conscripts whose hands were shackled. A slave driver stood next to her, wearing a thick glove so he could ram an iron poker into her flesh if she disobeyed.

A tear streaked down Genesta's face, and then Remy's resolve broke.

The enemy aithermancer used the distraction to his advantage and reversed the maneuver. With one hand he whirled Remy around and wrapped the cord around the human's throat and squeezed. Hard.

Remy could only focus on the elf woman who'd been his surrogate family all these years. And then darkness began to creep in at the edge of Remy's vision.

Chapter Twenty

Remy choked, gurgling and fighting for breath, but the garrote held fast.

Time seemed to stretch out for eternity as Remy stared at Genesta. She was chanting something. Remy tried to listen. He held his breath and ignored the pounding of his own pulse in his ears, but then remembered he couldn't breathe, anyway.

Why is my pulse racing—I'm not even connected to my body! Remy realized he only breathed and suffered from tunnel vision because he thought he should... He reacted in the way his physical reality had trained him to.

In that instant, Remy realized that he didn't even need to breathe—this was the aither. And then he relaxed, slightly. Gasping for breath didn't seem as imperative as it had a moment ago, and both his vision and hearing returned to normal.

The aithermancer still worked the garrote, and Remy assumed he had just a few moments before the fiend realized Remy had circumvented the attack.

He concentrated on Genesta, and her words finally reached him. They were whispered and manic, but Remy knew that they were meant for him.

"They know what I am... They know what I am," she said. Her eyes scanned side to side as if she was searching for him.

Remy's heart sank. If it had been discovered that she was a seer, Genesta was as good as dead—but not as an enslaved conscript for war!

It didn't make sense to Remy.

"They know what I am... They know what I am... Remy," she insisted. A tear streamed down her face.

And then Remy realized the play. Before they'd left for Hulda Thorne, Genesta had insisted that she would be free, even though she could not see Remy's outcome.

This was it... It's why she was so cagey with telling me the future! She knew that the only freedom she would ever gain was in death!

Remy argued with fate, screamed at it—or would have if his throat had not collapsed.

"They know what I am. They know what I am."

Remy recalled her last words to him in the garden before the wedding. *Whenever you hear my words, heed them.*

This was it... what she had meant.

His scowl gave way to resignation. Remy had concocted this plan to kill the aithermancer as soon as he'd realized what the ferrobombs were and how they worked. Genesta was telling him to follow it. Even if she'd seen the outcome. She knew.

And now, so did Remy.

Corax flew down and landed on Genesta's shoulder. The bird did not arrive as the menacing herald of an assassin this time. Instead, it came like a companion arriving to bring solace. Corax seemed to look directly at Remy, even though he knew it was impossible for the creature to see his projection into the aither. *Wasn't it?*

Remy scowled at the bird and then used the one hand that was already wrapped around the trigger cord. He yanked it. Hard.

In the back of the unseelie army, the bomb exploded in a deafening cacophony of noise and blinding pain. It blew a crater in the earth and scattered busted limbs and shredded torsos into the sky. Orcs and other tuatha screeched as iron shrapnel tore them to pieces.

The sudden confusion was just enough to let Remy turn his enemy aside. He sucker punched the aithermancer and then seized the remainder of the trigger cords as the elf recoiled.

The enemy looked at Remy, dumbstruck with awe. The astral human had no chance of overpowering the arcanist, not on this plane.

Remy winked at him as he wrapped the tethers around his hand.

Panic burned in the elf's eyes as he realized what Remy was about to do. The explosion could not touch the human interloper even though he stood directly next to a ferrobomb: Remy was a mere astral figure—just like the aithermancer... Except that the elf's body sat in the sedan chair only a few yards away.

Remy spared one glance back at Genesta and at Corax. Genesta had finally stopped her chant. She wore a serene look on her face. And then Remy yanked all the cords at once.

The detonation was furious, and it set Genesta free.

Chapter Twenty-One

Remy's soul flung back into his body like a stone from a sling.

He sat up with a ragged gasp, thirsty for air. After a violent fit of coughing, he cursed. "I *really* hate the aither."

The human leapt to his feet and ran to the hill's vantage on woozy legs. A massive fireball still expanded as it rose and washed over the busted remains of the orc army. Whatever survivors could still move sprinted away as far as they could.

Thumping sounds like a hailstorm caught Remy's attention. Chunks of metal and scorched flesh fell like icy stones all around. The patch of the burned and broken soil in a large zone all around was covered in iron fragments and flash boiled blood.

With the Demonsbreak army broken and Rhagathena's orcish corps of warriors decimated and scattered, Remy knew that this time it would take years before she could regroup and try again. And next time, Oberon would have a stronger garrison waiting for her.

At least her iron weapons had proved to be a failure, Remy told himself. With any luck, she would assume they had proved faulty or too unreliable. Certainly, a survivor would deliver that report.

Remy rubbed his jaw as he thought it over. She had likely sent the orcs on this assignment specifically to test her new weapon. Rhagathena must have suspected this was a possible outcome all along.

After cutting his horse free from its reins, Remy slapped its rump and sent it galloping away before he gathered up whatever items remained to him.

Besides his cloak and hood, there was not much left to him. Just his dúshlán. *Always my dúshlán.*

Remy could not escape the thought that whatever traumatic past had been stolen from him had been what birthed his mystic blade. He had no recollection of those memories—but he still wanted them back, even if they were nothing but pain. If for no other reason, they belonged to him.

He bent over and stayed low as he descended the hill, making for the iron seeded bridge. None of the fey could use it, and at least for now, and it had become unguarded.

The unseelie's forward troops that fled the burning ferrous explosions had been driven in one direction: directly into the waiting weapons of the seelie guards. But now, Summer and Winter's forces were on relatively even footing. If anything, Oberon's troops now had the advantage, since they controlled the bridge.

Remy slipped onto the vacant bridge and cut across it as quickly as he could. He paused halfway across. Winds whipping through the Solstox Canyon chilled him, but turned back to glance at the unseelie lands. They were the only thing he could remember.

He wished he could spot Genesta waving to him one last time. He would even have liked to see Corax flap his wings and ascend on an updraft.

Remy knew better.

He had watched the flames obliterate them both. They were dead, just like the life he was leaving behind.

Pulling the feathered hood from his pocket, he looked down at it. It was a symbol of what he had been… what he no longer was. Aderyn Corff. The death bird was no more.

He held the hood over the side of the bridge, and then let it fall.

Remy turned and hurried the rest of the way to the realm of Summer. He crossed unseen and hurried for cover immediately.

He was penniless. Direction-less. And he had no prospects. In a day or two, he would be out of food.

But Remy was free.

He turned on his heels, faced directly opposite from the unseelie lands, and began walking.

Bonus Story

Due to my successful Kickstarter which I helped to launch this new book series, I am including an additional story in this edition of Origins of the Cursed Duelist. The additional novelette takes place in between Remy's mission in the faewylds and his final visit to Arctig Maen which culminated in the orcish wedding, (Between Chapters 11 and 12).

CURSE OF THE FEY DUELIST
PREQUEL

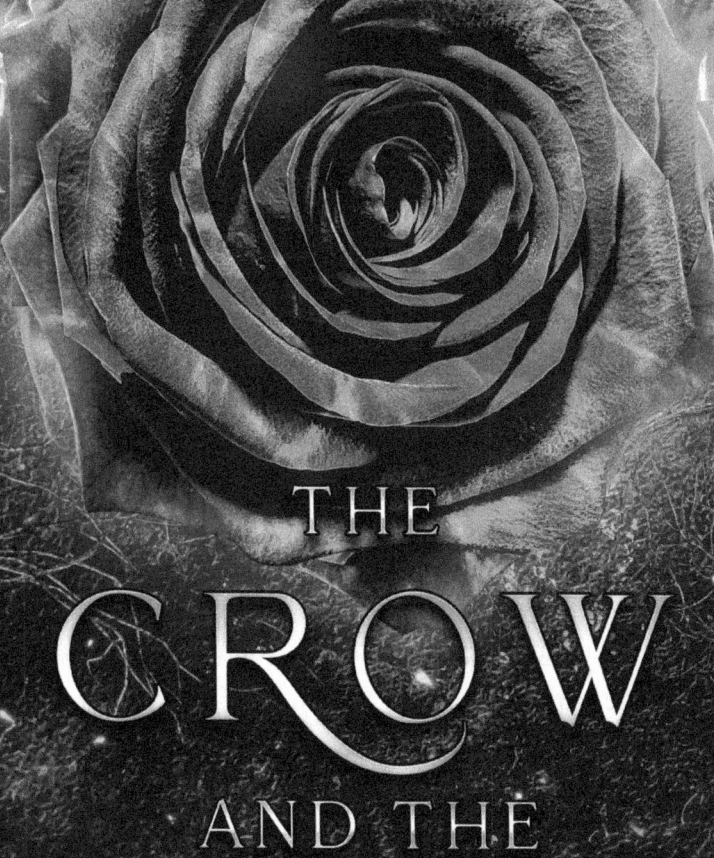

THE CROW AND THE TROLL

CHRISTOPHER D. SCHMITZ

The Crow and the Troll is a bonus story written in the prequel tales of the Curse of the Fey Duelist series. It takes place between chapters 11 and 12 and is one of the many missions Rhylfelour sends Remy out to complete as the orc warlord attempts to court the dangerous spider queen.

A contract killer. A gorgeous victim. And a mystic garden hidden beyond the Winter Court.

Remy Keaton is Aderyn Corff—the Death Bird—and a notorious assassin of the unseelie court. But what the fey don't know is that Remy is a human... and that Remy hates killing. Too bad he's so good at it.

When Remy is forced to track down and murder a beautiful sidhe Lady of the Court whose only crime is being more attractive than Queen Rhagathena, he must ask himself difficult questions. The orc warlord who pulls Aderyn Corff's strings demands blood, but perhaps there is some wiggle room in the spider queen's hit-list... and perhaps ascertaining that is the key to breaking free of the arcane vow that binds the human to the fey's service.

Can Remy defeat the oath that has bound him to the spider queen's service, or must he kill Lady Fenelope to satisfy the laws of his oath?

D EATH CAST ITS SHADOW across the hillside as a crow soared over the road upon outstretched wings. Aderyn Corff, *the corpse bird*, moved steadily towards the unseelie town of Rhosyn Glyn. The community lay on the eastern approaches to the Spinefrost Ridge, the domain of the N'arach and home of their leader, Anansi—a deadly female called Queen Rhagathena. The unseelie queen.

Below the crow's shadow rode a figure on horseback. Aderyn Corff was a human assassin trained by Rhylfelour, orc chieftain of the Broken Hand Clan and the foremost contestant to claim the Rime Throne. The orc was brutal, barbaric, and inhumane—the exact qualities that made him a viable mate for the unseelie ruler, Rhagathena, the spider queen.

Overhead, Corax the crow heralded the assassin. Corax had befriended the human before he'd earned the name Aderyn Corff. Remy still preferred his given name. His name was the only memory he'd retained since awakening in the mystic land of Arcadeax as a child; everything before that time had been lost when he'd eaten fruit from a tree that induced amnesia. *Remington Keaton*. Besides that, he had only glimmers of his past, seen like wisps of dreams after one's waking.

Aderyn Corff, Remy mused darkly. *The orc has tried taking even my name from me.* Remy acknowledged that the infamy brought by the name served him well when he needed it. It was a tool at his immediate disposal. All had heard of the Death Bird, a reputation Remy could thank Corax for. Like a grim portent, the crow would often follow and harass whoever Aderyn Corff had been sent to kill.

Presently, his target was a former member of the Winter Court, Rhagathena's gallery of wealthy nobles who controlled the unseelie realm. Warlord Rhylfelour had been given a list of the queen's political and personal enemies with a tacit understanding that the throne would be his once the list was completed. *When each creature named had met his or her end.*

Remy's horse plodded along and the rider surveyed the vale as it spread out before him. Rhosyn Glyn looked like a decent-sized town and was nestled between the foothills of two mountains. As the horse brought him nearer, Remy smelled the aroma of rose petals on the cool breeze.

The only thing he knew about the name Rhagathena had marked for death, a former Lady of the Court named Fenelope Rharra, was that the queen took offense to her several decades ago after Rhagathena's rise to power. Apparently, Fenelope was a beautiful sidhe, a member of the elven race, who were the predominant species of Arcadeax. According to the rumors, Rhagathena flew into a rage at the she-elf's beauty when it had overshadowed the queen's. The entire incident had been one of the spider queen's own imagining—but the execution order was very real.

Remy had met Rhagathena on multiple occasions, and knew that she was as beautiful as she was jealous and conniving. The queen was one of the most visually stunning beauties the human had ever seen. *At least,* he thought, *as long as one did not look below her waist.* At her hips, Rhagathena's body conjoined that of a giant spider in centaur fashion; her teeth were sharp, predatory, and feral—but Remy had rarely seen her smile.

"Sounds like this order is more of a personal grudge than a political hit," Remy grumbled, speaking to Corax. The bird was too far away to hear him, though Remy was reasonably certain the bird could understand him whenever he spoke.

Remy angled his mount towards Rhosyn Glyn and spurred it to a quicker pace. He grew eager to arrive after the journey.

Typically, Remy hated that he was forced to kill. But he was good at it. Until recently, Remy had invested his energies in helping raise a pair of young human slaves who'd suffered similar fates to Remy. The orc had tried to mold them into copies of Aderyn Corff. They'd both died at Rhylfelour's hands during the orc's "training sessions."

He would have killed Rhylfelour for it, but Remy was mystically prevented from seeking recourse on the orc, and anti-human sentiments prevented him from merely escaping the orc's clutches. However, when Remy was dispatched on assignments, he was able to experience some semblance of freedom.

Rhosyn Glyn lay at the base of the valley where the main road crossed through. Winds rushed down from mountainside, and looking up, Remy spotted a decrepit castle. Its crumbling stonework was in sore need of repair. A general lack of maintenance led to the structure's decline and cracks in the walls allowed snarls of thorny rose to bleed out from the once proud facility's walls. Remy guessed it was once the home of a sidhe who was part of the Winter Court, except the fierce disrepair made him wonder at that possibility.

Remy jangled the coins in his purse and tied a bandanna over the crown of his head to hide his shorter ears before spurring his horse towards the town. He was in sore need of a hot meal in the town and a rest for his saddle-sore legs.

Certainly, someone there would be able to help him locate Fenelope Rharra. He knew that information that could not be gleaned could always be purchased.

Remy guided his horse through a number of the town's streets. He criss-crossed Rhosyn Glyn to get an idea of the city's layout. A quick tour let him take the pulse of its people, and also plan an escape route if he needed one. Remy flexed his jaw at a memory when he'd needed exactly that after plans went sideways in the faewylds.

Rhosyn Glyn was much like many other urban centers he'd visited. It was a collection of various species, with the majority being sidhe. There were also other members of the various fey species, with all races collectively called the tuatha, and he saw a few stray humans who may have been free folk or slaves. Remy could not tell, but he didn't need that info.

He stopped near the center of town, where there was an active marketplace. The vendors' square was flanked by several inns and taverns, and Remy tied his horse to a hitching post before wading into the rows of vendors in search of food and knowledge. Corax descended and alighted on Remy's shoulder. The bird made an eager croak as the smells of food reached Remy's nose.

The assassin purchased a meal from a dirty halfling whose offerings smelled best; the halfling's wife tended a tandoori oven that looked comically large for her. Remy alternated between taking bites of meat and tearing strips for Corax, who greedily gulped them down.

"I'm a traveler," Remy told the halfling. "Is there somewhere that I can get information?"

"Depends on the topic," the smaller tuathan said. His words hinted that he could direct someone towards the more illicit realms of knowledge if plied with a coin or two.

"Nothing untoward," Remy assured him, which made the halfling slouch in disappointment. "I'm here on Winter Court business. Just locating a few old contacts on behalf of my lord. Do you know of Fenelope Rharra?"

The halfling gave him a quizzical look.

"She was the Lady of this region a few decades back," Remy said. "Was a part of the Court, even, until Queen Rhagathena stripped her rank."

He shrugged in response. "Probably best to ask Korgyn Chestra. He's the local magistrate."

As if in response, the street cleared suddenly. Vendors hurried out of the way and patrons jumped aside to make a path for an elf on horseback. He was flanked by two guards, also mounted.

Corax flapped his wings, but remained upon his perch as the arrogant sidhe forced his way through the crowd, making a straight line, despite the position of others. Stiff backed, and with eyes refusing to acknowledge the populace, he halted his horse when he came to Remy, who was in the way.

The assassin stood in the sidhe's path, and Remy refused to move. Filled with hubris, the elf looked down at Remy and met the human's hard-edged gaze. After looking into the eyes of a killer, he seemed to decide it was unwise not to force a confrontation.

One of the guards leaned aside, intending to dismount and rough up the traveler, but the elven leader waved him off. Instead, he set a new path and led them around Remy. His horse trotted aside, trampling the wares of an old she-elf who'd laid her bundled roses out on a tattered quilt.

She was old and ugly. Her bent back slowed her, and the hag was not quick enough to clear the space. Hooves crushed her bouquets and baskets into rubbish as she prattled curses at the rider.

"How's a fey supposed to make a living?" the old woman yelled at the arrogant sidhe who'd ruined her wares.

"Roses aren't worth anything," he scoffed. "Not in Rhosyn Glyn."

"Then why don't you risk the thorns and try picking them yourself," she growled at him.

The noble sidhe used a riding crop and cracked her across the face.

Remy tensed and stepped forward to defend her against the injustice, but the old she-elf stayed him with a hand. She kept her eyes downcast and the noble elf sniffed arrogantly, but then urged his horse onward. A few moments later, the trio of fey on horseback disappeared beyond the crowd.

Corax took flight as Remy hurried to the old she-elf and offered his assistance. "My name is Shue," she said after thanking him for the help. Shue sorted the ruined goods from whatever remained sellable despite the damage.

Remy offered her the remainder of his meal and Shue greedily accepted it. He wondered how long it'd been since she had a full meal. As Remy looked her over, he thought of Genesta.

Genesta was also a she-elf of advanced age, but Genesta had a secret. She was a seer, an elf with the arcane ability to see the future—but that gift also made her a highly coveted slave. Genesta had helped raise Remy. The fact that she continued to believe in the human and whatever destiny she thought he possessed kept Remy's faith alive, even when the darkness of his deeds threatened to consume him.

"Korgyn Chestra," Shue growled, touching the welt that blossomed angrily on her face. "I've known that capricious little shit since he was a pup." She stared in the direction Chestra had gone and sighed. "But if I was a hundred years younger and still possessed the beauty I'd had in my youth..." she trailed off. "A pity he's so handsome. He'll probably marry an equally icy bitch by this time next year."

Remy's brows knit. "Shue, if you've been around here all this time, can you provide me with information?"

She nodded, and Remy relaxed. Shue seemed like a better contact than the magistrate.

"I'm looking for Fenelope Rharra," said Remy. "She used to be the local Winter Court noble."

Shue laughed. "That's a name I've not heard in ages. She and her husband used to live in the castle on the hillside. I get my roses from the bushes that have grown wild there now, but it used to be grand. Supposedly she was in that castle since the height of Wulflock's power," she referenced the long lost unseelie king.

Remy's gaze pinched as he worked out the details. "She must have access to ambrosius?"

"How do you mean?" Shue asked.

"That's the food that keeps the sidhe young," Remy said. "It's why Oberon is supposed to look only a few years older than I. She must have some to remain so long lived"

Shue laughed. "If only I had some. I was once the great beauty of Rhosyn Glyn. If I had that back, I'd change my stars. But even the sidhe's beauty fades like a wilting roses... but I do hear that the nobility hoard the ambrosius for themselves. I'd do anything to get my hands on it."

Remy stared at the distant, crumbling castle. "You never tried to pilfer it from up there?"

Shue looked confused. "There ain't never been ambrosius up there."

He turned back to the old elf and relayed the story about the jealous spider queen as he'd been told it. The old crone laughed in response when Remy explained that Fenelope was supposed to be a great beauty.

"Fenelope Rharra ain't no sidhe," Shue wiped a tear from the corner of her eye as her amusement tapered. "I don't know who told you that tale, but they mustn't of been from the valley."

"If not a beautiful she-elf, then what is she?" Remy asked.

"Fenelope's not sidhe... and she's not a beauty, either," Shue said, pointing to the dilapidated structure in the distance. "She and her husband were trolls. They earned their position under King Wulflock for helping rally troll-kind under his banner during the Infernal Wars. They stopped an overthrow when Wulflock was away from the Rime Throne and at war against the demons. Foiled a coup, they did... too bad, whatever happened to him in the end... the kind, I mean."

Remy tapped a finger on his chin. "Something is amiss, then. Fenelope's name is on the list and the story came from a reputable source... someone who was at that first introduction between Lady Rharra and the queen." Remy swallowed the dryness in his throat. The information had come from Chokorum, Rhagathena's majordomo—no fey was as close to the queen as Chokorum was.

"If that's not what happened, then do you remember anything of that night?" Remy asked.

Shue did, though not many of useful particulars. "Rhagathena hadn't been queen long, and she was touring her domain. Around that same time, Fenelope's husband, the troll lord, Hexxar Rharra, had disappeared. After the queen left in a tizzy, she yanked the Rharra's title and court status; things shifted in Rhosyn Glyn, upsetting the power balance. None ever saw the troll lords again. I've no idea who Rhagathena met in their castle, but if it was sidhe, then it wasn't Lord or Lady Rharra." She shrugged and then added, "Ever since then, the castle has kind of... it's just fallen apart. Folk sometimes come and go, but none are trolls. Usually vagabonds, rakes, and the like. Trolls have some grudge against the queen, you know. Can't say I blame em."

Remy nodded, staring at the distant structure. He grumbled slightly. "I guess I'll have to investigate if I want to cross this name off the list."

Shue cocked her head at that statement. He'd not mentioned the purpose of his list. But before Remy would let her ask about it, he departed for the old castle of Lord and Lady Rharra.

Remy's horse seemed unhappy about being forced onto the road again so soon after arriving at a town. It had expected to be stabled and receive food, water, and rest. Remy glared at it whenever it neighed angrily. *Unseelie fey treat their mounts better than they treat humans.*

He wondered what he would find as his horse trudged up the slope to where the castle overlooked Rhosyn Glyn. Large stones had fallen off their perches and walls had succumbed to heaves. In random places they busted open, and from those cracks rose bushes spilled out, allowing the flora to invade the surrounding hillocks.

I wonder why nobody else moved in to take over after the previous owners abandoned the structure? Remy wondered. As he grew closer, he realized why. The castle's proportions had been difficult to tell from a distance but became clearer as he draw near. The place was sized for trolls and giants. Everything was enormous.

Although Shue had insisted the trolls had departed, Remy's horse became skittish. It sniffed nervously and faltered at the smells that only it could parse.

Just because an old she-elf hasn't seen *any trolls does not mean they are not here,* he reminded himself. Regardless, Remy assumed Shue was likely correct. Whatever activity *had* been seen in this area was probably due to a gang of highwaymen. Remy felt comfortable enough in his abilities that bandits did not concern him. All the same, he adjusted the bandanna around his head to keep his ears hidden.

There was more than enough room that Remy could have comfortably ridden his mount through the halls as he explored. However, the horse refused to go much past the main gates. Trolls were known to greatly enjoy the taste of horseflesh, and horses seemed to discern the creatures were a mortal threat.

After fighting the beast for a few minutes Remy relented and tied it to a post in a relatively hidden alcove. He felt keenly aware of Shue's comments that, while the place had fallen into disrepair, it was not altogether abandoned. After securing the horse, Remy set out on foot.

The courtyard he'd walked through was eerily empty, and its over-sized proportions unnerved him slightly. A breeze rustled leaves and provided an eerie ambiance. Flowering vines and thorny stems sprawled everywhere. Carpets of rose and bramble choked every area where their roots could find purchase. Greenery climbed up the stonework; they spilled onto catwalks and parapet before tumbling over walls and expanding beyond the castle's confines and into the unseelie.

Remy poked at a few leaves with his sword, half expecting the foliage to writhe, regroup, and attack him like some kind of carnivorous plant. But it remained inert. The plants were content devouring the stately, ancient castle rather than its inquisitive visitors.

"How long does it take to get so overgrown," he wondered aloud.

He ducked inside an old storeroom and found little but rot and mold. Remy explored a further, but he only uncovered more evidence of the place's long-term abandonment.

Methodically he worked through the rooms, hoping to discover either evidence of the Fenelope's fate or clues of recent usage so he could make contact and inquire about the castle's history.

Remy ducked through a collapsed door frame and found himself inside the gardens. Whereas the courtyard was merely overgrown, this place was a wild tangle of verdant life. Every inch was green except where vibrant colors of rose blooms exploded with crimsons, whites, yellows, pinks, and even one bush with ebony leaves as dark as the skin of the subterranean trow: the light-less elves of the under realms.

No wonder nobody remembers Rhagathena's visit, Remy thought, and then said, "This must have taken decades to get this overgrown."

"Five of them, in fact." A melodic, distinctly feminine voice pierced the air behind Remy.

He whirled to find a sidhe woman standing only two steps from him. She was perhaps the most beautiful creature he had ever seen.

Remy whirled, spotting the beautiful she-elf. With sword in hand, his mind raced, and he arrived at the conclusion that this gorgeous sidhe was his target: Fenelope Rharra. With so many of the particulars at play, he had to assume that she was not just his target, but a powerful spell-caster.

The assassin brought his sword to bear swiftly and struck with all his might. The blade met flesh and cleaved it cleanly, severing her head from body.

Surprise and betrayal frozen upon her face, Fenelope's head tumbled to the garden floor, propelled by a spray of arterial blood. It came to a rest near Remy's feet and the body of the sidhe beauty collapsed into a heap where it bled out among the roses.

Remy's chest heaved and a deep pool of guilt welled up within him as he stared at the corpse. Some days, he hated his job. Today was one of them.

I did what I had to do, Remy told himself. *If she was a powerful arcanist, as I suspected, I had to kill her before she could cast a spell.* He'd fought spell casters before. More recently, he had nearly lost his life outside Capitus Ianthe; were it not for a stroke of freak luck he'd be dead. *Luck, or maybe it was divine intervention? Whichever, I'll never let a caster get the drop on me again.*

He stared at the headless corpse a moment. What bothered Remy was how easy it was becoming for him to kill. With every body to fall by his efforts, it felt like a little piece of his humanity died, and it did not matter that he was forced into this life.

But the deaths of Rhylfelour or Rhagathena would not bother me… they deserve the blade and I would feel no remorse for delivering it.

Remy only wished he knew how to make that dream into a reality. He was oath-bound to the orc and the magic of Arcadeax forced his compliance. As a child, Rhylfelour had forced him to speak a vow in the olde tongue—which was the language of fetiche magic. Arcadeax itself enforced magical law as surely and as potent as any other force of nature.

Despite that, Remy felt certain he would find a way to defeat, or at least circumvent, those magical restraints which currently held Remy's knife from his master's throat.

Remy's heartbeat finally calmed as he stared at the cooling corpse. Silence again reigned. He turned and bent to pick up the severed head and examine it. As he did, something rustled in the nearby leaves.

The headless woman, only just murdered, stood back to her feet and shuddered, swaying on uneasy legs. A lumpy wad of congealed blood and mucus spurted out from the cut stump with vomitous rancor.

Remy recoiled with disgust and took several steps back to put some distance between them. His mind couldn't process what he was seeing.

Fenelope's body spasmed again and then a new head forced its way up from the wound like a baby animal emerging from its mother's womb. She shook the wetness from her head as her hair regrew to its previous length.

As terrifying as the scene was, she regained every ounce of what she'd been a few minutes prior. She was undeniably beautiful.

Beautiful creatures are dangerous, Remy reminded himself, and not for the first time.

"That was not very nice," she insisted, eyes focusing on Remy's hands, which gripped tighter upon his weapon. Fenelope flashed him a look of warning. "Please refrain from trying that again. We could do this all day... but it is rather painful and I would rather parley than devolve into violence."

Remy looked at her skeptically. He clutched his sword by the hilt and maintained a cautious posture.

She scanned him with wary eyes and seemed to arrive at the only valid conclusion. "So you have come to kill me? Fey knows I have tried unsuccessfully for years now. Surely, I know how, but cannot bring myself to submit to the flames."

Remy relaxed his grip and eyed her skeptically. "You are... you are not an elf?"

"No," she shook her head. "I most certainly am not. To be quite honest, I find my present form somewhat embarrassing."

The human assassin stared at the sidhe, who was not a sidhe. He put together what he knew of Fenelope, including the few details she had just provided. Facts merged, and in a flash of insight, Remy knew exactly what she was.

This stunningly gorgeous creature was neither human nor elf. Remy didn't know why or how she'd been stuck in this form, but the beautiful figure before him was some kind of troll.

"So you have already tried to kill yourself?" Remy asked. If she was a willing participant to her own death, perhaps he could satisfy the spider queen without tarnishing his own conscience. Remy thought about it for a moment. He decided it was an act of mercy to help those in suffering to end their afflictions.

Fenelope inclined her head gravely. "Understand that I have no wish to die. But after spending decades looking like—" she trailed off and motioned from her feet to her head with her pointer fingers. She finally said, flabbergasted, "I would rather die than continue on in such a... hideous form."

Remy stared blankly at her. Then he cracked up with such a belly laugh that he sank to his haunches and rolled onto his back.

The proud creature who looked like some sort of elf stood in the midst of the garden as still as a statue. She stared at the cackling human, not able to comprehend his amusement.

Finally, Remy calmed down and tried explaining his laughter. He wiped away a tear as he said, "A troll cursed with beauty," he chuckled some more. "You find *that* a fate worse than death." He tried to regain his composure, clearly finding no threat in Fenelope, even though trolls were known to be fierce, dangerous creatures.

Remy laid aside his sword and tucked his feet below him. Corax flew down and lit upon Fenelope's shoulder. The bird pecked curiously at the female's head and she shooed him away, sending him back into the sky.

She turned to match her guest's posture. As she rounded and sat, Remy noticed a tail, like that of a cow. It dangled off the female's shapely backside. Fenelope crushed flower petals below her and scowled at them, kicking them aside as she got comfortable.

"To answer your question, yes. I've tried to kill myself a few times in order to escape this curse," she said. "Though I'm not certain why one of the sons of Adam would be sent here to kill me."

Remy's expression softened at the creature's words. He'd half expected her to call him a ddiymadferth: an anti-human slur that many fey used when referring to humans. Remy judged the character of a person based on whether they used the term ddiymadferth, or the feys' colloquial reference to Adam. He removed his bandanna.

Her implied question was a fair one, and Remy assumed that, like most trolls, she could identify his species by the scent of his blood—that confirmed her claims to be troll-kind. Remy said, "Queen Rhagathena directs my master's hand and has compelled me to eliminate certain named enemies. Your name is among those who've slighted the queen."

Fenelope chuffed with amusement. "That pretender? I have no love for the spider queen to be certain, especially not after she stripped me of rank and title. That act sent me into this spiral of poverty and despair... though I suppose I am at least partly to blame for that as well. But for the life of me, I can think of no overt insult I've offered her."

Remy shook his head mirthfully. "When she visited here ages ago, Rhagathena felt your beauty overshadowed hers." He sighed. "It seems to me that she's ordered your murder because of a mere jealous grudge."

The shape-shifted troll rolled her eyes and shook her head. "I owed everything that I was, the position that I had arisen to, to King Wulflock, but it is some beautiful strumpet's curse that's undid me," she said. "Ironic."

Remy cocked an eyebrow. "I've heard of your devotion to the bygone king."

Fenelope tilted her head. "Do you know much about troll-kind?"

"I am no expert. But I have general knowledge. Neither more nor less than most citizens of the unseelie," he said.

"Then you know how devoted our kind is to the long-lost king, Oberon's brother Wulflock?"

Remy nodded.

"But you know that there are many subtypes of trolls?" she asked.

Remy waffled his hand back-and-forth to signal he had very vague knowledge in that area.

"I suppose I shall need to tell you my tale so that you might understand it," Fenelope said.

The human beckoned for her to continue.

Bards were held in high esteem in the unseelie. The troll smoothed her clothes and settled in, trying to appear presentable as a host thrust into the role of story-teller. She was hospitable, even despite her guest's clearly announced intention of killing her. The fey had protocols, after all.

She began her tale. "There was once a pair of powerful trolls named Fenelope and Hexxar. Both came to the aid of Wulflock during a dire hour as the Infernal Wars raged. Through many conflicts, those two trolls became something of a romantic item... at least as far as troll-kind goes, and we've established you know but little in that area, and I won't bother dredging up trollish mating rituals," she explained.

Continuing, Fenelope said, "When the day was won and the unseelie was saved, the two trolls were wed. To show his appreciation, the king rewarded Fenelope and Hexxar Rharra with a Winter Court title and lands near Rhosyn Glyn.

"Fenelope and Hexxar were happy for a time. A long time, in fact," she said. "Trolls are not specifically monogamous... though that does not mean we feel a lack of jealousy when a spouse takes another lover. We are fey, after all, and what are the fey except for jealous creatures?

"Hexxar had certain perverse proclivities. Not that I'm one to judge. We all have individual tendencies for certain…" she trailed off for a moment, looking for the right word, then found it, "kinks."

The beautiful troll smiled, almost bashful, despite her age and forthrightness. "Hexxar had a deep fondness for both the sidhe and for all things bovine."

Remy raised his brows and blinked, understanding that she was implying sexual deviancy.

"Don't judge," she said precociously. "Trolls like what trolls like. But I'll admit, the preferences of folks besides myself make little sense to me. Hexxar began meeting for a regular tryst with a huldra, which is a kind of troll subtype."

Remy had heard of them, but never seen one before. The connection suddenly snapped into place. Huldra look like beautiful sidhe but could be recognized by their cow's tail which they attempted to hide; they were generally viewed as seductresses.

He realized in that moment that he'd not actually confirmed the female's identity and thought he'd made a brilliant deduction. "You were that Huldra?"

"No. I was Hexxar's wife. Pay attention," she insisted.

"But you are Fenelope Rharra, correct?" he asked to make certain of it. He'd been fooled a few times already and wanted to ground himself in at least one fact.

The troll-elf-huldra creature nodded. "I am," she said, silencing him.

"Huldra have powerful magics. Though it took nothing more than her appearance to seduce Hexxar; no magic—just raw, animal lust. I discovered their secret trysts because of all these roses in the garden," Fenelope said. "The vile little thing had planted them before I'd realized it."

"I thought you said trolls were not monogamous?" Remy asked for clarity.

Fenelope shrugged. "We are not. And I would have allowed him his dalliances, but it became apparent to me that this tart had her eyes on more than just a roll through the rose petals with my husband."

Remy's brows knit with curiosity and he let her continue.

"It all started with one rosebush. You see, huldra love to be surrounded by beauty. They love to seduce, but they must employ deceit to do so. It is in their nature." Fenelope held up her bovine tail as if to accentuate the reasons for their trickery.

"I confronted the huldra about her ambitions. I detected no coyness in her and we determined that my husband lusted for such an appearance—I was willing to give Hexxar what he craved. She offered to grant me a boon with her magic: eternal beauty and the chance to win back the primary affections of Hexxar."

Remy scowled and shook his head, offering a humorless chuckle.

"I can see you understand where the story is going?" Fenelope said.

He nodded. "She fooled you?"

Fenelope bowed her head in recognition. "Indeed. That usurping strumpet played a trick on me. She used her magic to transform me into one of *her* kind instead of my own. I did not realize it until it was too late."

The female pointed at where the black petals bloomed. "She planted an enchanted rosebush at the center of my garden claiming that it was a fetiche. Pronouncing her curse, she asked me in the high speech, [Whoever owns this rosebush shall forever inherit the beauty that it brings; do you accept it?] I was a jealous, spurned woman, so of course I agreed."

Fenelope smiled uncomfortably for a moment. "Hexxar appreciated the new look. He *really* appreciated it." She fanned her neck at the memories her story elicited.

"While I was pleased that I could participate in my husband's fantasy, it was exactly that: fantasy. He was a Lord and I a Lady of the Winter Court. One cannot spend all their day playing," Fenelope said. "When I asked the huldra how I can revert to my true self or shift between shapes, she only laughed at me and responded with a deep and passionate kiss."

"Why would she do such a thing?" Remy wondered. And then he caught Fenelope's glare and realized that Hexxar was not the Huldra's prize... *Fenelope* was.

Their gazes met for a moment and the female seemed to know that he understood. "My fancies do not lean in that direction. Even if the harlot's loins burned for mine, I would not let her have me and so she left, abandoning me *as if she* was the spurned lover. Her departure left me forever cursed in this form."

Fenelope shook her head dourly. Her tale was layers of irony stacked upon themselves. "Perhaps the huldra thought she was doing me a favor, leaving me in the shape which Hexxar was so intensely infatuated with. Or maybe it was vengeful spite."

"What happened to the troll Lord?" Remy asked with genuine curiosity.

"Not long after, I killed him." Fenelope's words came matter-of-factly and with no remorse. Something about the tone warned Remy against inquiring further as to her and Hexxar's torrid relationship.

Fenelope said, "This all occurred about the same time as Rhagathena's rise to the Rime Throne. But in my state, I had no desire to present myself at court in Arctig Maen. Shortly after Hexxar's passing, the queen came for a personal visit." Fenelope frowned. "She is just another petty woman with wielding power like a cudgel, guided by wild winds of emotion." She fell silent for several moments.

Remy stood, understanding that the cursed troll's story had ended.

The human crooked his jaw. "Have you considered digging the flower up?"

Fenelope gave him an incredulous stare. "I'm not an idiot, child of Adam. Of course I tried that. I also tried to kill the plant using every means I can think of… but it is protected by an old magic—none of this modern glamour stuff. This is a true fetiche, and only something of a similar power will have any effect."

Remy frowned, but nodded. He glanced down at his sword and then used a toe to nudge the head he'd earlier severed from Fenelope's body, entertaining macabre thoughts. He figured he could end Fenelope's life with relative ease and quickness: he could behead her again and then burn her corpse so that would not regenerate. Fire was a particular weakness of the trolls; that fact was well known.

Fenelope looked up at the man sent to kill her. "What will you do now? You must follow the orders of your master, and I am prepared for whatever may come."

Remy scowled at his sword and then looked at the beautiful creature before him. "What if there was another way? Would you accept my help if I had a way to end your suffering and eliminate you from the queen's kill list without causing your death?"

Remy entered the unseelie town and could hear the shouting even above the clopping of his horse's hooves. He pulled back on the reins and stilled the mount in order to hear better.

At first, the voices sounded like heckling and insults, but it took a decidedly savage turn. "This will teach you to side with outsiders," a voice rasped.

There came a sound like a sharp crack. *Maybe a whip?* More likely, a riding crop across sidhe flesh, Remy realized. A feminine voice cried out in painful response.

Remy slid off his horse and hurried around the corner of the building separating him from the altercation. He dashed out into Rhosyn Glyn's market square where he'd been earlier and spotted the conflict in a nearby alley.

Korgyn Chestra's two goons were assaulting Shue. The old she-elf laid out on the ground where they'd tossed her after roughing her up. One cheek was rosy and brilliant where she'd been struck with the magistrate's riding crop. A thin trickle of blood streamed down.

Chestra's goons had ruined the remainder of her wares and thrown her quilt into a midden heap where local farriers scooped animal refuse for later transport as fertilizer.

In a rage, Remy drew his blade and rushed forward. Before they could strike the old elf again, his sword flashed, spraying a gout of crimson and killing one of the two ruffians.

Chestra was not physically present. Only his riding crop represented him; it was in the hand of the remaining thug. That elf whirled in surprise. He recoiled and put some distance between him and Remy.

"Do you know what you've done? I will tell the magistrate—he'll bring a hundred fey after you!"

Remy glared at him with hard eyes. His gaze did not waver in the magistrate's thug wilted.

"Do you know who I am?" Remy asked.

The elf merely blinked.

"I am Aderyn Corff." As soon as Remy spoke, Corax dropped from the sky with flapping wings. The crow alit on the assassin's shoulder and croaked.

The elf's eyes widened. He had obviously heard that name spoken before. Remy's fame, embellished though it may have been, had reached as far as Rhosyn Glyn.

"If you bring me one hundred men, I will give the magistrate one hundred corpses," Remy threatened.

Chestra's henchman turned on his heels and sprinted away, practically wetting himself.

Once Remy was certain the sidhe was gone, he helped Shue to her feet. The old she-elf was more upset that they'd ruined her quilt and wares than that they'd struck her bloody.

"My body will heal in time," she grumbled. "But it will take me the better part of a day to recover my stock of roses."

Remy looked down his nose at her. "Do folks really pay you for those flowers? I've been to the old stone walls where the rosebushes spill over in great torrents. Any person could go pick their own."

Shue fixed him with a pinched gaze. "It ain't about the value of flowers, young man-it's about pride. I ain't gonna beg, and so I've got to offer *something* in return for a little coin... the flowers may be free, but I'm providing the flower picking service rather than a product. Fey knows that the only thing I've left of any value is whatever time I've got left on Arcadeax... and at least I'm still capable of picking flowers."

Remy looked her over for a few more moments and then nodded. He asked her, "did you mean what you said in our earlier meeting? Would you really give anything to be young again?"

She gave him a quizzical look. "Is this some sort of test?"

Remy shook his head. "It is an offering. An opportunity."

He stared at her, awaiting an answer.

Shue spoke hesitantly. "I would, I think. But such bargains always come with a price. I should know the cost before I give my answer."

"Wisely said," Remy told her. He extended a hand. "Come with me. We shall learn it together."

Shue stared at the Rharra's massive garden drenched in shades of green. She said with awe, "I've never actually been *inside* this place. I've only cut roses from the outside."

Remy used his pair of dúshláns to work the soil around the base of the ebony tinted rosebush at the center of the grounds. Its flower petals were satin and blacker than night.

One of the two dúshlán blades belonged to the human. The second one was the property of an orc who he greatly respected: an orc who'd defied Remy's master, Rhylfelour. His name had been Warchief Krogga. Krogga was another orc chieftain who opposed Rhylfelour with every fiber of his being... an orc who Remy had been forced to murder out of obligation.

Despite the human's orders to kill him, Krogga had first given him the dúshlán, a magical blade forged from a raw need for vengeance—a mystic weapon that cried out for revenge. It was empowered by the fundamental arcana of Arcadeax itself. Krogga's intent had been clear: he hoped Remy would use it to someday kill the orc who'd oppressed them both.

Dúshlán's were olde magic—they were fetiche weapons. Knowing their nature, Remy had correctly ascertained that a dúshlán would be capable of disinterring a mystic plant such as what the huldra had planted. As Remy dug away soil from the roots, Fenelope explained the bargain to Shue.

"I am unsure how to break the curse upon me, and I greatly desire to be rid of this terminal youth." Fenelope shuddered. "I'm not certain why folks are attracted to the shapes and appearance that this huldra put upon me, but I'll be glad to be rid of it."

"So you are merely transferring the curse rather than breaking it?" Shue realized.

Fenelope nodded. "I think that the fancy dagger the human carries could kill the plant if you would rather... but for some reason, he collected you and thinks this might be a better way."

Shue visibly panicked at the notion that the plant might be destroyed. Once Fenelope explained what the black rose did, Shue had remarked that it was a better deal than the highest casted nobility who regularly consumed the legendary ambrosius to retain their youth.

Finally, Remy finished unearthing the bush. He ripped it out from the dirt and exposed the lumpy ball root below the thorny stems. Once it popped free, all the remaining roses seemed to wilt at once.

The human winced as a barb bit his flesh, and he dropped it.

Fenelope intervened and picked it up. Sharp spines drew blood from her hands as she seized it, but she shrugged off the nuisance wounds. After all, she was a troll and would heal quickly. The former Winter Court Lady placed the bush into a planter and clutched it tightly.

She glanced back at Remy and explained, "I needed the blood for the spell, anyway. Fetiche magic always demands a payment."

Fenelope turned to Shue. She spoke in the olde tongue. [Shue, do you freely accept this gift and all its consequences? Whoever this rosebush belongs to shall forever inherit the beauty that it brings; do you accept ownership?]

[I do accept it as mine,] Shue responded in the arcane language.

Fenelope nodded and turned over the plant.

Shue grabbed a hold of the plant and let the thorns cut into her flesh and draw blood, linking her to the ancient magic.

Fenelope looked relieved to be done with it. "Make sure you plant that thing properly within the next day or so."

"What will you do now?" Shue asked her.

Fenelope shrugged. "I am departing these lands in search of something better… in search of the lost brother of Oberon. Perhaps I'll venture through the faewylds… I hear queen Mab is amenable to troll-kind."

"It's Maeve, now," Remy said. "Queen Maeve. Mab is dead, and Queen Maeve now rules in her succession." A mischievous light glinted in the assassin's eyes. "It's not much different."

Fenelope nodded her understanding. "I feel the change coming." And then she collapsed to her knees.

Remy put a shoulder under her and helped Fenelope into the shade of the castle's tall walls. They made it just in time as her transformation began in violent fashion.

She arched her back and her limbs stretched and grew. Joints popped as bones expanded and stretched flesh. The pale white skin of her huldra form shredded like a too small husk for a creature in molt. Her troll form returned in hideous fullness.

As soon as the change was finished, Fenelope stood. She towered above Remy and he took in her gruesome visage. She was terrifying... at least to the humans perspective. But Fenelope seemed greatly relieved to be in her own flesh again.

Shortly after, Shue also underwent her own metamorphosis. Unsure what to expect, she quickly disrobed as the transformation gripped her.

Her aged epidermis sloughed off like blistered skin after a bad sunburn finally healed. She rubbed it free like polished rind and revealed a taught sheath of fresh skin. Shue was filled with the glow of vibrant young life.

Shue was physically gorgeous, still like the sidhe in *almost* every way. And she was nude, revealing the only significant difference of her new body. Her now-shapely backside had sprouted the bovine tail of a huldra.

Remy blushed and turned away so that the cursed beauty could wrap herself in her old, ill-fitting clothes once again. To Remy, Shue looked uncannily similar to Fenelope's huldra form, but was different enough that she could not be mistaken for the same person.

With her beauty restored, Shue bounced with joy and embraced Remy happily. She planting a kiss upon his cheek. "I shall never forget this gift, young human." Shue picked up her potted bush and made to depart.

Remy called after her. "Where will you go now, Shue? What will you do?"

She turned back and flashed him a dangerous smile. "I am going to remake my life locally. It won't take long, and then I'm going to find Korgyn Chestra and then play upon his desires. I will make him fall in love with me."

Remy cocked his head.

Shue laughed, and then hissed, "Once I have accomplished that, I can truly make him the most miserable sidhe in all of Arcadeax." She wrinkled her nose playfully, and then departed.

Remy watched her go. He reminded himself again, *Beautiful women are dangerous women.*

Remy picked up the severed head from where it lay in the undergrowth. It still retained the visage of Fenelope's huldra form, even after her return transformation to troll form had completed. He felt the troll's eyes upon him as he stuffed the macabre trophy into the sack.

"I'm sure you won't mind if I take this?" Remy told her.

Fenelope shrugged. "As I said previously, I don't openly judge another person's... kinks."

Remy open his mouth to argue, but then he closed it. Fenelope had promised not to attempt explaining the sexual dynamics of trolls, cows, and fey. He figured he could reciprocate as much and leave the topic alone. He didn't want to open the door to such conversation, not even to defend himself.

"You are truly leaving the unseelie?" he asked instead.

She nodded, keeping to the darker sections of her keep so that the sun could not harm her. Dusk would arrive soon and allow the troll freedom to leave. "The heart of troll-kind has long departed from the realm of Winter."

"You *really* can't stand the spider queen, can you?" Remy asked.

A knowing glimmer sparkled in the troll's eye, paired with a grin. "It is true, what you told me about trolls enduring the sun in the faewylds?"

Remy nodded. "I have seen it with my own eyes."

"Was that before or after you murdered Queen Mab and deposed the ruler of the Briar Throne?"

This time, it was Remy's turn to grin. "You apparently hear all the important news out here, even despite how far Rhosyn Glyn is from the center of the unseelie," he remarked.

The troll winked. "I've not been completely without visitors." She smiled. "How else do you think I've stayed fed?"

Remy gulped. He knew only the basics about trolls, including their dietary preferences. Remy did not ask if her prior visitors were traders who brought her food, or if they'd *been* her food. If Shue's initial guess of bandits in the castle ruins were true, her previous guests had likely never escaped.

Fenelope sighed. "But you are correct. I may not remain in the unseelie so long as Rhagathena holds sway; Fenelope Rharra is no more. We trolls remain ever hopeful of Wulflock's return—when he does, I might come again. Perhaps after the faewylds I shall go below ground to the realms of the dvergr or the trow. Maybe the Spring and Autumn Courts will be kinder to an old troll?"

Remy nodded, wishing her luck as she pursued a new and optimistic future. He headed for the castle gate where he'd left his horse.

Fenelope waved as Remy exited the collapsing fortress. Until the curse was lifted, it had still been a home. Now, it was little more than a heap of stones its owner would abandon as well.

She called after him, "Good luck, Aderyn Corff. We'll not likely meet again."

Remy returned her wave and then leapt into his saddle and departed.

Rhylfelour barked at Remy as soon as the human had returned to the orc's compound. "The deed is done? I am eager to cross another name off of this list."

Remy nodded at him. He pulled Fenelope's decaying head from the sack which he had wrapped it within and threw it to the cruel warlord.

The severed flesh had begun to turn, and the skin developed a kind of sickly slime that coated it in a greasy sheen. Rhylfelour fumbled the slippery, cadaverous head, and it fell to the ground.

Rhylfelour picked it up by the hair and examined it. "She looks like she might have once been a true beauty," he said.

"She was," Remy said. "And I ended that."

The orc detected no hint of the humans doublespeak.

"Fenelope Rharra met with a swift end to my blade. I later confirmed her identity," Remy said earnestly.

Rhylfelour glowered at him and motioned with his hands.

Remy knew what the orc wanted. He repeated the statement verbatim but spoke it in the high speech, the olde tongue of the fey in which it was impossible to speak falsely. Of course, one was still capable of lying, just so long as the letters of the words were true, even if the spirit of them was false.

The human relaxed somewhat as his orc master accepted the statement as truth.

Remy felt at ease deep within regarding the mission's outcome. His conscience finally allowed him a moment's respite. Remy had discovered a way to obey both his master's orders, but avoided murdering folk for the sake of the spider queen's twisted demands.

Rhylfelour stopped the human before he could depart to his quarters for rest or visit with the elf seer, Genesta, who Remy was close with. "Speak your oath," the warlord insisted.

Remy grit his teeth but complied. He spoke like a clockwork automaton, or one of those akasha powered mechanical contraptions. Using the olde tongue, Remy said, [I swear my allegiance to Rhylfelour, son of Jarlok and warlord chief of the Broken Hand orcs.]

He said the words with his mouth, but in his mind, Remy insisted on a different oath.

One day, Rhylfelour... someday soon I will end your life and gain my freedom! I shall defeat your prison of mystic words and end you... I already have an idea how, and my encounter with the troll makes me believe all the more that it will work.

What Comes Next?

I first explored the world of Arcadeax in an overlapping multiverse of interconnected Urban Fantasy books: *Wolf of the Tesseract, The Casefiles of Vikrum,* and *The Hidden Rings of Myrddin the Cambion.* The paranormal investigator Vikrum Wiltshire, who connects the worlds falls into Arcadeax and has to flee the spiderqueen, Rhagathena.

The world is ever expanding. Parts of Remy Keaton's story truly begins when he enters the seelie in *A Kiss of Daggers*. The sequel is, *Of Mages, Claw, and Shadow.*

Keep up to date and stay in touch with the author at this link: https://www.subscribepage.com/duelist

and add your email to be added to the newsletter list!

CURSE OF THE FEY DUELIST

Wolves of the Tesseract
1. Wolf of the Tesseract
2. Gate of the Multiverse
3. The Architect King

The Casefiles of Vikrum Wiltshire

Curse of the Fey Duelist: Origins of the Fey Duelist

Curse of the Fey Duelist: A Kiss of Daggers

Glossary

Aes sidhe – a class of magic wielding seelie fey

Aes sith - the equivalent of aes sidhe, but these fey are all wildfey

Aderyn Corff – "the death bird," a feared unseelie assassin who disappeared after defying the unseelie queen

Akasha – "magic in a bottle," a magic-based power source available to non-casters

Anansi – the title given to the ruler of the unseelie giant spider-folk known as N'arache

Aither – a spiritual realm composed of pure thought and power

Aphay tree – a tree whose fruit erases memories

Arcadeax – the world of faerie-kind which coexists with Earth, the Infernal Realms, and many others

Bruscar – low class tier of Arcadeaxn society

Changelings – half fey, half human

Coroniaids – often mistaken for dvergr who are the subterranean version, these are dwarves

Cù-sìth - a kind of hellhound

Cupronickel – a common metal alloy used so that no iron is present

Dagda – the chief deity of Arcadeaxn religious thought

Ddiymadferth – the chief insult among the fey: a derogatory word for human

Dream Hallow – a type of drug that causes euphoria and sends its users into the aither

Dúshlán – a kind of fetiche item given by Arcadeax itself, it is a boon for its recipient to right a great wrong with an act of vengeance

Dvergr – often mistaken for coroniaids who are the above-ground version of dwarves

Ellyllon – a wildfey variant of the sidhe with a slightly more feral appearance, typically thinner limbs, and longer, more narrow ears

Faewylds – any part of the world not claimed by the seelie or unseelie courts

Fetiche – Arcadeaxn magic that predates the aes sidhe; it is the magic of the gods

Fey – a word used to describe anything with Arcadeaxn origins

Frith Duine – a fey alliance dedicated to the eradication of humans living among them

High speech – also called the Olde Tongue and denoted by [brackets] when it is being used… oaths and commitments made in this language cannot be broken

Ina aonar – a house-less, ronin status for duelists who belong to no specific guild

Maven – politically aligned mages who govern factions of magically gifted citizens

Méith – the elite class of the Seelie society

N'arache – the giant spider folk of the unseelie; they live mostly in the Spinefrost Ridge mountains and have elf-like bodies fromt he waist up and giant spider bodies on their lower half much like centaurs

Olde Tongue - also called High speech and denoted by [brackets] when it is being used... oaths and commitments made in this language cannot be broken

Oibrithe – middle class of of the Seelie society

Powrie - a goblin-like race of tiny unseelie creatures who wear red caps and have generally murderous intentions

Saibhir – upper class of of the seelie society, but not méith

Seelie – the summer court: one of the kingdoms of elves ruled by Oberon and Titania

Shade – a kind of animated corpse under the control of a necromancer

Sidhe – members of an elvish species of the fey folk

Teind – the "hell tithe" which rulers of Arcadeaxn realm must pay to infernal forces to keep shut the gates of hell

Trow – beneath the seelie and unseelie realms are subterranean kingdoms of under-elves which make up the autumn and spring courts

Tuatha – creatures or "people" native to Arcadeax; includes the sidhe but also other sentient beings such as fauns, dvergr, etc... can be a synonym for fey in certain contexts

Tylwyth Teg – a type of elf from the faewylds and considered uncivilized and barbaric by their seelie and unseelie counterparts; looked down on by other sidhe

Vantadium - a metal alloy made of vanadium and titanium so that no iron is present

Wolfranium - a metal alloy made of tungsten and titanium so that no iron is present

Wulflock – the long-lost rightful king of the unseelie

Map

- Wildfell
- Draenen
- Fiáin Vale
- Dant
- Frosthorn
- Brialtholme
- Solstox Cliffs
- the Selvage
- Vale Rhewi

The Unseelie

- Fiacail
- Icedinas
- Grimming Wood
- Crafangu
- Clawdale
- Faewylds
- Gaeafdale
- Coldhome
- Demonsbreath Enclave
- Hulda Thorne
- Gwylltown
- Iâ Tre
- Hestref
- Eira Cartref
- Lloches Oer

About Author

Christopher D. Schmitz is an indie author from the fly-over states who dabbles in game design. He has published award winning science fiction, fantasy, and humor. He's written and freelanced for a variety of outlets, including a blog that has helped countless writers on their publishing journey. On any given weekend, he can be found at pop culture and comic conventions across the USA or playing his bagpipes for people. You can look him up at:

www.authorchristopherdschmitz.com.